The Pa

the Loyalist

Angela K. Couch

The Patriot and the Loyalist

White Rose Publishing, a division of Pelican Ventures, LLC
www.pelicanbookgroup.com PO Box 1738 *Aztec, NM * 87410

White Rose Publishing Circle and Rosebud logo is a trademark of Pelican Ventures, LLC

Publishing History
First White Rose Edition, 2017
Paperback Edition ISBN 9781611168891
Electronic Edition ISBN 9781611168877
Published in the United States of America

What People are Saying

A poignant blend of adversity and love set against the gritty backdrop of war, Angela Couch skillfully weaves a redemptive story that will keep fans of historical romance turning pages and rooting for a happily ever after.

~Heidi McCahan, author of Unraveled and Covering Home

From the descriptive pen of award-winning historical author Angela K Couch comes an intriguing tale of lies and deceit that will keep you turning the pages way into the night. . . I always enjoy Angela's stories where history meets fiction. The Patriot and The Loyalist was no exception.

~ Marion Ueckermann, USA Today Bestselling Author

The Patriot and the Loyalist brings readers a Revolutionary War historical that will keep them reading both for the romance and the intrigue.

~Janet Ferguson, author of Leaving Oxford

Angela K Couch delivers once again. The only problem with The Patriot and the Loyalist—it is impossible to put aside. Filled with realistic characters, its wonderful storyline stays with you long after you finish reading.

~Lucy Nel, author of The Widow's Captive

1

South Carolina, November 1780

Daniel Reid slowed his horse and sucked air into his lungs as he reined to the road's grassy edge. Blood pulsated behind his ears but in no way drowned out the pounding hooves of the approaching soldiers, the green of their coats almost deceptive. He was used to scarlet, but no doubt they were British. He'd been warned of Colonel Tarleton and his Green Dragoons.

With a smile pressed on his lips, Daniel nodded to the commander of the orderly column. The gesture was not returned, only the narrowing of dark eyes—like a snake seeking the next target for his wrath. The colonel looked to the cane fastened to the side of the saddle. Stale breath leaked from Daniel's lungs, and he laid his fingers over the brass handle, hoping they believed he had need of the cane as he surveyed the rest of the well-armed cavalry.

Mud and manure-ridden boots. Dark scuffs across legs and sleeves. The acrid aroma of smoke. Horses walked with heads down, weary like the men who rode them. Obviously, they'd already had a long, productive day, and yet their polished blades glinted with the late afternoon sun, and the barrels of their muskets did not carry the stain of powder.

As the last soldier passed, Daniel pulled his bay mare back onto the road and encouraged her pace. He raised his gaze to the strip of blue high above the treed

1

banks of marsh and swamp. Sweat tickled the back of his neck. Nervousness, or the heavy humidity? Not that it mattered. He'd volunteered for this.

Thin swirls of smoke rose from the horizon, the first a mile off. Maybe two. Daniel spurred his mount in that direction. He'd never find Colonel Francis Marion if he avoided the prospect of danger.

The trees thinned into farmland and opened into fields left barren from harvest. The sky hazed behind the dissipating smoke. A crumbled barn, not much remaining of it but charred boards and glowing coals, stood not far from a grand house. Was this Tarleton's work? Or Colonel Marion's?

"Mama!"

The panicked cry followed a boy as he darted into the brick edifice he no doubt called home—much different from the two-room cabin Daniel had been raised in. Moments later, several young faces appeared in the crack of the open doorway. Dirty, tearstained faces. None were older than ten. Surely this was the work of the British and not the man he sought. Daniel had lost the taste for such deeds years ago. A man should be able to leave his woman and children safely at home. War belonged to men.

The oldest boy, a sandy-haired lad, stepped back out onto the porch and folded his arms across his chest. "What do you want here, Mister?"

Daniel swung out of his saddle and held his hands away from his sides. "Where are your folks?"

The scowl only deepened on the boy's face as he widened his stance. "You have no right on our land. You'd best get back on that horse of yours or I'll—"

The door pushed wide and a woman appeared, a lady, despite her disheveled appearance. "Hush,

James. We have no means of knowing who this man is."

"But Mother." He spun to her. "You should not be up. I can take care of this."

"I know you can, James, but I will be fine." With a hand on her son's shoulder, she gazed at Daniel. Though her chin showed confidence, her eyes pooled with the pain she tried to keep contained. "Who are you, sir?"

"I was passing by when I saw the smoke. Who did this?"

She straightened, wincing as she did so. "You have yet to answer me, sir."

Daniel couldn't help but glance around. This far behind enemy lines...yet to complete his mission, how much did he dare reveal? If only he could be certain Tarleton had done this misdeed. But he couldn't. "I am Sergeant Daniel Reid."

"Sergeant?"

He met her gaze, trying to read it. Not a single clue. "Of the Continental Army."

Her shoulders sagged and trembled. "Praise the Lord."

Daniel's hands dropped to his sides. "So the British are responsible."

"Yes." She stepped around her son and sank to the top step. "My husband was General Richard Richardson. He was taken prisoner by the British because he refused to support them. He'd resigned the army already, but because he couldn't be bought, they hauled him away, keeping him locked up until he was ill. They let him come home to die. He passed away a couple of months ago."

"I'm sorry."

She shook her head as though to wave away his condolences, while glancing to the small family cemetery across the road. A mound of dirt stood dark between the headstones. "Tarleton dug up his body. He gave some excuse, but really he was treasure hunting." Her fingers hid her eyes. "What sort of monster digs up a man's grave?"

The boy set a protective hand on his mother's head. "Or burns animals to death."

Daniel cringed as he looked back at the remains of the barn. That explained the more pungent stench wafting on the air. "Do you know how to find or contact Colonel Marion?"

"No." Mrs. Richardson blinked hard. "I knew the British hoped to attract him here, so I sent one of my boys to warn him away. Who can say where he's gone."

James nodded. "Though, if he had come, the British wouldn't have had the nerve to flog a lady."

Daniel's gut twisted. The attractive, middle-aged woman was obviously used to a genteel living despite being displaced this far from a town. "Are you all right, ma'am?"

"I will be fine." Her jaw stiffened and raised a degree. "I only wish I could speed you on your way with the Colonel's location. You could ask at his plantation. Or check at Port's Ferry. Rumor has it he camped there most of last month." The lady waved him nearer and lowered her voice. "Or Thomas Amis's Mill. The Colonel has been there, as well." She pushed to her feet, her hand braced on the railing. "You are from the North?"

"New York."

She looked his homespun up and down. Not near

as fine as the uniform he'd worn the past three years. "I thought as much. Do not get lost in the swamps trying to locate him. Go to Georgetown and find Mister Lawrence Wilsby. He was a friend of my husband's and true to the cause. He might be able to help you."

"Thank you, but..." Daniel glanced to the barn, and then back to the three young boys who had made full appearance behind their mother and older brother.

A woman, her skin shades darker than his own tanned face, now stood in the doorway with a scowl.

Two men, their complexions even darker, moved around from the back of the house.

Slaves, probably—something quite foreign to him. In the Mohawk Valley, a man labored with his own hands, not someone else's. Daniel dragged his focus back to Mrs. Richardson. "Is there anything I can do?"

Her lips tightened as she shook her head. "I have the help I need. May God speed your way, Sergeant. And may scum like Tarleton reap His wrath."

Amen. Daniel mounted his mare.

The oldest boy moved to his side, eyeing the cane. "What is that for, sir? You don't seem to have a limp?"

Daniel gave the cane a pat. "This is to keep the British from asking any pressing questions about why I don't fight for them." He winked, and then with a tip of his hat, reined toward the road. "Thank you, ma'am."

He fought to keep his mind in the present as he encouraged his horse to a faster clip. But, as always, the image of a barn left in ash accompanied a spade full of guilt and the memory of a woman with hair like new corn silk.

Rachel Garnet.

He had prayed that three years would be enough

to rid her from his mind.

"Come on, Madam!" He nudged the animal with his knees, craving speed, as though the wind could snatch him from the past. Besides, if he kept up the pace, he could reach Georgetown before nightfall.

~*~

"Miss Reynolds, be reasonable. Let me send for our carriage to take you home."

Lydia shook her head and pulled up the hood of her cloak. "No, Mr. Hilliard." She slipped the letter he had given her into her reticule and tightened the strings. "It's not far, and I do not want anyone to know of this. Not yet." She needed time to think and make a plan.

Ester Hilliard stepped around her father, catching Lydia's arm before she could turn away. "Do not be foolish."

"With the British's presence in Georgetown and Major Layton billeted in our own home, it has never been safer," Lydia replied. But then Ester, three years her senior, always had been overly practical and reserved.

Lydia threw a farewell wave into the air and hurried out the door. Blackness had spread itself across the town, with nothing but the flicker of a few lamps illuminating the barren streets. The odd scarlet-clad soldier still stood watch, but the townsfolk appeared to be retired for the night. Lydia quickened her steps with the hope that everyone at home had done the same. If Charles found out she'd sneaked out alone instead of going to her bed with a headache as she had insinuated, she'd never hear the end of it. Especially if he knew why. She needed to determine how to confront him. Soon.

The methodic plodding of hooves on the next street only brushed her mind. Raucous laughter startled her and jerked her attention to the Coat of Arms Tavern. Men's and women's voices mingled together. Lydia frowned and pulled her cape closer around her shoulders. She could not understand what would drive a woman to degrade herself so, flinging her attentions at a man for the sake of her purse. She hurried past the establishment and to the end of the block. Even for the sake of a roof over her head she would not concede—though more and more it seemed that was where she stood with Charles, her late sister's husband. He would no doubt extend an offer of marriage, but Lydia had no desire to sell herself in any form.

She tightened her grip on her reticule. The letter within represented so much more than a new life. It was freedom. A surge of anticipation propelled her forward, and she darted across the road—directly into the muscular shoulder of a horse.

Snorting in surprise, the animal reared.

Lydia scampered out of the way. But not fast enough to be missed by a sharp hoof. Pain seared her shin and she fell on her backside with a thud.

"Madam, whoa!" The man reined his horse back a few steps before flying from the saddle and to Lydia's side. He reached for her arm. "I am so sorry, miss."

She warned him away with a glare and the wave of a hand, and then pushed to her feet, careful to avoid putting her weight on her injured leg as she smoothed her skirts over it. "I can manage on my own, sir. You would do well to watch where you lead that beast."

"Pardon me, but it was you who walked into us."

She glanced past him to the horse that stood with head low, looking far more apologetic than its master. Or perhaps the animal was merely weary from a long day and many miles. Sweat shimmered on the heavy coat in the dim light of the nearest lamp—a coat ready for a colder winter than Georgetown, or anywhere in South Carolina, would know.

"That may be, sir, but..." Lydia looked back to the man.

His clothes, from the knee-high boots meeting his breeches, to a homespun shirt and woolen coat, were nondescript, but that could be said of little else concerning this stranger. He towered over her. Dark waves descended from under his tricorn hat to where they were tied at the nape of his neck. The whiskers shadowing the attractive slope of his jaw showed a week's growth—if her brother-in-law's face could be any means of measurement. And his eyes appeared black like coals.

The pain in her leg pulled her attention back to the present. "Here in the south a gentleman does not place blame on a lady for something when they share equal fault." Though, who could say how far from a gentleman this rogue fell?

He swept the tricorn hat from his head and offered the slightest bow. "I do apologize. And you are correct. It was my fault entirely." His words came with neither humor, nor the attempt to patronize. He seemed as weary as his horse. Which begged the question why? Obviously a northerner, what were his affiliations with the south, Georgetown in particular? Where did his loyalties lie?

"How far have you come today?"

The man shoved his hat on his head and turned to his bay mare, his large hands working to straighten the reins across the animal's shoulders. "Probably fifty miles."

"And the day before that?"

He glanced back at her with raised brow. "A ways."

"And have you reached your destination, or do you have farther yet to go? Perhaps Charles Town?" Did he side with Britain, or the rebels? Something about him suggested the latter.

"That will be determined by what tomorrow brings." He nodded to her. "But for tonight, I should leave you to continue home, while I find lodging."

The noise spilling to the street from the tavern drew both their gazes.

"Good evening then, sir." Lydia took a step away. Her bruised, and possibly cut, shin spiked pain through her leg and she bit back a surprised gasp. Powerful fingers wrapped around her arm.

"You're hurt."

"It is nothing." She started walking, trying her best not to limp, and very aware that he hadn't yet released her. She swatted his hand away. Were all New Englanders so brazen?

"If you won't let *me* help you, then at least allow Madam to make recompense."

She kept walking.

He continued to follow.

"Madam?"

"My mare." His chuckle held no mirth.

She glanced back at him. "You named your horse *Madam*?"

"As a filly she was particularly…haughty. And my

sisters disliked the name." He cracked a smile. "I assure you she is safe to ride and can carry you wherever you need."

"I do not need to be carried anywhere." Lydia again quickened her pace despite the discomfort. "My home is not much farther."

"You expect me to simply walk away after trampling you with my horse? That would hardly be the gentlemanly thing to do." He continued to keep pace with her, his gait smooth.

"And I would hardly mistake you for a gentleman." She sensed him stiffen beside her, but if he was determined to see her home, she would resume her interrogation. Maybe this northerner had information useful to the British. "I would guess farmer or laborer. Or soldier? But then why would you ride with no uniform?" She turned to him so she could see his face clearly in the light of the lamp they approached. Ignoring the ache in her leg, Lydia flashed him a smile. She leaned closer and lowered her voice to the breath of a whisper. "You are a Patriot, aren't you? A spy?"

2

Daniel froze at her words. A Patriot? A spy? One of those could be refuted. He'd been sent to deliver a message, not size up the enemy's positions. Despite his surprise at her turn of questioning, he held his stoic expression—though perhaps his eyes narrowed a little before he managed a laugh. "Is that the usual occupation of strangers to Georgetown?"

The young woman relaxed back a step, the pain of her leg evident in the motion. "It is not so easy to ascertain."

He again allowed a throaty chuckle. "I would think a town serving as a British stronghold would ward off traitors to the crown, and spies..." He looked about, taking in the patchwork of light and shadow cast upon the streets. "I'm sure talk of such is unsafe, even for a girl of the town."

Her chin rose at the use of the term "girl", much like Fannie or Nora's did when he teased them. Susanna and Rose on the other hand, only seemed to enjoy his playful harassment. The image of his sisters pinched in his chest. More than three years since he'd been home. Three years since he'd ridden away from the Mohawk Valley and his family to join the Continental Army. Three years and, instead of returning as he ought, he'd only distanced himself more.

"Now you insinuate that I might be disloyal?"

Fine lace cuffs hung like banners from the maiden's elbows as she folded her arms.

Daniel peered at her all the harder, not sure how to interpret the underlying tone of her words. Perhaps she was a Patriot as well. Perhaps she'd be able to help him.

But, in the middle of Georgetown, with British sentinels within a block of where they stood, the risk was too great until he could be certain. He shook his head. "Of course not. You have given me no reason to doubt your devotion to our King." With a smile, he gestured ahead of them. "But 'tis late, and I've come a long way. Let me assist you onto my horse and deliver you safely home."

Light from the nearest lamp flickered in her eyes. He couldn't make out the color but they were pale. Very different from his sisters', or even Rachel's—he chastised his thoughts for their betrayal. The young woman's hair appeared as dark as his own. Too bad the sun wasn't bright overhead. He would have liked to see her in the light of day. As it was, the shadows lay across the delicate features of her face, leaving much to his imagination.

After a moment of deliberation, she sighed. "Very well. Since you are responsible for my predicament."

Daniel stepped around her, leading the mare to her side.

She winced as she lifted her foot to the stirrup.

The mare nudged his arm with her nose as though also placing blame on him. More likely Madam only wished for him to speed things along. It had been a long day for them both. Quick enough to not give the woman time to protest, Daniel set his hands to her waist and boosted her atop.

She gasped and worked to tug her full skirts over her legs.

Turning to grant her some privacy, Daniel waited a minute and then clicked his tongue to encourage Madam to follow. "Which way?"

"Right at the next corner, and then go straight."

He answered with a nod, though his legs protested against moving. He almost needed the cane strapped to his saddle for more than his deception, but he decided against the effort of utilizing it. There were not many King's soldiers out tonight, and a bit of a limp came naturally with his muscles so stiff. He needed a walk after endless miles astride a horse. Hopefully, another day and he'd complete his mission.

But then what?

Daniel frowned. He was officially discharged from the army. Would he enlist again for possibly another three years? He'd be nearing thirty by then, with no land, wife, or children of his own. He had nothing. But what other option was there? Return to the Mohawk Valley and join the local militia? He could help on his parents' farm, and do his best to stay clear of Rachel and her husband. Not so easy with Fannie now married to Rachel's brother and them having a young'un.

"So what does bring you to Georgetown?"

Daniel blew out his breath, wishing it were as easy to empty his mind as his lungs. "Land." He'd rehearsed his story well. "I'm tired of harsh winters and short summers."

"You want to buy a farm?"

He glanced back. "Is that so surprising to you?"

She settled into the saddle and shrugged. "I suppose not. The area has been in such upheaval the last few years, but I suppose you cannot put aside your life forever." Sorrow tugged at her last few words.

Daniel paused to look up.

She stared at her hands resting over the pummel, the tie of a fancy pouch woven between her fingers.

"I just realized I don't know your name. But I would like to."

Her gaze dropped to his. Hesitation. She shifted in the saddle. "Such an introduction would hardly be considered proper." She tugged her hood to better hide her face as she glanced left and right. "Lydia Reynolds."

He inclined his head in a nod. "*Miss* Reynolds?"

"Yes."

Daniel couldn't help a smile from easing onto his lips, though her marital status should mean nothing to him. "'Tis a pleasure." He turned and started walking again.

They didn't go far before she spoke. "And what of your name, or do you purposefully desire it to remain a mystery. I must admit to not being fond of secrets."

"Daniel Reid."

"And you were a farmer up north?"

"I was."

"But the winters are too cold and summers too short?"

"That they are."

"It is a strange time of year to be seeking land, is it not?"

His smile stretched into a grin. This was almost as much fun as bantering with one of his sisters. "I don't think so. I finished harvest at home in time for winter, sold my crops, and now here I am. If all goes well, I'll be ready to plant by spring."

"I suppose so." The old saddle squeaked as she shifted.

His hand tapped out his thoughts against his leg. Maybe he would be able to ask her for more help, after all. "Are you familiar with a Lawrence Wilsby? I am told he might know of some land for sale in the area."

"I am acquainted with Mister Wilsby. Though, I was unaware he had any dealings with the buying or selling of farms."

One step closer to finding Colonel Marion. Daniel kept his eagerness contained, his tone casual interest. "Then perhaps you would be willing to introduce me to him tomorrow? I'd be indebted to you."

"Hold up here."

Not quite the answer he expected. He surveyed the stable to their right. "I find it hard to believe you reside in a livery."

Without waiting for his assistance, she slid from the saddle with only a short groan when her feet met the ground. "I do not. You might find one useful, though, and there is an inn across the way." She brushed past him with a definite favoring of her left leg. Maybe he needed to offer her the use of his cane.

"But what about you? And of Mister Wilsby tomorrow?"

She didn't look back. "If I can get away, I will meet you here at noon."

Then, like a phantom of the night, she vanished between two buildings. Gone. Still, his smile remained.

~*~

"Say nothing of this to Master Selby." Lydia winced as the heavy binding tightened around the

15

bruised scrape on her leg and Molly tied off the bandage, her dark fingers nimble. If Charles did ask, Lydia would make up some excuse like walking into... She glanced around her bedchamber. The stool at her dressing table seemed the only likely object she might have cracked her shin against.

The girl stood and folded layers of petticoats down over the bandage. Though she attended Lydia, Molly, like all the slaves attached to the estate and shipping company, now belonged to Charles. Except Eli. She hadn't known it until last night, but the aged Negro had remained her grandparents' property even though they had sent him to America with Lydia's mother upon her marriage. And now, with the passing of her grandparents, and she the only heir, the slave belonged to her. As did the cottage near Brighton.

Lydia scooted to the edge of her bed and smoothed the pale blue fabric of her gown. "Thank you, Molly." She stole one last glance to the pillow concealing the letter Mr. Hilliard had received from the officiators of her grandparents' modest estate. She'd read it over and over last night after she'd sneaked back into her room, and then again this morning. She could not hesitate. Now was the time for action— before anyone thought to question her tardiness for breakfast.

She opened the door to infectious giggling coming from the nursery. The baby's chortle drew her across the hall. It was all too easy to picture little Margaret with her wispy curls and full cheeks. Lydia forced herself to turn away. No attachments. Especially when she would be leaving so very soon. Her leg felt much better than last night, and she made a quick retreat, descending the stairs and pushing into the dining parlor.

Charles already sat at the head of the table, the place that had been Father's before the *Magellan* was sunk by Continental Navy's frigates. Even three and a half years had not made her brother-in-law's place as the head of the family and sole owner of the shipping company any more acceptable to her. Especially now that her sister, poor Margaret, rested in the cemetery with Mother and the boys. Lydia sat in her chair, her enthusiasm draining away. Only she remained of the South Carolina Reynolds. Her family had helped build this town, this colony, and soon she would also abandon it. Just as well. Neither Georgetown nor South Carolina held anything for her now.

"Good morning, my dear," Charles crooned, his blue gaze following her to the table. "I do hope you feel better this morning."

"Yes. Quite." She glanced around. No other place settings were present. "Where is Major Layton this morning? He is not joining us?"

Charles sipped his wine, waiting to answer. "Colonel Tarleton asked for him to take his regiment north toward Camden, if I heard correctly. It appears that rascal Marion has been playing a sly fox again and giving the colonel quite the hunt."

Over the past year, Francis Marion had become quite the nuisance to the British and Loyalists, and she hoped Tarleton found him—though she didn't care for the man's manners. Thankfully, the officer who billeted with them did not let his eyes wander *quite* so freely.

"You look far too relieved by Major Layton's absence." Charles set his fork beside his plate and touched the napkin to the corners of his mouth.

"I am merely glad for a moment to speak to you of something." She paused as her plate was set before her.

"What would that be, my dear?"

Lydia steeled herself against the urge to cringe. He'd taken to titles of endearment the last little while, and it made her skin crawl. Her sister had passed away only eleven months earlier. Had he no respect for her? Or patience? "I want to go to England."

His golden eyebrows shot high while the corners of his mouth twisted downwards. A broken laugh issued from his throat. "Really, Lydia, now is not the time to indulge your appetite for society, with French ships and privateers making such a trip treacherous."

"I care not for society, or the French."

His frown deepened. "It would be very different for you in England. Here you have wealth and prestige. There you have neither name nor title. You would be nothing to them."

"I do not care." She slid her napkin onto her lap and measured her breath. "I received news that my maternal grandfather left my mother the cottage near Brighton. There is no other heir, so it is mine." Unlike everything her Father left. This grand house, the ships—all included with the company—had become Charles's, as partner in the company and the husband of the eldest daughter. "I want to live there. I am finished with this place."

"You cannot be serious." He pushed up from his chair and circled around the table toward her. "I will not allow it."

"And pray tell, how will you disallow it?" She surged to her feet. "You do not own me."

She could see him thinking, frustration lighting sparks in his eyes. Then he pointed a finger. "The allowance you receive now is not required of me to give."

Lydia forced her lungs to take breath despite the heat burning within and the snugness of her stays. She couldn't risk making an enemy of him. "Charles, please. Have I asked for anything? A small living has been left me. Enough to get by comfortably. When I am gone, you can find a new mistress for this house. I know you have plans to remarry someday and—"

"And there is nothing wrong with the present mistress." His voice mellowed as he reached for her hand. "Your father would not want you to leave. Margaret would not have wanted it." He raised her knuckles to his mouth and pressed a kiss. "There is no reason for it."

"I cannot marry you, Charles."

His spine stiffened. "I have not asked you..." He shook his head. "What I mean to say is, yes, I had intended to ask you to be my wife...soon. Maggie needs a mother and it is only right that—"

"I will not replace my sister. I cannot." Lydia pulled away from him. She didn't want to be a mother. Not to little Margaret or any child. Ever. She wouldn't risk it. There was so little of her heart left that if broken again, she might not survive. "Please, let me go. All I ask is passage on one of my own father's ships."

Charles released her. "I am sorry, Lydia. But I cannot allow it."

3

Daniel leaned into the wall of the inn, cane in hand. Despite a shave and wash making him more presentable to the public eye, his presence garnered many a curious gaze from the locals. The British soldiers passing also gave him long looks, but he merely nodded to them. Sometimes he saluted. Usually, one glimpse of his cane and the apprehension or mistrust slipped from their faces. Still, he hoped Miss Reynolds stayed true to her word. Already past noon, the sooner he left Georgetown and its English proprietors, the better.

A carriage hesitated in front of the inn, and its door swung open. "Hurry and come aboard, sir." Lydia appeared, waved him forward, and then dropped back into her seat.

Daniel utilized his cane to step onto the street and climbed inside. As soon as he sat across from her, the coach lurched forward. "I didn't expect quite this much courtesy," he said, laying the cane across his knees. Looking at her now, he wondered why she had seen fit to offer him assistance. The quality and fashion of her gown, the perfect ringlets gracing her slender neck, the way her gloved hands rested demurely on her lap—everything about her bespoke a lady in the fullest meaning of the word. He'd found pomposity another common trait among such women.

"The least I could do to repay you for the ride you

provided me last evening." She gave the smallest smile. "And I wish to speak to you at greater length."

He returned her smile, but with more ease than she had managed. "I'm glad to hear you arrived home all right. How is your leg?"

"Much improved, thank you." Her bluish eyes glinted. "I remember seeing that cane fastened to your saddle, but you seemed to fare well enough without it last night. You do not really require it, do you?"

Daniel kept his smile in place, not sure what game she played. "On the contrary."

She matched his expression. "But not for walking."

He fought the urge to raise the thick velvet curtain from the window. For all he knew she was hauling him to the British to turn him over as a spy. Would they shoot him right away, or interrogate him first? Fortunately, no matter what they did to him, he could give little to assist them against the rebellion's efforts in South Carolina.

"Tell me who you really are." She inclined toward him. "Why are you in Georgetown?"

Daniel folded his arms and attempted the nonchalance that often drove his sisters mad. "I already told you who I am."

"But you are not a farmer."

"But I am."

She set her jaw. Her eyes, hints of green mingling with the blue toward the centers, narrowed. "You do not have to play games with me. I want to help you."

He raised a brow. "You're already helping me by introducing me to Mister Wilsby. Or are you also aware of land for sale in the area?"

~*~

Lydia huffed and settled back into her seat. The New Englander sat there looking all too confident and sure of himself. Nothing she hated more than an arrogant man. Except perhaps an arrogant rebel—so certain breaking with England was the only way. They were instead destroying the colonies with this war and murdering good men. Like her father.

She lifted a corner of the thick velvet curtains. Only two and a half blocks to go. She'd suspected Wilsby of his inclinations toward the rebels for a while now. The arrival of Daniel Reid seemed only to solidify both their guilt, and if she was wise, she could use them to her advantage. "We'll be there soon." Lydia dropped the folds of crimson curtain.

"Regretful."

She met his gaze. "Why do you say that?"

He shook his head and looked to his cane. "No reason."

"I do wish you would be more forthright, Mr. Reid, before our journey comes to an end. I can help you."

"How, exactly?"

She gave him a knowing smile. "Before I incriminate myself, tell me truthfully that you are a Patriot."

He studied her for a full minute or more, the methodical plod of hooves and the squeak of the axels marking the passage of time. He sighed and raised his hand. "All right. Now tell me how you plan to assist me?"

I knew it. She grinned and slid to the edge of her seat. "We have a British major billeted with us. And my sister's husband is very loyal to the crown—an outspoken man. You would be surprised how often our table is laden with talk of military strategy and plans." She tipped her head slightly to one side, feigning the look of innocence. The bait was laid for him. The question remained as to whether he would bite.

The carriage lurched to a stop, and Lydia glanced out the window at the modest home of Mr. and Mrs. Lawrence Wilsby. She touched Daniel's arm. "Please do not mention me or my name to the Wilsbys. Not yet."

"Why? They have nothing to do with this. But if they did, why would you be willing to share information with me and not them?"

"Because the fewer who know of my involvement, the better. Not only because it endangers myself, but my whole family. If the British discovered…" Lydia let her words melt away and gave the tiniest shudder.

"Might they not recognize your carriage anyways?"

She shook her head, pleased at the measures she had taken. "I hired this one. These are dangerous times, Mr. Reid." Lydia pulled a handkerchief from her reticule and began to wring it—anything to convince him how frightened she was at being discovered, to get him to trust her. "My family…" She honestly wasn't sure what Charles's reaction would be, but uncompleted thoughts couldn't hurt her pretense. Daniel's mind would hopefully paint a much more horrific picture of consequences than reality.

Two thin creases formed between his eyes as his expression softened. "Your secret is safe, but what proof have I that you speak the truth?"

Lydia's pulse quickened. She could think of no harm that could come by divulging the direction Major

Layton had taken, but if she was mistaken... "I overheard Colonel Tarleton is quite frustrated chasing Colonel Marion and requested Major Layton to head north toward Camden. That's all I have at the moment."

"I will see what I can find out about your major, but for now," one corner of his mouth twitched upward, "I do need to go talk to a man about some land."

Lydia relaxed into her seat. "How do you think you will take to our southern crops? I hear indigo is one of the most common this year. Indigo and rice."

His dark eyes lit. "I admit I have a lot to learn, having spent my youth growing wheat and corn. But I enjoy a challenge."

"I do not doubt it."

Daniel scooted to the edge of his seat and gripped the door handle. "I know your name but not where you live or how to safely get a message to you."

Lydia again kept her desire to grin suppressed. She'd spent some thought on this, as well. "In the livery, your horse is boarded in the third stall."

"How did you—?"

"I will tuck a small pouch on the inside, under the manger with a note. No one should notice it, but it would be unwise to use names or divulge information. Just when to meet. The location will be in the woods southwest of town. Toward the center is an ancient oak. Trust me, you will not mistake it. I will be there."

Daniel climbed down from the coach. His gaze met hers once more before he closed the door. The carriage pulled forward once again, and Lydia sucked a breath to her deprived lungs. Now to meet with Major Layton when he returned and convince him she had an asset worth bargaining for.

~*~

Daniel leaned into his cane as the carriage turned down the next street. He'd know soon enough whether or not he'd just hanged himself or gained a useful ally for South Carolina. Miss Lydia Reynolds seemed sincere, but something left him unsettled. Maybe he simply wasn't comfortable risking her safety.

He pushed the thought aside and turned up the cobblestone walk to the comfortable cottage on the northern outskirts of town. A string of laundered sheets waved in the breeze along the side of the property, and a handful of chickens pecked at the ground. A fine home in his opinion, but he couldn't help but wonder what a lady like Miss Reynolds thought of the place. Likely she considered such an existence below her. And if she did, how much harsher would she judge his family's log cabin in the wilderness along the Mohawk?

Yet again Daniel forced Lydia from his mind and rapped his knuckles against the door. Footsteps approached, and a moment later the door opened to an older woman, a generous amount of gray pulled up under her linen cap. The wrinkles at the corners of her eyes deepened as she looked him over. Her gaze paused at the cane before returning to his face. "Good day, sir. What is it I can do for you?"

"I am looking for Mister Lawrence Wilsby. Is he at home?"

"Aye. He's sitting down to his dinner."

"Though I hate to interrupt a man's meal, I do need to speak with him."

The woman stepped aside and waved Daniel past her, through a poorly lit hall, and to the right into the small dining room. "This man is here to see you," she told the white-haired gentleman seated at the head of the table, knifing butter across a thick slice of bread.

He set both the bread and the knife down and rose to his feet. "Am I mistaken in assuming we haven't met?"

"Not at all, sir." Daniel stepped forward to extend his hand. "This is my first time south of Virginia."

"Though from your speech I place you farther north."

"New York."

"Aye, that sounds about right." Wilsby shook his hand and then pulled him toward a chair. "Have a seat. Would you care for some soup?"

Daniel took the chair but waved aside the offer of food. "I was told by Mrs. Richardson that you might be of assistance to me."

"Oh?" Dark eyebrows rose, creating a field of furrows across his forehead. "The general's widow?"

Daniel nodded. "The same."

"And what did she think I could assist you with?"

He leaned forward with a glance behind to make sure the woman, though probably Wilsby's wife, had left. He leaned his arms across the worn-smooth boards of the table and lowered his voice. "Finding Colonel Marion."

The man sat back. "Marion?"

"Yes."

Lawrence Wilsby stood and shuffled to close the dining room door, before rotating back to Daniel. "I think it is time to tell me exactly who you be and why I should help you."

4

Daniel glanced to the sun's colorful retreat below the horizon. His muscles tensed. After a full day of riding across unfamiliar terrain and trying to avoid swamps, all the while searching for the man known as the *Swamp Fox*, he could well understand the British soldiers' frustrations. Even with the names and directions Wilsby had given him.

"Ho there," a voice rang from a thicket, followed by the rustling of brush. Three men on horseback emerged from the trees and curtains of moss, pistols aimed.

Daniel raised his hands enough to be easily seen. "What do you want?"

The youngest, still a youth, kicked his horse near enough to seize Madam's bridle while the others kept their weapons trained on Daniel. One, half hidden behind a monster of a beard, wagged the barrel of his pistol. "Your horse, guns and any powder you have."

"First, inform me to whose cause I'm contributing."

"To the Continental Army and Colonel Francis Marion's brigade." A straight line of yellowed teeth showed. "Now get down from your mount and don't try anything. We'll give you a voucher to redeem after the war."

Daniel didn't move. "You can have what you've asked for and more. I'm coming with you. After you've given me some proof that you are, in fact, Colonel Marion's men."

The men looked to each other and laughed. "You're a Patriot?"

"I am. Why else would I wander alone in these marshes? I've been searching for Colonel Marion for two days now. But again, how can I be certain you are his men?"

The man waved toward the youth. "Why, this is the Colonel's own nephew, Gabe Marion."

Not exactly evidence, but Daniel didn't doubt their word. Their tricorn hats sported the white cockades Marion's men were becoming known for, and there were too many things about them that screamed 'desperate Patriots who had spent far too long hiding in the back country'. "Then take me to him. I have messages for the Colonel from Colonel Sumter and General Washington."

Gabe's head jerked to him. "General Washington?"

"Yes."

"Well then, let's get back to camp." Gabe released Madam's bridle and reined his horse. Daniel followed suit, matching pace. The others trailed behind. They rode for a while, before plunging back into the forest. Branches brushed Daniel's arms and legs as they moved through the deepening shadows to the edge of a swamp. The surface glistened in the descending light. Then the water swirled as something moved. Daniel pulled Madam to a halt as a set of large eyes appeared in the ripples.

The others paused ahead of him and looked back.

"Is that a…"

Two nostrils appeared as well.

Gabe twisted in his saddle and chuckled. "Aw, that's just a little alligator. He won't bother you as long as you don't stop." He nudged his horse, water spraying as hooves sank into the marsh.

The other two men waited, watching Daniel.

He swallowed. The alligator hadn't moved, but, though most of the body remained under the water, it appeared anything but little. Still, not much choice remained but to follow. He'd just make sure Madam kept her pace and her distance. Daniel didn't look away from the long snout of the overgrown reptile as he entered the marsh.

A second set of eyes rose—even closer.

Daniel laid his heels to Madam's ribs. With his luck one of those massive jaws would take off his boot, foot included. His head felt light with relief as they reached the next swell of dry land. Unfortunately, that was not the only marsh they had to pass through, and with each the sun sat lower, making it impossible to tell if there were more alligators. The only comfort he had was that Gabe rode on ahead and seemed confident in his path. Finally, glints of fires flickered between the trees, and the way opened up to a small clearing filled with men and horses. Most paid the newcomers no heed, while others shouted greetings.

"Young Gabe." A lean man, not overly tall, pushed up from a fallen log and circled a smoldering fire. He took hold of Gabe's horse. "Anything?"

The youth swung down. Likely thirty years separated them in age, but they shared the same prominent nose and dark, low set brows. "No. Tarleton's burning the countryside, though. Any known Patriot farms between here and Jack's Creek." He turned and motioned to Daniel. "And we met this man on our way. He insisted he needs to speak with you."

Daniel took that as his cue and joined them on the ground. He saluted. "Colonel Marion?"

"Yes." Francis Marion returned the gesture. Though not a large man, the way he carried himself denoted command. "You are?"

"Sergeant Daniel Reid. I fought with the Connecticut Line, Sixth Regiment, until two weeks ago."

"And what brings you this far south, Sergeant?"

"General Washington wanted to let the remaining troops in North and South Carolina know that he is not unaware of your situation here. He plans to send General Greene to take over leadership of the area. I have letters from him and also Colonel Sumter. I reported to Sumter first, and he requested I bring them on to you."

"Very well, Sergeant. That is good to hear." Marion smiled and then waved to one of his men. "Morgan, take care of Sergeant Reid's horse," he ordered before turning back to Daniel. "Why don't you come rest yourself, and let us know how the war goes in New England. This past year has left us feeling rather detached."

The man took the reins from Daniel's hands and led Madam away. Uncertainty sank to the pit of Daniel's stomach, residing there even as he found an unoccupied length of log.

The Colonel crouched beside the fire and speared what appeared to be a potato. He passed one to Gabe, who also plopped down, and a second to Daniel. "You are in time to join us for supper."

The vegetable's hot skin burned Daniel's hands,

and he dropped it to his lap while he drew his knife. Pa's knife. The blade had been a gift the evening before Daniel left. How did his family fare now? Last winter had been especially cold. Did they have enough food put away for the one approaching? Was Pa's leg allowing him to keep the farm going? Daniel eyed the knife. It was wrong of him to stay away for so long.

Marion's voice pulled him from his mulling. "So, Sergeant Reid, what do you think of our fair South Carolina?"

Strangely, Lydia Reynolds came to him.

Gabe chuckled. "He wasn't so sure about the 'gators."

"Only because I've never seen the likes of them before," Daniel mumbled, digging into the pale orange flesh of the sweet potato.

"You don't have to worry about them unless you plan to pause and have a chat." A smile stretched across Colonel Marion's face. "You said you are not with the army anymore? How did you get enlisted to mail service?"

"I volunteered." Daniel took another bite, the texture a little dry from roasting over coals, but the flavor and his hunger more than negating that. "I finished my three years of service, but wasn't ready to head home."

"Well, you are in good company, Sergeant. Most every man here is giving his time freely. The men will probably return to their farms in a few weeks, but you're welcome to join as long as you have the mind. That is, if you're done delivering messages."

Daniel stabbed his potato and reached with his free hand to yank off his boot. He rolled down his sock, baring the letters, and passed them to Marion. "Now I am." He pulled his boot back on.

"And do you have something waiting for you up north, or will you consider lending us a hand?"

Daniel glanced into the fire, his mind on the larger ones spotting the countryside. How many more had he seen over the past three years? And before that? Farms and homes that had taken months and years to build up reduced to rubble in under an hour. Weariness laid itself over him, but the thought of home brought no comfort. And who knew, maybe he'd be able to help turn the tide of the war down here. If Miss Reynolds told the truth and was willing to feed him information about the British...

And, he couldn't deny the urge to see her again.

"Well, it looks like you're at least considering it."

"No, I'm not, sir. I mean, I already have. I think I just might have something to offer South Carolina."

~*~

The cuff of her gown cascaded with ripples of lace from her elbow. Lydia set a hand against her abdomen, her stays cinched far too tight, and managed a shallow breath. Adorned in folds of crimson muslin–one of the last gowns her father brought her from France–she'd wasted no efforts in dressing for dinner. Major Layton had returned, and she had a proposition for him.

Both Charles and the major, with their powdered wigs and fine coats, stood as she entered the dining parlor. She gifted the latter, clad in red, with a smile. Charles would learn his best efforts to thwart her independence were in vain. She'd find passage to England without his help.

"You look most lovely, my dear."

Lydia sent him a glare and tipped her chin away.

"Quite correct, Mr. Selby," Major Layton agreed. "Your sister-in-law glows this evening."

The look in his eyes as they toured her from head to hem and back unsettled her stomach, but at least she had his attention. She sat and dinner began, both men conversing over the shipments expected in the next few weeks and other items of business. Lydia only partly listened as she picked away at her food, more than her stays constricting her appetite.

"So what will Colonel Tarleton do now?"

Lydia's attention perked at Charles's question, and she slipped a tiny cut of roast into her mouth as she listened for the answer.

"I am honestly not sure. He was so frustrated after trying to catch that fox, Marion, that he had us burning houses and barns across the countryside to warn rebels. When I left Colonel Tarleton, he was on his way back to Camden and felt quite confident that the rebels were subdued for now—wrote as much to General Cornwallis."

"You sound less than convinced, Major." Lydia set her fork beside her plate. There was no way she could eat another bite.

"Marion has a loyal following among the planters in the area," Major Layton replied. "Burning barns will not endear Colonel Tarleton to anyone. No, we need to strike at the heart, root out the leaders of the rebellion and the others will simply follow like sheep."

"Hard to do when you can't find the leaders. When they are as sly as a fox or, what was it Tarleton called Sumter? A gamecock?"

He chuckled. "Yes. Colonel Tarleton does seem to enjoy comparing our enemies with animals."

"The problem remains." Lydia glanced to the large clock hung over the fireplace as the door to the dining parlor sighed open and Eli stepped in. His timing was perfect.

Eli glanced to her with the a subtle nod before approaching Charles. "The Captain of the *Zephyr* is here to see you. He waits in your study."

Charles pushed up from his seat. "Excuse me, I am sure it is nothing." He gave a slight bow and followed the slave out.

As soon as the door closed, Lydia turned her full attention to Major Layton. It would not take long for Captain Hues to question why he had been sent for. He would inform Charles about the note sent to the *Zephyr* and Charles would return with questions, but hopefully no way to attach the deed to Lydia.

"Major." She gave Major Layton a smile as he looked her way. "Tell me, what would information regarding Marion's camp, his plans, and his tactics, be worth to His Majesty's army? Or to you?"

"A great deal. But why the interest?"

"Would it be worth passage for myself to England?"

His look of surprise melted away to disbelief. "You want to trade information of Marion and his brigade to me for passage? Pray tell, how are you to acquire this information?"

Lydia raised her hand, flattening her palm to him. "I will not tell you. Not until you agree to my terms and conditions. I will not allow you to shove me aside and leave me with nothing. I will find that sly fox, Francis Marion, and you will find me a way back to England."

"So it's passage you desire?" Major Layton sat

back in his chair and gave her an appreciative look. "You know, we needn't complicate things. I am sure there are other exchanges that could be made to pay for your passage. A beautiful woman like you need not resort to a dangerous game of spying to get what she wishes."

Skin crawling, it was all she could do to not grab her goblet and splash its contents into his face before storming out. "If I were not repulsed by such an arrangement, I might not be as anxious to leave Georgetown." Though that was not fair, nor completely true. Charles would marry her and provide for her.

Major Layton's brows rose, then he laughed. "Ah, that explains why you have come to me in the first place. Your brother-in-law owns two fine ships, and yet here you remain."

Lydia dropped her gaze. Her stays bit into her ribs. "Just tell me if we have a bargain. I give you information, and you deliver me safe and sound to England's shores."

Footsteps in the hall announced Charles's return. He strode across the room, his pointed glare on Lydia as he lowered himself into his chair at the head of the table. "The *Zephyr* sails tomorrow and Captain Hues wished to know if I had any last minute instructions."

"I preferred Captain Ross." The one who had served her father. "I do not understand why you replaced him with Hues."

"Hues is a good sailor and a good man."

Lydia couldn't argue the first point, but to her he seemed…secretive. Devious, even.

Charles took a drink of his wine. "Did I miss anything, *my dear*?"

"No." Major Layton touched the corner of his mouth with his napkin. "Miss Reynolds was telling me how well she loved the South Carolina countryside. And how she would hate to leave." He looked to her with a nod. "Someday you will have to accompany me on a ride and show me what secrets this land has to offer."

5

Daniel approached the morning fire, bedroll tucked under his arm.

"Good morning, Sergeant," Marion greeted from his place near the fire. "Have some breakfast."

"Thank you." Daniel took the sweet potato, their staple food the past week, and sat down on the log, letting his bedroll drop behind him. Dawn hugged the horizon, slow to dissipate the haze of blue still draped over the forest. A bird or two announced the day, but most of the men still slept. "What's our next move?"

Before the Colonel had a chance to answer, Gabe stepped over the log and lowered himself beside Daniel. He wore a big grin, though his eyes remained glazed from lack of sleep. "Poor little lizard." Gabe chuckled.

Daniel shook his head. Of course the kid had to remind him.

"What lizard?" The elder Marion leaned forward so he could see his nephew on the other side of Daniel.

"Just a little one looking for a warm place to sleep. Nights are getting cold out here. Seems Sergeant Reid isn't one for sharing, though." Gabe nudged Daniel with his elbow.

"First of all, it wasn't that little of a lizard, and second of all, I like sleeping alone."

"That explains why you're out here with us," the lad shot back.

His uncle gave a laugh, and then a censoring look. "Young Gabe."

Daniel peeled off the blackened surface of his sweet potato, dug out a chunk with the tip of his knife and took a bite of the lukewarm mush, reheated from last night's dinner. "No, it's fine. In a lot of ways he's right."

"You are unmarried?"

As always that word beckoned thoughts of Rachel Garnet. Standing before her on the land he had worked so hard for, the little cabin in the background, the stream running behind him. The moment had been perfect, as though God Himself arranged it just for them. The ground had been soft under his knee when he'd slipped down to ask her to be his wife. Their one kiss still haunted him—that moment she'd softened in his arms, only to pull away and ask for time.

Time.

He'd been such a fool. She'd never felt anything for him. Friendship, perhaps. But not love. Daniel cleared his throat, and attempted the same with his mind, refusing to give her more thought. "No. I'm not married. The only woman I wanted chose a British captain instead." He no longer held anything against Andrew Wyndham—except for the fact he lived the life Daniel wanted, on his land, and with the woman he'd loved.

"Ouch." Gabe grimaced beside him.

"That was a long time ago." And he needed to move on. Thankfully, only two men witnessed his confession. Daniel took another bite, minding the glinting edge of his knife as he pushed the sweet potato into his mouth. "What is the plan for today, Colonel?"

Marion rested his elbows on his knees and extended his hands toward the fire. "It's been a busy week for the British and Tories, but for now we'll sit low. Day after tomorrow we'll start toward the Black River through Williamsburg and then on toward Georgetown."

Daniel brought his head up. "Maybe I should ride on ahead and into Georgetown. My...friend there might know what the redcoats have planned. Besides, if I keep up appearances, they might decide I'm harmless enough."

Gabe nodded to where Daniel's saddle leaned against a tree, the walking cane still strapped across the side. "Your limp better be as good as your story."

"I've seen how it's done most of my life," Daniel said, not letting the guilt linger as he had in the past. "My pa had his leg crushed under a felled tree when I was a boy. He's struggled with that limp for a lot of years now. That cane is supposed to be for him." He'd wanted his father to have something nice. "But I imagine it'll serve me well enough while I'm here."

Colonel Marion didn't look as confident. "I would feel better if you could tell me more about your *friend.*"

"I would sir, but..." Daniel glanced around. Lydia had asked him not to reveal her identity to anyone, but surely her secret would be safe with the colonel and his nephew. He was already prepared to trust them with his own life. "If you could first promise me no one will hear her name besides yourselves—"

"Her?" Marion raised a brow but nodded. "You have our word."

"Miss Reynolds. Lydia Reynolds." Daniel liked the way her name felt on his tongue. The way it sounded. With her dark hair and brilliant eyes, Lydia suited her well. "Her family are Tories, and she fears for both them and herself if anyone were to know of her true loyalties. They have a British officer quartered in their home."

Marion stood. "All right, Sergeant, ride ahead and meet up with us as soon as you can. You know our route."

"Yes, sir." He finished his potato as Marion moved toward the horses.

Other men rose from their bedrolls and hurried to light fires. Daniel chuckled to himself. He'd heard more and more grumbling as temperatures dropped, but he didn't understand it. Sure, the damp air made the chill penetrate his clothes a little more, but otherwise it wasn't much colder than a late summer morning in New England.

Gabe picked up a stick and rolled another sweet potato from the coals. The corners of his mouth twitched upward. "So, this friend—the one who says she can get you information from the redcoats—is she pretty?"

Daniel tossed the charred skin of his sweet potato in the fire and gave the lad a pointed look, and then clapped him on the back. Daniel took his bedroll to his saddle and tied it into place. *Yes.* Though nothing like Rachel Garnet, he could not deny that Lydia Reynolds was indeed a beautiful woman.

~*~

Lydia left the door open as she stepped into what had been father's private library, his refuge when home from voyages. They had made no changes to the room since his death. She breathed deeply of the sweet, musty smell of paper, and brushed her fingertips over the embossed leather spines of books. Morning light filtered through the large windows and past heavy maroon drapes, while dust motes danced their welcome. She'd avoided this room since Father's death three years earlier. Though he'd often been gone on one voyage or another, she'd still loved him with all her heart. Just as she had loved Margaret. Mother. Little David and Martin. Everyone gone...but her. They had left, leaving her nothing but fear. She would never let herself hurt like that again—pain that still haunted, tearing through her whenever she thought of her family.

"What do you have for me?"

Lydia spun to Major Layton as he sauntered into the room. She laid her hand to her collar and caught her breath. "Nothing as of yet. I had someone watch the livery, and the rebel returned to Georgetown last night. I was about to write a message asking him to meet me."

He walked to her father's desk and perched on the corner. "Then why did you ask to speak with me?"

She forced her hands to relax at her sides. She couldn't have him know how nervous this whole affair made her. Her success was too vital. "If I am to be a spy *for* the rebels, I need information to give them. Something they can prove true, but inconsequential at the same time."

"Ah, I see what you mean. To gain their trust."

"Precisely." She couldn't very well tell Mr. Reid everything she'd overheard at the dinner table. That would only make her a traitor, too.

The major stood and paced the distance between the desk and the door, his polished boots beating out his steps. After a couple of minutes, he turned to her and straightened the crisp scarlet coat, a sharp contrast to his white breeches. "I have it. The Allston's plantation. But timing will be vital. Today is the thirteenth. We can't have him passing along this information until the fifteenth."

"What information is that, sir?"

"Tell him that you've learned Loyalists have pitched camp at Allston's plantation. Make it sound like a small group."

"But not until the fifteenth."

"Yes." He gave a smile. "By then a larger company will be on their way there. You see, it is perfect, Miss Reynolds, the information you give will be accurate, just incomplete. Something they cannot fault you for."

But would deceive them nonetheless. A trap. Lydia's stomach tightened without the assistance of her stays. What had she been thinking when she'd conceived this plan? "But how will I hold him off for that long?"

Layton chuckled, circling her. "This is your game, Miss Reynolds. But I will give you some advice. If you want to truly gain his trust so he'll offer you information, you need to do more than spy for him. You have a lot of charm when you want to. Use it."

"Sir, I..." Lydia raised her chin. Though her words faltered, her gaze did not. Major Layton needed to accept that she would never lower herself to the level of a tavern maid. She may not be a lady of name, or title, or even wealth anymore, but she had been raised a lady.

He only smiled. "Try your hand at getting this rebel to give you information, but if it does not work, as I highly suspect it shan't, then I shall take over and show you how to properly get information out of a man." He leaned near, his breath hot on her neck. "If you cannot break him with pleasure, then we will have to try pain."

Lydia hastened back a step and gripped the edge of the bookshelf. "I will get the information. Do not concern yourself about that, sir. And this way you can use him to feed the rebels bits of news, as well. How much more useful will that be? Just see that you are ready to keep your side of our bargain. I am already packing my luggage. I will not stay here longer than I absolutely must."

"Of course." His tone still conveyed doubt.

"I will find Colonel Marion's camp for you."

"The *Swamp Fox*, Miss Reynolds. If you are to walk with the rabble, you should be careful to talk like them. That's what the *Patriots* have begun to call their Colonel Marion." With a shallow bow, he turned, strode to the doorway, and then looked back. "I must say, Miss Reynolds, I always found you a handsome woman, but this new side to you, the fire that ignites your eyes..." He saluted. "I almost feel sorry for the poor rebel. But yes, I will stand back and allow you to try it your way first."

Lydia leaned into the shelves of books as Major Layton's footsteps bade her farewell. Good riddance. She filled her lungs to their full capacity and slowly released the breath. She had a limited time to prove productive in her interrogating, but she would not fail.

Seated in her father's chair, Lydia withdrew a sheet of stationary from the top drawer, filled the ink well, and picked up her father's quill pen. His favorite. She slipped the silky feather between her fingers, an ache rising in her chest. Mother had given the pen to him the year before the smallpox epidemic that had taken her and the boys.

Lydia hurried her motions, not caring about the ink blots she dribbled across the page, or giving it enough time to dry sufficiently. She blew on her scrawled letters once, and then rolled the note into a small pouch.

~*~

Daniel tucked the note into his pocket, the muscles in his cheeks contracting at the corners of his mouth. He wasn't sure why he wanted to smile, but for some reason the thought of Miss Lydia Reynolds evoked the reaction. With his weight on his cane with each step, he made his way to his saddled horse and passed a coin to the stable boy. "Thanks."

Getting into the saddle while feigning his injury was not easy, but he had practiced. Madam shifted under him, anxious for his command. A click of the tongue was the only encouragement required. Perhaps she sensed his own eagerness.

Outside of town, Daniel slowed his mount. He needed to get his mind straightened out. This was not the time or place for developing attachments, and Miss Reynolds was not the woman. Though it didn't bother him that she was well bred and probably more educated than him, the fact that such might bother her, bothered him. He'd been foolish enough where Rachel was concerned and they'd been cut from the same cloth, their families homesteading the Mohawk Valley together. He wouldn't set himself up for failure again.

Daniel rode west a short way, before turning south into a thickly wooded area. Towering trees spread almost naked branches overhead, only a few gold and brown leaves left clinging. Rays of sun danced across him, and the mat of moss and freshly fallen leaves silenced the usual plodding of Madam's hooves, leaving the rustle of the breeze and the twittering of birds the only insurgence against complete serenity. But how was he supposed to find one specific tree in the middle of—

Daniel reined Madam in at the sight of a great trunk. Branches, like huge arms, extended in every direction, a couple bending low against the earth as though the tree had become too weary to hold them up anymore. Daniel swung from the saddle, not bothering with his cane. No one was likely to see him out here and he was honestly too mesmerized to care. Up north he'd cut acres of evergreen and cottonwood, and even some oak with Pa, but he'd never seen anything like this, even in the back country of New York. He'd already been impressed by the cypresses along the marshes, the growth no doubt the result of ample water and warmth, but this...

"Beautiful, isn't it?"

Daniel's head jerked to where Lydia walked around the broad base of the tree, ducking under one branch that rivaled her for thickness, and stepping over another. "Yes, it is."

"Even more so in the summer with everything brilliantly green."

"I imagine so." Daniel wrapped Madam's reins around the smaller end of a limb, his gaze never deviating from Lydia.

She sat on the branch she had crossed over. Though more than a foot and a half in diameter, the massive limb swooped to run parallel to the earth a short distance before drooping against the leaf-littered ground.

"I got your message."

"I gathered." Her hands were clasped together on her lap as she watched him with those lake-green eyes. "I am glad you returned when you did. I have news."

6

Lydia stood as Daniel secured his mare to a smaller branch and walked to the wide base of the oak. He laid his hand over the ridged bark and filled his lungs. "This tree is magnificent. How old do you think it is?"

"I am sure I do not know. But yes, it is magnificent." A loose strand of hair tickled her cheek as a breeze stole through the grove from the nearby bay. "I love it here." Something she would miss when she left South Carolina, but undoubtedly England also boasted beautiful forests.

Daniel turned to her, but his gaze only skimmed over her before he looked up at the expanse of branches above them. "What have you found out?"

"Colonel Tarleton has given up pursuit of Colonel Marion for now." She gave him her most winsome smile. "Once again the Swamp Fox has outwitted the English hound."

Daniel's mouth pulled up at that.

"Tarleton is tracking Colonel Sumter now. Up by Camden." Common enough knowledge. Nothing that would hurt the British. "I also know groups of Loyalists are gathering in the area at some of the local plantations. I did not have a chance to find out which ones, but tomorrow Major Layton has guests—officers. They often become quite free with their conversation, so if you can wait another day…"

Daniel rapped his knuckles against the tree. "I suppose a day won't hurt."

"When does Colonel Marion expect you back? You found him?" Lydia held her voice even though her heart did little skips as she turned the questioning.

"Yes, I found him. And I told him about you."

Her chest seized. "Surely you understand it is not safe for me? If anyone else found out—if the wrong people..." There were those who knew exactly where her true loyalties rested.

"Only the Colonel and Gabriel Marion, his nephew. No one else knows. I trust the man. With my life."

"And with mine, it seems."

"Yes."

Lydia gave a sigh. There was nothing for it now. She did not know Francis Marion personally, so as long as he kept his silence and trusted Daniel's opinion of her... "And the nephew?"

"Cut from the same cloth." Daniel shook his head and gave a bit of a chuckle. "He's a good lad. Young, but on fire with our cause. Already a lieutenant. He'll do his family proud. The Colonel is unmarried and has no children, but I get the impression that's how he feels for young Gabe."

"*Young* Gabe?"

"Gabriel's a family name. His grandfather, and father, I think. Or another uncle."

The man was talking, but saying nothing she could use. Lydia took a step closer. "His parents must worry for him, camping out in the swamps. Some of the areas near the Santee River are not very welcoming. Any number of places might make for a perfect hideout, but goodness knows what conditions you would have to endure."

A nod was all Daniel gave.

"Where have you been camping?"

He shrugged—cursed man. "Here and there. Only spent two nights in the same place so far. Too much to do to settle in, I reckon. Maybe once winter arrives." He flashed a boyish smile. "If it ever does."

Lydia hid her hands behind her back so he could not see them work the fabric of her gown, the only exit she had for the frustration heating her blood. She had to keep her expression soft. "What are the Swamp Fox's plans now with Tarleton and his Dragoons no longer breathing down his neck?"

Again a shrug, but Daniel only lifted one shoulder this time. "That probably depends on what I learn from you."

"Where are you to meet up with him? Do you have far to go?"

"Depends how long it takes me to get that information about the Tory camps."

Lydia turned, stepped back to the low sweeping branch, and sat down. It was either that or strangle the man. Why could he not give her a direct answer for once? Would she risk raising his suspicions by asking any more questions?

Daniel regarded her much too closely. "It's a little nerve wracking, isn't it?" He folded his arms. His rich brown eyes bored right through her.

"What?"

"Spying."

The blood drained from her head, almost making her swoon. "Excuse me?"

"Having a British major in your home, and your family looking over your shoulder as you sneak letters and meet in secret."

A gust of air huffed from her lungs. She hadn't been discovered. Still, her hand trembled as she raised it to her chest.

"I'm sorry." Daniel dropped to his knee in front of her and cupped her elbow. "I didn't mean to upset you. I only wanted you to know how much I respect what you're doing for our freedom. Your bravery is inspiring. You should know that." His hand slipped to hers, embracing it with warmth, his callused palm creating a perfect cocoon. "I will do everything within my power to make sure no one ever suspects you."

She tried to work moisture into her dry mouth. "Thank you."

Daniel's gaze held hers a moment too long and she looked away, glancing to his hands. He quickly withdrew. "I'm afraid that was rather presumptuous. Forgive me. I…" He shook his head as he backed away. "If you have nothing else right now, I should go. I'll keep my head low and meet you back here tomorrow evening."

"No. Not tomorrow," she said too quickly. He couldn't have the information until the fifteenth. "Um…I shan't be able to get away after dinner. If anyone saw me…it might be considered suspect. I will meet you here the next morning."

"All right." He collected his reins and mounted. A single nod and he was gone.

"Oh, God, help me." Lydia glanced heavenward through the canopy of bare branches. Mother had been religious, but Father had never had the time for "such nonsense" after her death. Lydia had not bothered with prayer either, but perhaps it was time to start.

~*~

Daniel applied pressure with his heels, encouraging Madam's gait. Away from Lydia Reynolds. As much as he wanted to look back, Daniel wouldn't let himself. It had felt too good to wrap her hand in his, the urge to protect her surging through him. Irrational. That's what any attraction to her was. He'd already made one disastrous mistake with love, and he wouldn't do it again no matter how much her smile reminded him of home, or her patriotism stirred him. Or how the dark fringe of lashes, contrasting the paleness of her blueish irises, made her eyes appear so large. And innocent.

A scoundrel. That's what he was. Daniel slowed his horse. He was within sight of the road and needed to clear his head before he entered the village. Georgetown. A hornet's nest of redcoats and Loyalists and he was letting a wide-eyed girl risk everything spying for him. Maybe he should stop her before she stepped too far into harm's way. What if he were cursed to hurt every woman he learned to care for?

"You don't care for her. Not like that." Daniel spoke the words out loud, needing to hear them. His attraction to the young woman was undeniable, but it could go no further. He only felt protective of her because he had sisters. He wouldn't risk one of them this way.

A narrow cart drawn by a single horse rattled down the road past him on its way into town. The farmer guiding the horse gave Daniel a passing glance. Pushing reservations aside for the time being, he moved onto the path—at the same time a troop of King's soldiers emerged from between the buildings ahead, coming toward him. Daniel stiffened but kept true to course. Technically, he was no longer in the Continental Army, and nothing should lend suspicion to his affiliation with Marion or Sumter. For today Daniel was just another British colonist.

The stocky, scarlet-clad officer led his six men around the cart, but slowed as they approached Daniel. With the raise of his hand the officer drew to a halt, and his troop followed. "Good day, sir. I'm Lieutenant Mathews. You have business in Georgetown?"

"I do."

"You look an able-bodied man. Why are you not serving your king?"

Daniel leaned back and gave his cane a pat. "Who's to say I haven't already given the king what I can?" Like a fight the king and his men would not soon forget. King George deserved a fervent rebellion against his tyranny.

"Where did you fight?"

Daniel smiled. "New England. Albany. Saratoga. I'm not much use to them anymore, so I came south. I heard the king still had a strong hold on South Carolina, so I decided this might be the place for me." A place he could show the king and his troops that the Continentals weren't about to roll over and submit.

Lieutenant Mathews settled into his saddle. He seemed harmless enough. Not the same cunning as men like Tarleton. "What is your trade?"

"I was a farmer," Daniel said. "Or planter, as I hear them called around here. I'm looking to get myself some land." Someday. Somewhere. Like that valley near the Mohawk that had been his for a whole two months.

"The indigo and rice grown in this colony feed the

war." The lieutenant waved to Daniel's leg. "But can you manage a farm?"

Daniel thought of his father. Benjamin Reid needed his cane for over a decade now and it hadn't stopped him from braving the wilderness, clearing land, planting fields. A man could do whatever he had the mind to. "I get by. Especially if I get some healthier bodies to do the work for me." Though he smiled and chuckled, the thought of owning another man, no matter what his color of skin, didn't sit well. Maybe that's what it took to build and maintain the stretching farms and huge houses this colony boasted, but he'd be happier with a few dozen acres and the simple frame house he'd promised Rachel the day he'd proposed marriage.

"Good to hear it. I'll let you about your business, then."

"Thank you, sir." Daniel snugged down his tricorn hat and nudged his horse forward with his "good" leg. Madam gave the bit a chomp and a tug, then nickered low and started forward, weaving past the soldiers. More streamed from the town—a whole company. The commander's shoulder bore the insignia of a major. Lydia's major possibly? Daniel refused eye contact as the man looked him over. Not quite the serpent Tarleton was. More like a vulture. A red turkey vulture with a powdered wig.

Just before entering town, Daniel glanced behind at the lobsterbacks. The soldiers continued on while the major and lieutenant paused with their mounts off to the side of the road, eyes on Daniel.

So much for keeping his head low.

7

Lydia flinched as Charles took her elbow, slowing her descent down the stairway. He circled in front of her. Now a step lower, their gazes were level. "I know you are up to something." Even with his voice hushed, it held an edge. A sharp one.

"I do not know what you are talking about." She jerked her arm away.

"Yes, you do. But it is no good. Major Layton has nothing. He has worked his way up ranks because he cannot afford to buy a commission. I have made inquiries. His family resides on the fringe of society. Barely more than peasants. To attach yourself to such a man would—"

"You think I intend to marry him? I assure you I have no such plans or thoughts."

Charles folded his arms. "Then perhaps you play a more dangerous game. I implore you, Lydia, if only for the reputation of your family, do not—"

"I assure you I would do nothing to damage my family's memory, or my own reputation." She shook her head at him. "And I have no idea where the basis for such insinuations has come from."

Charles's expression remained as staunch as ever. "I've seen how he admires you, which cannot be faulted. But for you to return his sly glances. And the meetings in the library? I have a mind to suggest the major take his residence elsewhere. Hushed conversations. Passed notes. And you deny all of this?"

Had she really been so obvious? Lydia set her hand to the polished oak banister. "I deny nothing—our interactions are simply not what you assume them to be. If you must know, I have of late taken a keen interest in the war efforts and the state of Georgetown, and the major has merely been keeping me informed." She raised her chin at Charles's look of disbelief. "You may ask Major Layton himself. You may even join us in the library after supper if you care to."

Taking her skirts in hand, Lydia brushed past him. The fullness of her gown forced him to shuffle aside. Inviting him to join them might prove a mistake, but she already knew what the major wanted her to tell Daniel, and it would give her opportunity to lay Charles's concerns to rest.

Major Layton and the several lower officers he'd invited upon her request already visited in the dining parlor as she entered, Charles at her heels. The officers stood.

"Good evening, gentlemen." As Lydia moved to her seat, she trained her expression to one less severe than she had a mind for. The food was served, and she busied herself with the meal, letting the hum of the men's conversation remain a buzz in her ears. She really had little interest in this war. Why should she when England would soon be her home?

"It is difficult to be sure of our true allies with the ebb and sway of people in the area."

The major's statement brought up Lydia's head. There was something about the way he said it, as though the words were discreetly aimed at her.

"Like that man you questioned coming into Georgetown yesterday, Lieutenant Mathews." Major

Layton looked to Lydia, an intensity darkening his eyes. "A New Englander in want of some land. He has a lame leg he claims is a result of fighting for the Crown, but how can anyone be sure in a case such as this? As a peasant farmer, he has no documents confirming the fact."

Lydia dabbed her napkin to the corner of her mouth before replacing it to the table beside her plate. Was the major inquiring if the man were *her* Patriot? She swallowed past the tightness in her throat. It should hardly matter if Daniel Reid was known to the British—Major Layton had already promised he would let her handle the rebel—but the thought left her uneasy. "Does anything make you doubt him?"

"Not offhand. But this past week I have found myself watching newcomers like this man with extra suspicion. How can we be certain how many spies we have in our midst?" He gave a half-smile and took a sip of wine.

Lydia made no reply, returning her attention to her food. She ate quickly and excused herself. Leaving was expected of her anyway so the men could have more time for their talk.

"Before you go, Miss Reynolds," Major Layton called and raised his wineglass. "Gentlemen, let us toast the health of our lovely hostess."

They all rose and drank, and she curtsied her reply before again turning to the door.

"Colonel Tarleton will be joining us in three days," the major continued. "I told him you and Mr. Selby would be pleased to hold a dinner in his honor."

Lydia glanced back and smiled, refraining from the shudder that always rose at the thought of Tarleton. Rumor had it he was quite the scoundrel when it came to women. "Of course. Good evening, gentlemen." She sped to her escape.

The hinges on the library door creaked as she pushed it open. A testament to the room's lack of use. The sun dimmed in the window, but Lydia didn't bother with a lamp or candle. She sat in her father's chair and leaned her head against the tall back, the leather stained a dark brown—a similar shade to her New Englander's eyes. She smoothed her hands over the arms and focused instead on the wall of books. Encyclopedias, histories, novels and ship records. Leather-bound and pristine. Father had collected them one by one and read each in turn. He'd been proud of his library for that reason. Not as extensive as others she'd seen, but Martin Reynolds had been able to boast what few others could.

Meanwhile, she had read very few.

Lydia ran her fingers along the stained wood of the desk. The quill pen and ink pot remained where she'd left them after writing Daniel the note to meet. What sort of man was Mr. Reid? He seemed intelligent enough—he'd easily sidestepped every one of her questions. A man with confidence. Too much, really, walking into the lion's mouth here in Georgetown. Major Layton watched for him and possibly even knew his identity. Was Daniel aware?

He was a fool, and that would be his downfall.

Lydia traced her finger down the drawer on the right side of the desk, and then eased it open. Inside were papers, untouched for three years, another quill, and a book lying face down. Perhaps the one Father had been reading before he left on that last voyage? She withdrew the volume and turned it over in her hands. *The Holy Bible.* That made no sense. Her father disliked religion. Yet memories stirred, faded and abstract. More a sensation of familiarity. She opened the cover. Elegant script marked the first page.

My darling Louisa,

May God hold you in His kind palm as you travel those great waters to your new home in the Americas to be with your husband. Be safe and forever in our prayers.

Your mother.

The ink blurred, and Lydia blinked to clear her vision. This book had been her mother's, a parting gift from her grandmother. How long had the Bible been tucked away? Lydia stared at the page for a long time before closing the cover and lowering the book to her lap. She took up a blank piece of stationary and the quill. A dab of ink.

Dear gentlemen,

I am weary and have decided to retire for the evening. We shall continue our conversation about the war at a later date.

Lydia Reynolds

Not wanting to pass by the dining room and risk being detained, she tucked the Bible under her arm and took the back stairs up to her chambers. The note remained behind on the desk where Major Layton or Charles could easily find it.

~*~

Daniel paced near the base of the ancient oak. He'd waited for almost an hour and his patience was spent. Miss Reynolds had promised him information this morning, but how much longer could he delay? If all had gone according to plan, Colonel Marion would be only a few miles north of Georgetown.

The swish of fabric and scamper of feet turned him toward town. The form of a woman appeared between the trees, rushing in his direction. She slipped the hood of her cloak from her head as she slowed her approach. "I came as soon as I was able."

His edginess ebbed much more than it should. "What have you found out?"

"Allston's Plantation, just north of here. Loyalists are camped there."

"How many?"

"From what I understood, only a few, but they have been collecting gunpowder. I do not know specifics." Her eyebrows pushed together forming a single crease between. "I wish I had more. I had hoped to be of greater help to you."

Daniel's feet rooted to the ground at the regret in her voice. And those eyes of hers, so open and disarming. But she'd given him a location, and Colonel Marion would soon be deploying his troops. Daniel patted her arm and forced himself to where Madam pawed the ground, not as quick to recover from impatience. She disliked being tied in one place for too long. "Thank you for trying. Even that one location should help." Daniel pulled his foot in the stirrup and swung his other leg over the back of the horse. She nickered low and tried to sidestep. He tightened the reins. "I shouldn't keep the Swamp Fox waiting."

"Where is he?"

Daniel glanced down at her. "A very good question." But hopefully it wouldn't take too long to find the colonel.

"What direction are you headed?" Lydia had followed him and stood only feet away, her dark tresses piled in elegant knots at the back of her head with only a few strands laid across her pale skin. The darker blue of her irises merged with a hint of green toward the centers. The beauty of innocence.

Daniel fixed his grip on the reins. The less Lydia knew about what went on outside of Georgetown, the better. Too much knowledge was never safe.

"Do you have far to go?" She was a curious little thing.

"Thank you, Miss Reynolds." He tugged Madam's head around and spurred her into a gallop, directly west. He'd give Georgetown a wide berth before circling north.

~*~

Lydia clenched her teeth until her jaw ached. If she could breathe fire, no doubt flames would flare from her nostrils. Daniel Reid would be the death of her by pure frustration. Maybe she hadn't given him much information he could use against the British, but the least he could do was answer one of her questions.

As she neared the house, Lydia slowed her steps and her breath.

Lieutenant Mathews's stout form stood on the veranda with a dozen men in red already mounted nearby. Major Layton likely waited in the library for any information she had gleaned. If he suspected her failure, he would step in and get the information from Reid using his own methods, and she would be left with no passage to England.

Cursed New Englander!

Lydia walked past the men without a word. The less anyone knew about her involvement the better. She went directly to the library.

The major stood from Father's chair. "How was your morning stroll, Miss Reynolds?"

"Fine, thank you." But she wasn't there to mince words with him. "Your fox is hiding somewhere west of here. Not far. Either way, I'm sure they will make their way to Allston's Plantation."

His mouth stretched into a smile. He slid his hands into white gloves, and started past her. "Well done. I shall go a-hunting." He walked to the front where his men waited.

Lydia stepped forward and closed the door of the library, shutting herself off from the rest of the house—the rest of the world. If the kind God her mother believed in did exist, maybe they would run the Swamp Fox to ground, Lydia would be given the credit, and a way would be prepared for her to escape this place. And the memories that pressed over her with the weight of millstones. She glanced at Father's chair and its dark leather.

If the British had success today, perhaps she could also be done with spying, lies...and all-too-confident rebels with rich brown eyes.

8

"Sergeant, where have you been?"

Daniel reined Madam alongside Colonel Marion's mount. Two miles north of Georgetown, they hadn't been difficult to locate. "I'm sorry, sir. I was waiting on information."

"And?"

"The Allston Plantation. That's where a group of Loyalists have set up camp."

Marion rubbed his palm over his day-old stubble and glanced around. "Do you know how many?"

If only. "I'm afraid not, sir, but it didn't sound like a lot."

"Good. Colonel Horry has already started toward the White Plantation with a couple companies. Word has it a large band is forming there." He twisted in his saddle. "Captain Melton."

A burly man nudged his mount forward to join them. "Sir?"

"Take your patrol down Sampit Road, and find out how many men the Loyalists have gathered at Will Allston's place."

Daniel nodded to the captain. "I can go along if you want me."

"I'll come too," Gabe boomed, pushing his horse to the front of the lines. "Better than waiting around here to see if we'll get in on the action."

Daniel chuckled at the elder Marion's censoring

glare at his nephew.

"Permission granted." The Colonel sighed. "Just don't be telling your mother when you go home next week."

The youth grinned and gave his horse a kick. Daniel did likewise, taking the place beside Gabe. The boy had an energy that made him a pleasure to be around. As the animals matched strides, Daniel couldn't help wondering what it would have been like to have a younger brother. He loved his sisters but enjoyed the camaraderie another male provided.

He chuckled to himself. Taking into consideration his own temper and all the mischief he'd gotten into at Gabe's age, perhaps the Lord knew what He was doing sending him sister after sister after sister. That didn't mean Daniel couldn't enjoy his nephew someday, as Colonel Marion seemed to.

His nephew. Joseph and Fannie's boy. Strange to think of the child, because he'd never seen him. Little James Garnet, named for Joseph and Rachel's father, would be almost two now, and, according to the last letter from home that had reached him—almost six months ago—Fannie was already expecting a second babe.

Men surrounded Daniel, yet loneliness spiked through him. What was he doing down here, hiding after so long? The war raged just as fiercely in New York as it did in South Carolina. He had to leave the past in the past and be open to new possibilities. Pale blue-green eyes rose in his mind along with a pretty face framed with dark hair. *Lydia.*

"I see you're clean shaven again," Gabe said with a long, sideways glance, saving him from stray thoughts.

"I believe that is civilization's mandate." Daniel smoothed a hand across his jaw. He'd shaved every morning he'd been in Georgetown. "Be glad you don't have to worry about that yet."

"I've shaved," Gabe protested.

Daniel cocked a brow at the youth. "Just for the sake of it?"

He shrugged and they both laughed.

"Remember, hot water makes all the difference," Daniel said.

"As does having someone who appreciates it?" Gabe's grin returned. "Like a beautiful woman. Though you never said whether or not she was pretty."

"For all you know she might be a sixty-year-old grandmother."

"But she isn't, is she? I've heard enough fire-side conversations. I can tell when a man is attracted to the subject, *Sergeant*."

Daniel shook his head, suppressing the urge to smile at the lad's use of his rank. It was easy to forget that the boy was indeed his superior. With the young Marion it seemed to give them leveler footing. "Then I guess there is no denying it to you, Lieutenant."

A chortle broke from Gabe's chest. "Maybe you should consider settling here once the redcoats have gone home. How do you like South Carolina so far?"

"It's warm."

Gabe looked at him, his puzzled expression making Daniel want to chuckle.

"Honestly, I'm used to a good dump of snow by now and below freezing temperatures. If this is the best your winter has…" His thoughts faded as Captain Melton waved the troop off the main road.

Trees loomed around them but the way lay open

enough to pass unhindered. Moss draped across the branches above made up for the leaves that now padded the path. The noonday sun glimmered, and long strands glowed with tones of gray-blue. After a while the ground sloped. Mud clung to the horses' hooves. Marshes stretched out before them.

"Can you ride anywhere in this area without swimming?" Daniel had to ask.

Gabe's throat rumbled with a laugh much like his uncle's, though adolescent. "Hardly swimming. Your boots aren't even getting wet."

"Not yet. I'm just waiting for one of those alligators I'm sure is lurking below the surface to grab hold of my boot and take me for a swim."

"Don't worry." Gabe clapped him on the back. "If one does, I'll shoot him before he can take off your whole leg."

Not very comforting. "Thanks."

"Besides, in the winter they're less active."

"But possibly more hungry." Cold weather had that effect on most creatures Daniel knew.

As they rose from the swamp, a rustle drew his gaze from the murky water to the men and horses becoming visible through the trees up ahead. Scarlet coats stood out among the earth tones worn by the Tories. A shout rose from both sides at the same time, and men grabbed for their guns.

Daniel snatched his pistol from his side and fired at the nearest enemy. The air erupted around him, cracking with the discharge of muskets and clouding with smoke. Daniel didn't watch to see whether or not his target fell as he scrambled for another ball and his power horn.

Madam jerked her head and pawed backwards as

the British rushed them. As he brought his pistol back up, she lurched sideways, and then dropped out from under him. Her body pinned his leg, crushing his ankle into the ground as she spasmed. Thick blood poured from her neck.

A musket ball dug the earth a foot from Daniel's head. He jerked his pistol toward the charging Tory on horseback and fired. A miss. Daniel pressed himself to the dirt and covered his head with his elbows as the animal leaped over him. The sharp edge of a hoof scored his sleeve. He dropped his pistol and clutched his thigh. He had to get free.

A bolt of agony ripped up Daniel's leg as he writhed his foot out of his boot and from under Madam. Her body still trembled with life, but he could do nothing for her now. He rolled out of the way of the battle and into the embrace of the marsh. The slimy, cool water swallowed him as he slid toward a cluster of dead reeds. No one seemed aware of his departure, but he took his knife to hand, the only weapon remaining to him. His pulse filled his ears as he watched the Patriots attempt a retreat. The scarlet-clad soldiers and their allies swarmed them with at least three times the men.

Daniel sunk into the reeds and grass rising from the shore, submerging all but his head below the surface. His chest compressed as numbness set into his body, stealing some of the pain. He was helpless to do anything but sit silent as one of the British officers rode past and put a ball into Madam's head. And the heart of one of Captain Melton's wounded men.

Daniel wiped a wet hand over his face and glanced heavenward. Would there ever be an end to such brutality? Already a cry of triumph wafted from the main group of Brits. They had given up chase and were returning. Daniel hunkered down lower, depriving his lungs to keep their motion slow. If he were killed, how long before Mama and the rest of his family knew...or would they ever? Would they be left to wonder why he hadn't ever returned? There'd be no record of him after he left his regiment in New York, and only a handful of officers knew of his mission to South Carolina. If he survived this, he needed to write his family.

They deserved to know where he was. Mama deserved a lot more than that.

A cry of pain and a pleading voice pulled Daniel's focus back to the enemy and a prisoner. Daniel squinted through the reeds, blinking the droplets of muddy water from his eyelashes. A group of Tories thrust the young man forward, beating him down with the butts of their muskets.

Homespun breeches and light blue shirt, light brown hair falling over his face...Gabe.

No!

Daniel's fingers ached from his grip on the knife. He couldn't sit here while that boy—

"He's one of Marion's own kin."

The cry rose loud and multiplied. Before anyone else could react, a man stepped forward and laid the barrel of his musket to Gabe's chest. The boom reverberated through Daniel's core and he sagged back, burying his face with his hands. "Oh, God, no." *Not that boy, Lord. Not Gabe.*

~*~

A soft glow of moonlight stretched across the

room and the quilt covering her legs. Lydia set the lamp aside and slid the Bible onto the stand. Smothering a yawn, she laid back and sank into the pillow. Her gaze remained on the book. Its words seemed both foreign and familiar—rhetoric she had heard on occasion—and were accompanied by the strangest feeling of belonging.

The rush of heavy footsteps to the front door was followed by rumble voices. Then the slam of the door. Her mind followed the voices through the house and back, to the bottom of the stairs.

Major Layton. He'd returned. But what had happened today?

Pushing the blankets aside, Lydia rose and wrapped in a robe. Feet bare, her steps were silent as she crept to the head of the stairs. She froze.

Major Layton peered up at her, Lieutenant Mathews at his side. The lieutenant averted his eyes while the major smiled her way.

She slunk back a step to conceal her feet.

"You did very well, Miss Reynolds. But our arrangement might have to be adjusted." He raised his hand, his fist wrapped around a cane. The brass handle glinted in the lamp light. "If my suspicions are correct, your rebel informant may no longer be of use to you."

"What is this?" Charles joined her at the top of the stair though his hands still worked to fasten the ties of his midnight-blue robe. His eyes glowed almost as dark. "What arrangement did you have? A rebel informant? Tell me the meaning of this, Lydia."

His words bombarded her, but she couldn't look away from the cane. Did that mean Daniel Reid was dead? The thought screamed so loud as to drown out whatever else was said. She hadn't meant to be the cause of his death. Or anyone's death. She just wanted a way to leave this place. She tried not to think about it—about him. Every day battles raged throughout the colonies, and every day men died. Even her father had. The rebels were responsible for that.

"I'm going to bed," Lydia mumbled and turned back to her chamber. There would be enough to deal with in the morning and her head already spun.

"Not before you tell me what this is all about, Lydia."

She glanced at Charles and shook her head. "My private affairs are none of your business. Nor are my dealings with Major Layton." There. She'd said it, the words liberating. Charles was Margaret's husband. Lydia would not let him dictate what she did. He'd already refused to help her, so she had little reason to reside under his thumb.

"Lydia."

"Goodnight, Charles." She wanted to be alone and find a way to forget Daniel Reid. She had to believe that was possible. If he was dead, it should mean little to her. The war was at fault, and the rebels who had started it. Daniel had not even belonged in South Carolina. He should have stayed in the North. Then she wouldn't have met him, or had this awful, and so familiar, pain creeping through her center.

Lydia climbed into bed before realizing she had not removed her robe. A wave of nausea kept her from getting back up. She pressed a hand to her stomach and clamped her eyes closed against the weight crushing her. With the understanding that if Daniel was dead, she had likely killed him.

9

Shivers vibrated through Daniel's body, making each halted step all the more difficult. Whether a result of his wet clothes and the frosty bite to the night air, or the throbbing agony of his ankle, he couldn't be sure. The makeshift crutch he'd whittled out of a branch made walking possible, but barely. It was the first time he actually needed the cane he'd been toting for the past month, and the British removed that option.

Daniel paused against the hewn rails of a fence and dropped his head forward to catch his breath. The dim outline of a small house, not much bigger than his parents' cabin, beckoned him forward. But what good would it do him? The home wasn't his—that was hundreds of miles from here—and he couldn't risk pounding on the door of a Tory. Not in his condition. Not here. They would easily guess where he'd gotten his injuries, and he wasn't about to press that gun to his head. He'd keep walking.

Marion's band had probably retreated back toward Snow Island or Indiantown, and Daniel was in no state to follow. Georgetown was closer. If he could get to Wilsbys', surely they would give him a place to rest and help him secure a new horse.

Just a little farther. The crutch dug into the tender flesh under his arm as he hitched it into place and maneuvered his weight. One step at a time. He'd already come a couple of miles. He could make it the last few yards. Daniel was almost grateful for the physical pain. The greater it became, the less potent the image of Gabe's murder. He almost felt responsible. He'd pointed them toward Alliston's plantation.

The Wilsby cottage sat silent and still, not a light in the windows. No wonder, though, being well past midnight. Dawn probably sat on the horizon's doorstep.

Daniel leaned into the doorframe and tapped a knuckle to the wood. And waited. He knocked a little harder. "Please." He pressed his forehead into the door.

It cracked open to the flicker of a candle and the old man in his nightshirt.

Thank you, Lord.

"Reid? What's happened to you?"

"There was a skirmish. I need a place to hide for a few days."

Wilsby gaped for a moment, and then shook his head. "I can't keep you here. Much too dangerous." He stepped out and closed the door behind him. "My daughter is staying here with her husband. He's a Tory."

Daniel shifted the crutch. "Where am I to go?"

The breeze snuffed out the candle's tiny flame. The older man looked down. "Maybe..." He shook his head. "I wish I could do something for you, but tonight—"

"A message." Daniel had no other choice. "That's what you can do. Send a message to Lydia Reynolds. No name. Just write *meet me*. She'll understand." God willing.

Wilsby nodded. "I can do that. But are you sure about Miss Reynolds? Her family has always been stringently loyal to the Crown."

Daniel pushed away from the wall. "I'm sure." He clamped his jaw against a surge of anger and the pain spiking through his ankle as he attempted a shuffled step.

"What happened to your foot?"

"Don't let it concern you. Go back to your Tory family," Daniel growled. How could this man think to judge Lydia for her family when the loyalties of his own were equally contemptible?

"Wait here."

Daniel paused and let his eyes close. They burned.

Behind him the door opened and closed, the man going inside. The action repeated as he returned moments later.

"Take this." Wilsby handed over a crutch. "I've had trouble with gout in my foot from time to time."

The smooth sway of the armrest fit comfortably under Daniel's arm as he traded his branch.

"Why don't you spend the night in the smoke house? There's nothing in it but what's already been cured. You can rest and we'll think of something in the morning."

Oh, to lie down and prop up his foot, but frustration at Wilsby's lack of welcome spurred him on. Which was probably for the best. Once Daniel stopped, he'd likely not be able to move again. Not anytime soon. "I'd best get where I'm going before dawn."

The man voiced no real argument but mumbled under his breath as Daniel started away.

One step at a time. One more step. Daniel's good leg threatened to buckle with each movement, the muscles almost useless after coming so far, but he was determined to make it the remaining distance. The first light of day glowed through the trees as he leaned against the base of the huge oak and let himself sink to the ground.

~*~

Lydia stepped from her bedchamber and halted at the sight of little Margaret. She gripped her father's fingers, walking with him down the short hall to the nursery where the nursemaid waited at the door.

Charles looked up at Lydia and frowned. "I wish to speak with you. Meet me in my study after breakfast."

She nodded and hurried to the stairwell, only glancing back once at the full-cheeked cherub, her dark hair beginning to form a crown of ringlets...as her mother's had. A family trait. Even little David and Martin had dark curls, though Martin's hair had been so fine. At eighteen months he'd still been such a baby when he'd died.

Lydia hastened her steps as though she could escape feeling. If she had truly succeeded in closing her heart, why did she ache with thoughts of the dark waves on the head of a man she'd hardly known?

A rapping on solid wood saved her from the downward spiral she'd been fighting all morning, and Lydia stood back as Eli answered the door. From her angle, she could make out the boy delivering a slip of paper. He said something and was gone.

"Who was that?"

Eli turned and stepped to her. "For you, Miss Lydia."

She took the worn note, its end jagged as though

ripped from a larger piece of parchment, and nodded her thanks to Eli. She waited for a moment before unfolding it, smoothing the crease between two words.

Meet me.

"What is that?" Major Layton's voice boomed behind her.

Lydia twisted. "Nothing." But who would want to meet with her and be confident she knew the location? Unless… "Miss Hilliard wants my opinion on something. The affairs of women—I am sure it would bore you." She folded her arms behind her as she took a step away. Lydia tucked her fingers around the note. "I am afraid I must leave directly. Could you inform Mr. Selby, if you see him, that I will be taking breakfast with the Hilliards?"

"Of course." His eyes narrowed, but she simply smiled and retreated.

She would discuss their arrangement later. She needed to see if this meant what she hoped. Lydia gathered her cloak, chiding herself. *Hope* wasn't the right word. She was merely curious. She refused to attach emotion to a rebel—or any man, for that matter. She couldn't let herself hope.

Her breath showed in the cool morning air as she hurried down the steps and around the back of the house. She would go on foot. The grove wasn't far and waiting for a mount or carriage would only delay her. Hitching up her full skirts, she ran in short bursts, part of her wanting to race all the way to the ancient oak, while another part wondered if someone might be watching. Or if she was going in the wrong direction. What if Daniel hadn't sent the note after all? What if he were dead? But if not him, then who? Again, the sensation of hope rose within her. She wanted it to be him. Lydia slowed her pace, though her heart continued to race. She could afford no attachments.

The monster of an oak sat silent in the morning light. Mists wafting off the bay gave a serene haze. No one stood by.

Lydia reached out and let her fingers trail along one of the lower branches as she followed it to the massive trunk. No Daniel. Either he hadn't come yet...or he would never come.

But then, who had sent the note?

Grabbing onto a branch level with her head, Lydia ducked under. A gasp clogged her throat.

A corpse.

No. His face was pale and lips tinged with blue, but his chest rose and fell with breath.

She crouched, her outstretched hand not quite touching his shoulder. "Mr. Reid?"

His sudden jerk awake made her startle and almost landed her on her backside. Lydia grabbed the tree and steadied herself. "What happened to you?"

Daniel moaned as he pushed himself up. "I—" A cry broke from his chest. Both of his hands pulled his right foot in front of him, his teeth gritted at the motion. The swollen ankle had no boot but had been bound in a dirty cloth, like a...shirt? She glanced to his bare chest, a wisp of dark hair showing from under his coat.

"What happened?" Her mind already formulated a reply. She recalled Captain Layton's cocky look of triumph. They hadn't gotten the Swamp Fox, but they were not unpleased with the way the battle near Alliston's Plantation had gone.

"They met us in the marshes." Daniel peered at her, the muscles in his jaw flexing. Mud colored the side of his face. "There were too many."

"I told you I did not know their numbers."

"But you inferred a few." He glanced away and wiped his palm across his mouth. "They massacred us."

"I am so sorry." The apology tugged at her, but she refused to heed it. She had to remain detached. But what would she do with him? Lydia glanced around. "Where is your horse?"

Daniel stretched for the crutch leaned at the base of the tree. "Dead."

"Oh." Hence the crutch. But what a loss. Madam had been a beautiful animal. "How awful."

"Awful?" He heaved himself upward, releasing a short gasp as he maneuvered his injured foot. Standing, he leaned into the oak's mighty trunk. His nostrils flared. "No. Awful is watching a boy plead for mercy while he's clubbed with muskets." Daniel looked past her, his knuckles showing white as he clenched his hands. "Watching helpless while someone fills that boy's chest with buckshot, the barrel close enough to ignite his shirt." He plowed his fist into the rough bark. Multiple times.

Lydia flinched back a step. She stared at his knuckles, scraped and bleeding, then glanced to his face and the naked rage that burned like live coals in his dark eyes. What was this man capable of when driven by anger? If he ever discovered her deception…

The fury melted from him. His eyes dulled, his shoulders slumped and he let his bloodied hand fall to his side. "They killed Gabe Marion. What is the life of an animal to the life of a…man? Any man. I'm so tired of this killing. This…waste of life." His gaze found hers, his brow ridged with questioning. "When will it stop?"

Lydia straightened, hardening her spine against the plea in his voice. It did not matter if the war ended. Lives would continue to hang in the balance. Disease, accident, and even giving birth to another life, would always be there, waiting to kill.

10

Daniel released a breath as Lydia's expression hardened. His knuckles stung, momentarily rivaling the pain in his ankle. His temper was the curse of his existence. After all the damage he'd done and the hurt he'd caused at home, he'd spent the last three years trying to gain more control of his anger. Unsuccessfully. The war had only added fuel to that fire. But seeing the fear flicker in Lydia's eyes...

His head throbbed along with his foot, and he lowered himself back to the earth.

"What are you doing?" The hem of her pale blue gown swept the ground as she stepped closer. "We should take you to the inn or somewhere you can rest and heal. Out of this cold morning air. You look terribly ill."

"I can't show myself in Georgetown." A pained grunt squeezed between Daniel's teeth. "The British know my face, and I don't hanker to spend my life rotting in a British galley." He leaned his head back and clamped his eyes against the growing ache within his skull. Standing had been a mistake.

"I don't believe the British have true galleys anymore."

Her statement offered no relief. "Then they would probably dangle me from the end of a rope." He glanced up at her. "They still have those."

"But..." Her hand rose to her throat. "You—you

cannot possibly remain out here. Your foot looks…well, it looks frightful and probably requires a physician's care. What of Wilsby? Could he help you?"

"No good. He might as well be a Tory."

"Surely there is someplace that—"

Daniel shook his head. "Don't worry yourself."

"But…" Contrary to his words, her concern appeared genuine. Her fingers resided over her mouth, and a wrinkle formed between her lovely eyes—eyes that drew him deeper every time he looked into them.

"I wasn't thinking properly when I asked you here. There's nothing you can do for me that won't risk your own safety. I don't want that."

She met his gaze. But only briefly. Lydia rotated away and took two steps. "There must be some place I can take you. Somewhere you can rest and let your foot mend." She glanced over her shoulder at his wrapped foot. "It is unfortunate the British know your identity. Faking your limp would have no longer been necessary."

Daniel tried to chuckle but fell short. "Until someone noticed it's the wrong leg. I was limping with my left leg before." And he no longer had his cane.

Arms folded across her abdomen and lips pursed, Lydia turned back. "There must be somewhere…" Her eyes lit. "My father has a storehouse—three actually, but the larger two are still in use. The smaller one should be empty. They haven't needed it since…" Her fingers crept to her arms as though chilled by what she'd been about to say. Then she cleared her throat. "Since the *Magellan* was sunk."

"The *Magellan*?"

"One of my father's ships." Dark eyelashes flittered low, concealing sea-blue irises. "Charles keeps the building locked, so no one would find you in there."

"But if it's locked —"

"There is an extra key in Father's library. In his desk."

As much as Daniel wanted to argue with her, and not let her take the risk of smuggling him anywhere, he could not come up with an alternative. The chill in the air last night had wrapped itself around his bones, draining his strength. Plus, he had no food. The thought of it pinched his stomach and thirst burned his throat. And what if he was discovered out here in the open so close to Georgetown?

She must have sensed his contemplation. "What other choice is there? If you think you can make it as far as the road just east of the woods, I'll bring a carriage to meet you. I know who I can trust."

Daniel didn't share her confidence. "If you are sure."

She smoothed her palms over her skirts, her spine like a ramrod. "I am."

~*~

If only Lydia felt as much assurance as her voice conveyed. But, though she had no interest in his politics, she couldn't walk away and leave him there. Neither could she turn him over to Major Layton. She wanted to remain detached from any sense of responsibility for what had happened to him and his friends, but she could not. The Major thought him dead, and she would leave it at that. If Daniel gave her information that would lead to the Swamp Fox, she would try to buy her freedom with it. Otherwise, as soon as Daniel Reid was healed enough, she would see him off and find a different way across the ocean.

"I will need one hour before I come with the carriage."

Daniel's head dropped forward, and his chest heaved a sigh. "All right."

She hesitated. The poor man looked no better than the corpse she had first mistaken him for. "It's not far, but are you sure you'll be able to reach the road?"

"I'll manage."

Fortifying herself with a breath, she hurried back into town. An hour later, as promised, the carriage was ready, and she had Eli drive slowly down the road along the edge of the woods.

Nothing.

"Stop here," she called through the small hatch above her head. Lydia braced herself as the carriage jostled to a halt. She searched the trees for any sign of Daniel.

Still nothing.

She shoved open the door and climbed down.

Daniel hobbled from behind a tree.

She waved to him to hurry, and then remembered that was not possible. The thought of him being seen drove her to his side. They had passed a British patrol on the way here. Though headed in the opposite direction, she couldn't guarantee a different troop wouldn't ride around the bend and catch her with this rebel.

"Let me assist you." Lydia hesitated to touch the filthy sleeve of his coat and tried to hide her grimace as he glanced to her face.

He didn't seem any happier than she, but he lifted his arm so she could prop him up and hasten him to the closed carriage. Eli jumped down from his perch to help boost the rebel inside and out of sight.

Daniel didn't even try for the seat, just dragged himself to the wall and leaned his head back.

Lydia stepped over him to the seat as Eli climbed back up top. An instant later the carriage jerked forward and Daniel moaned.

"Is your ankle broken?"

"I don't believe so," he said through gritted teeth. "Hopefully, only badly bruised and sprained." He winced as he shifted his foot, so rudely wrapped.

"All the same, maybe it would be best to have it looked at by a surgeon."

"No. Can't be trusted. I'd rather heal on my own than in a British prison." He shook his head and coughed. "Though, I probably don't have to worry about that. Tarleton's quarter is more likely what I'd get."

"Tarleton's quarter?"

Emotion mingled on his face, sorrow and anger fighting for dominance. "Same as they gave Gabe Marion."

"You said he was killed. That's not giving quarter." Prisoners weren't supposed to be shot after they surrendered. But that is what Daniel had said happened to the Swamp Fox's nephew. Was that the terms Colonel Tarleton offered? And the rest of the British?

Lydia didn't want to think about any of that right now. Needless killing. No mercy. She brushed at dried strands of grass on her shoulder, moist where his arm had rested. She bent over and touched the corner of his coat. "Your clothes are soaked through." More than a heavy morning dew could be responsible for.

"Sat for over an hour in a swamp waiting for one of them big lizards to come looking for supper." His lip curled with the hint of a smile. "If one had come along, I don't know which I would have feared worse, the British muskets or those teeth. I'd probably take my chances with the first. At least then I'd know what I was up against."

Though Lydia held no affection for alligators, after what he'd just told her, she questioned his choice. "I imagine you have faced the British often enough."

"Spent the past three years battling them in New England, but it's not like they left us alone before I joined the army. I saw a lot of good men die in skirmishes and raids near my home."

"Where is your home?"

Daniel's expression softened, the curve of his mouth becoming more genuine. "Prettiest valley on this continent, I reckon. A small farming community along the Mohawk River, central New York." Daniel studied her. "You haven't heard of it, have you?"

"I've heard of the Mohawk River." She honestly couldn't imagine why anyone would want to settle any distance from civilization. And farm? She remembered how hard those first years were after Mother died, and she and Margaret were left alone in a small house to fend for themselves while Father buried himself in obtaining that first ship. The *Zephyr*—the Greek god of the west wind—had taken him and Eli away for weeks at a time. Sometimes months.

A flock of mean-tempered chickens and an ornery milk cow resided in the barn behind the shack, and they had been her responsibility until she'd turned ten and Father moved what remained of their family into Georgetown and a bigger house. If all chickens and cows were like the ones she remembered, she'd be better off spying for the British.

"So you spent a while in the Continental Army. What rank are you?" She would probably never offer it to Layton, but it was the kind of information he would want.

"Sergeant. Not as lofty as your usual guests, I'm sure." He paused to cough into the crook of his arm. "You are probably used to entertaining men far more sophisticated."

Lydia straightened her cloak around her. They would soon be to the storehouse, where she would hardly be *entertaining* this rebel sergeant. The carriage halted and she reached for the door latch, not waiting for Eli.

"Mornin' Lieutenant," he called out.

"Is Mr. Selby inside?" Lieutenant Mathews's voice murmured, approaching.

Eli's boots hit the ground. "No, sir. Just Miss Reynolds."

Lydia glanced to Daniel. If anyone found him now… Heart rate skittering, she eased the door open and filled it with her skirts. The Lieutenant stood with a handful of his men still mounted, back-dropped by the tall masts of vessels loitering in the harbor. They weren't yet at the storehouse.

"Miss Reynolds? What brings you out here this morning?" Mathews craned his neck to see past her. "When I saw the carriage, I expected Mr. Selby. I was told to assist him with—"

"As Eli said, he is not with me." And she had no desire to balance here discussing her brother-in-law. "Perhaps he is already onboard the *Americus*."

Lieutenant Mathews tucked his hat under his left

arm as he wrinkled his brow. "The *Americus* has not yet reached port. We are still waiting on the supplies and ammunitions she carries."

That wasn't right. "Is she not due?"

"Of course. Major Layton—"

"Is he here?" The mention of the man spurred Lydia's pulse. As did the memory of him flaunting Daniel's cane as a trophy.

Lieutenant Mathews shook his head. "He's meeting with Colonel Tarleton right now. Which is why we had hoped to have news from the *Americus*. With the rebels so near Georgetown and only eighty regulars posted here and—"

"Good." She pasted on her most pleasant smile. Daniel didn't need to hear the full state of the British Empire. "I will leave you, then. Until this evening."

He nodded, set his hat back on his sandy head and mounted his horse. As soon as the soldiers focused forward, Lydia drew back and closed the door. She dropped onto the padded bench.

Daniel's face appeared even whiter than before. "It's a good thing you wear so many petticoats, Miss Reynolds."

Lydia widened her eyes at him.

Color must have reached her cheeks because he shifted and cleared his throat. "Forgive me, Miss Reynolds, I'm afraid being raised with four sisters has not…" He shook his head. "I mean no disrespect."

Lydia tugged at her skirts to make sure they hung properly over her laced boots. The carriage jostled forward again. Four sisters? In a rustic cabin in back country New York? "How many siblings have you?"

"Only the four who lived past infancy. All girls." His gaze settled on her again and he cracked a smile.

"You remind me of them." Daniel turned his head and coughed.

"In what way?" Other than the fact she was also female.

"Little things. The color of your hair. Complexion." He winced as the carriage dropped over a rut and rolled to a stop. "Your eyes are different, though. My family all have the same as me. Plain old brown. I like the blue in yours."

Eli opened the door, saving Lydia from the uncomfortable turn of their conversation and the intensity of eyes she would never consider plain or old. They were vibrant, rich, and much too penetrating.

~*~

Cold sweat seeped from Daniel's skin and the back of his throat ached from thirst by the time he reached the ground.

Lydia hurried to the door of the smallest of three brick buildings and stuck a key in the lock.

The wiry Negro assisted Daniel. *What was his name?* Daniel scraped through his memory. *E something. A Bible name. Eli.* "Thank you, Eli."

The man started as if surprised, but he nodded.

Set behind the larger storehouses, a row of trees kept this storehouse tucked mostly out of sight of the road, but after their recent meeting with the British, Daniel sped his steps as best he could.

The scent of molasses and honey saturated the musty air. With the door left open, Daniel could make out barrels stacked high, bearing the markings of their contents, while smaller crates held wines.

Lydia paused in front of them. "I thought this

place was supposed to be empty." She ran her hand over the layer of dust coating the top of one of the crates. "It was empty the last time I was here, just after the *Magellan* went down. Charles said it wasn't in use."

Eli, helping Daniel, continued past her to the back wall where sacks of grain were piled high. He released Daniel long enough to rearrange them. A groan mingled with a sigh as Daniel lowered his body onto the makeshift bed. At least he didn't have to worry about starving.

"We will need to bring some blankets," Lydia said, with barely a glance toward him. She stepped back to the door and waited for her servant. "I doubt I shall have time to return today with a dinner to prepare for, but I will send Eli with what you need."

Daniel pushed aside a twinge of disappointment. "Colonel Tarleton will be joining you for supper, I assume?"

Her dark lashes lowered. "Yes."

"Then perhaps you will be able to confirm the numbers the lieutenant was kind enough to offer. Give me something to take back to Colonel Marion."

"You are hardly in the position to worry about helping Marion take Georgetown. I doubt you will be leaving here for a while."

"On the contrary. I won't stay for more than a day or so." Just enough to sleep off the intense exhaustion. "It's a horse I need." And another boot, but he'd settle for not having to walk.

Lydia merely looked at him as though he were insane, and then pulled the door closed, plunging the room into darkness.

The clicking of the lock resounded in Daniel's head. Though he trusted Lydia—she'd already had opportunity to betray him to the redcoats—he couldn't shrug off the feeling of entrapment.

11

"Lydia, may I have a word with you?"

She paused on the bottom step. "I have so much to prepare for this evening, Charles. Now is not a good time."

"I asked you to meet me after breakfast." He strode to her from the small room he had made his office after the shipping company had fallen to him. "Where have you been all morning?"

"I was visiting with Ester Hilliard. Major Layton agreed to inform you."

"And he did." Charles crossed his arms. "But I called upon Miss Hilliard and her father myself this morning, and she told me she had not seen you."

Lydia braced to keep her expression from flinching. "Why did you call upon the Hilliards?"

"I had business with John and to invite them to join us this evening."

"Of course." She flashed a smile, but her lips fought the upward curve. She stepped off the stairs. "With Ester and her father coming, I must change the arrangements for the dinner." They were more neutral in their political views and could not sit by just anyone. She tried to turn, but he caught her arm. "Charles, let me go."

Instead of heeding her, he dragged her to his office. He shoved her inside and slammed the door. "What are you up to?"

She spun to him, rubbing where his fingers had bruised her arm. "I do not know what you speak of."

"What exactly is your arrangement with Major Layton? He said something of a rebel informant. I believe those were his words. And the cane? Whose cane was that?"

Lydia backed away from the anger in his eyes. "Why not ask the Major?"

"I did. But I want to hear it from you. You have knowingly endangered this house. Your family."

Heat spiked up her spine. "I have no family!"

Charles relaxed a step and lowered onto the corner of the desk. "What about your sister's daughter? Does Maggie and her future mean nothing to you?"

Lydia stood for a moment, heart pounding. She did not want to consider the question, afraid to answer truthfully even to herself. With quick steps, she made a break for the door.

Pain shot up her wrist as Charles caught hold of her. "No more, Lydia. No more sneaking around. No more risking your life and reputation."

She glared at him and jerked away. "You do not own me."

"But everything else, I do own. Without me you have nothing. No allowance. No hope of a future. The very roof over your head I provide out of respect for your father and sister. The law does not require such generosity."

Is that what he had discussed with Mr. Hilliard? "Are you threatening me?"

"I am warning you. If you cross certain lines, I cannot protect you. And I will not allow you to risk..." Muscles danced in his jaw. "Everything." The word squeezed between his teeth.

Lydia twisted away. She charged up the stairs, almost tripping over the hem of her gown. From the nursery, a soft lullaby was joined by a child's cooing. Her legs lost strength. Truth be admitted, little Margaret already held too much power over her heart. Better to keep her distance until she could leave this place. Charles's warning weighed Lydia's steps. In her bedchamber, she paced. What were her options? She had to get to England or remain under Charles's thumb forever. Unless she married. But Charles was the only one who had expressed any honorable intentions. There were no prospects in Georgetown, and even if there were, she didn't want marriage.

She spun on her heel and started back across the thick woolen rug and its extravagant pattern of reds and blues. Her parents' marriage had been one of love, and losing his wife had almost destroyed her father. It was as though he had shriveled up inside. And then he lost himself at sea, returning only for short periods to check on his daughters and supply for their needs.

Of course, marriage didn't require love.

Lydia shook the idea from her head. Marriage of any kind often brought children, and in many ways she feared that the most. To give birth to a sweet infant, feeling a mother's love and to risk losing that child to complications, accident, or disease. She had only been six when her brothers died, but the memory of their motionless little bodies and Mother's screams still haunted her.

No marriage. No children.

Dropping onto the edge of her bed, Lydia pressed her palms against her face. Another bargain with Major Layton seemed the only realistic option. She couldn't bring herself to use Daniel as she had, to set an ambush, but surely he still had information that would be worth something to the Major. He knew how to find Colonel Marion. That was all she needed.

Daniel Reid was still the key, poor man.

Lydia pushed back to her feet. Her thoughts in a tussle, she could not bear to sit a moment longer. Maybe if she spoke with Daniel again, she would glean something more from him. Something useful. And she hadn't had a chance to send Eli back with blankets or a change of clothes. She would see to that.

Course set, Lydia slipped past the happy noise coming from the nursery and into Charles's chambers. The room still carried the memory of her sister. The dressing table against one wall, the silver-handled hairbrush, the cream drapes Margaret had chosen. Lydia did not allow herself to linger. She dug out a pair of breeches and muslin shirt that would probably not be missed. Though similar in height, the breadth of Daniel's shoulders was her main concern as to whether the clothes would fit. After creating a bundle with a spare blanket and tucking it under her cloak, Lydia crept down the stairs and out the back of the house.

The servants, busy with preparations for the evening, seemed not to notice her.

Keeping out of sight of the roads, she wound her way through the trees toward the bay. She knew the path well and within ten minutes she came to the small storehouse. The door creaked as she pushed it open, and daylight spilled across the dirt floor. She hadn't considered how dark the interior would be without a window. A lamp hung from a hook on the wall, and she hurried to light it so she could again close the door.

"I wondered if you'd thrown away the key and decided to forget about me." Daniel pushed himself to his elbows. "Your man, Eli, never came back."

Lydia thought of the hustle and bustle of preparations for the dinner in a couple of hours. Time was short. "Just a few delays."

Daniel swung his booted foot to the dirt floor and leaned forward on his knee.

"I brought you some dry clothes to change into." But he needed much more than that. She made a mental list of things to send down with Eli as she laid the bundle beside Daniel.

"Thank you."

"And your ankle should be seen to." His foot was propped up on the sacks of grain, and she motioned for him to unbind it. "What happened?"

"Madam crushed it when she fell."

Lydia cringed as he unwound the tattered shirt, and then drew off the long stocking. A deep purple and black bruise stretched across the outside of his lower calf, and his ankle appeared badly swollen. The thought of that beautiful animal tugged at her heartstrings, as did the image he had lodged in her mind of a lad having his chest ripped through by a musket ball. If only the rebels would admit their defeat and end this horrid war.

Daniel moved his toes and gave a grunt. "As frightfully painful as it is to walk on, I don't think the bone is broken."

"All the same, you should wrap the ankle with something besides your shirt and..." She lowered her gaze to the tall boot his other foot sported. "I will try to find you a new pair of shoes or boots."

"That would be appreciated. As are these clothes. Your weather is mild compared to New England's, but sitting wet to the bone last night—" His voice broke with a cough. "Pardon me."

"I will send some tea. You look quite ill."

He waved her off. "Other than the foot, I am fine. Besides, I've given up drinking tea."

Lydia opened her mouth to argue, but clamped it closed just as quick. She had forgotten many of those opposed to the Crown had traded their tea for coffee. "Understandably. But something warm to drink would do you no harm."

"I'd not be against warmth with some substance to it. Sitting amongst all this food does nothing for the hollow pit my stomach has become." His fingers worked to unbutton his coat, bearing his chest inches at a time. "I hate to burden to you, but give me one day and I will be off your hands."

Lydia had no reply as he pulled off his coat and laid it aside. Warmth rose through her core as his chest was bared. Had he no sense of decency? Had she? She needed to look away, but fascination kept her attention from wandering as he plunged his arm into the cream-colored shirt she'd provided. Only then did she notice the wide scar marking the other arm above his elbow. An ugly bruise resided over it.

"I should think that is also quite painful?"

Daniel glanced at her and then followed her gaze. "The bruise? A little. Not as much as it did when the horse's hoof first made contact. And the scar—long healed."

"What is it from?"

The wound vanished inside the pale muslin shirtsleeve. "Tomahawk. We were on our way to relieve Fort Schuyler along the Mohawk. Walked into a British and Tory ambush." His chest deflated. "I was blessed to walk out of that ravine. A lot of men didn't.

Eight hundred marched that day, and only half left Oriskany alive." He fastened the buttons, and then brushed his hands down the front. His jaw tensed.

"Is something wrong with the shirt?" It seemed to fit him well enough, though perhaps a little tight across the chest.

"Nothing's wrong. It's fine."

"Good. I will leave you to finish dressing, then, and send Eli back with something for your foot and for you to eat." Lydia hesitated before turning. She had forgotten to ask him more about the Swamp Fox and his movements. But how to go about it when all of her previous attempts failed? Unless… "Perhaps if I bring some parchment paper and ink, you would like to send word to Colonel Marion. You could tell me where to take it."

Daniel's deep brown eyes seemed to peer through her. "I would like to send word but not to Colonel Marion. That would be too dangerous. Would you bring the ink and paper, all the same?"

"Of course." Lydia forced a smile and walked to the door. She needed to hurry back to the house and dress for dinner. The rusted hinges sang at her departure. Despite the cool breeze rising off the bay she felt overheated. She should hurry to find Daniel a horse as he'd mentioned earlier. The sooner he left Georgetown, the better for both of them.

She took three steps.

"Good evening, Miss Reynolds."

Lydia jerked at the deep voice and scarlet coat emerging from the shadows of the nearby trees. "Lieutenant Mathews? What are you doing here?"

"Wondering what you are doing away from your home with guests soon to arrive."

"I...was checking on something." She retreated a pace. "I mean, I forgot something for the dinner this evening."

The lieutenant strolled forward, studying her. "What exactly? Or were you making a delivery instead?" He paused only a foot away. His voice lowered. "What was in that bundle you brought with you? Blankets? Food, perhaps?"

Lydia's mouth went dry. If she tried to deny Daniel's presence, she would only be aligning herself with him. How much did the Lieutenant already know?

She caught the soldier's sleeve and drew him away from the storehouse and out of earshot. "I have an agreement with Major Layton."

"As I am aware." He looked behind them to the building. "That is who you have in there? Major Layton suggested he was dead."

And he nearly had been. The image of Daniel lying under the ancient oak clenched her stomach.

"What are your plans with him?"

"As long as he has not overheard us, he believes me to be sympathetic to their cause, I will continue to garner what information I can."

"Good." Lieutenant Mathews narrowed his gaze at her. "But why the secrecy? He was with you in the carriage earlier today, was he not?"

"Yes, but I could not very well have introduced you, could I? And I need time."

One of the lieutenant's pale eyebrows peaked.

"His ankle is hurt. I know how impatient Major Layton can be, but we did have the understanding that he would leave the man alone until I was finished with him. Of course, that was before the Major almost killed him."

"Even the Major has little control over what happens in the middle of a skirmish."

"All the same..." She let the sentence die, not sure what more to say. "Have you told anyone of your suspicions?"

"Not yet." Lieutenant Mathews gave a thin smile.

"Then wait. Please. Let me speak with the major first."

He crossed his arms and then nodded to the path she had taken. "Let's walk. You will soon be missed."

Hardly an answer, but she kept pace beside him as he started toward her home.

"Tell me, Miss Reynolds, why are you so anxious to return to England? What awaits you there that rivals the life you have here?"

"A cottage near Brighton."

His feet faltered. "In Sussex?"

"Yes."

"My family is in Worthing, a village west of Brighton. Must be a mighty fine cottage to make you want to leave the estate your father built."

Lydia kept walking. From the description, the cottage that awaited her was comfortable enough and had rooms to spare, but not near as grand as her present home. It would easily meet her needs, though. That was what mattered.

The brick walls appeared through the trees and she paused. "No one knows I left, so it is best we part ways here, Lieutenant. And please, wait to report anything about the...storehouse to Major Layton."

"I shall wait. But be wary, Miss Reynolds. The major is a shrewd man. Your brother-in-law and his ships are a boon to our position here, but there is only so much protection that will grant you. If Major Layton comes to suspect your loyalties…" He shook his head. "This is not a threat, ma'am. Only a warning. I do not know all your reasons for keeping the rebel hidden, but be sure you do."

Lydia hurried to the back door, her thoughts on his warning—the second one she'd received in as many hours.

12

Daniel sat on the edge of the sack of grain, clean breeches in hand, the deep voice that had faded with Lydia's still rumbling in his mind. If only he had made out the words. Eli had likely been the one to meet her. The alternative...

Pushing aside the sinking sensation in his gut, Daniel focused on the dry change of clothes. As with the shirt, the quality of the breeches chafed his pride. While Lydia might share some of his sisters' features, her upbringing was far displaced. The sooner he left the better.

The single lamp lit the dark of the storeroom, but after he finished changing his clothes, little was left for him to do except sit and glare at his offending ankle. It still throbbed with each pulse of his heart, but that no longer held his thoughts. Gabe's pleas, and the sudden explosion of the musket laid to his chest echoed in Daniel's mind, tormenting. That and the understanding that soon Tarleton, Layton, and other British officers would sit around the Reynolds' dinner table discussing their victories and possibly their plans. What he wouldn't give to listen in and garner the sort of information that could bring about their fall.

But he was left to trust Lydia.

Daniel tapped his fist against the side of the grain sacks beneath him. *Lydia.* The image that name conjured settled over the anger burning in his chest.

Bright blue-green eyes. Chin set with determination. And a pair of the prettiest lips he'd ever been drawn to. Daniel groaned and pressed the heels of his palms over his eyes. Hadn't he learned his lesson?

An hour or so later, the door creaked open and he tensed. The man who entered appeared almost invisible in the shadows except for the whites of his eyes and the gray in his hair. His arms were laden. A pail of water, towels, bread and a small pot of warm soup, more blankets, and socks.

"Thank you."

The man said nothing, his expression stone as he made his delivery and picked up Daniel's lone, muddy boot.

"What are doing with that?"

"Miss Lydia asked me to fetch it." Eli pushed the boot into a canvas sack and left.

The hairs rose on the back of Daniel's neck. Though taking the boot made sense so a suitable replacement could be found, he wouldn't make the mistake of figuring Eli as a complacent man. He appeared as intelligent as any. He might do Lydia's bidding, but to what point? Were his loyalties to her, or her family? Or the King?

Given the choice, Daniel would make plans for leaving that very night, but unfortunately his ankle wouldn't take him far. He didn't even have boots. And the door was again locked.

~*~

Twenty-one people in attendance, almost half of them British officers, and the other half Tory leaders and their wives. The walls vibrated with conversation of the war, the last set of skirmishes with the Swamp Fox's men, and the terrible plight of keeping up with England's latest fashions.

Lydia sat on the settee beside Ester Hilliard, not really listening to the middle-aged woman across from them as she continued bemoaning their displacement from society.

A hand brushed Lydia's arm and she looked to Ester, who leaned nearer. "Are you feeling unwell?"

Lydia pasted an affable smile on her face. "Perhaps a little weary," she whispered in return. "But I am fine." Another lie. She glanced to Lieutenant Mathews only to find his gaze on her. He raised a brow and glanced to Major Layton in his scarlet uniform, who stood in conversation with Colonel Tarleton. And Charles. Though his back was to her, she knew the blue coat. She gave a slight nod to Mathews. She needed to get Major Layton alone so she could reason with him properly.

With a "pardon me for a moment," Lydia rose and circled behind the settee. As much as she wanted to wait until the morrow before speaking with the Major, she doubted Lieutenant Mathews would afford her that option.

Lydia's hands trembled at her sides, and she pressed them into the generous folds of her gown, the same crimson one she wore the evening she had first negotiated with Layton. Though her stays did not constrict her lungs as they had, she still couldn't manage a full breath as she stepped to join the threesome. Colonel Tarleton's admiring stare made her skin crawl.

A hand gripped her elbow. Charles. "Excuse me, gentlemen," he told the officers. "There is a matter I must speak of with Miss Reynolds."

"Most unfortunate," Tarleton answered, "but hopefully you will not keep her long. I am growing weary of all this talk of stratagem."

Lydia let Charles lead her away, almost grateful for the escape. Until he drew her from the parlor and paused outside the door.

"Tarleton is a pig when it comes to women," he whispered in her ear, "and Layton is little better when in his company. But that should be the least of your concerns if you are not careful." Charles released her and strode back into the room, going to Mr. Hilliard's side.

Lydia steadied herself with a hand on the doorjamb. She wasn't sure she wanted to consider what he referred to. And Major Layton had started across the room toward her.

Lieutenant Mathews watched.

"You are again a most congenial hostess, Miss Reynolds," Layton said as he approached. "Though I must say Mr. Selby does not seem himself this evening. I hope there are no difficulties between you."

"None that cannot be easily resolved by my departure."

"And I had even written to General Cornwallis about our agreement, but have you anything left to offer?"

The words momentarily clogged her throat, but she forced them out. She no longer had a choice. "He is not dead."

"Your rebel? Really?"

Lydia smiled at Charles as he glanced their way. She lowered her voice more. "Yes, he is quite alive." Even now she felt the relief of it.

A gust of a chuckle carried the major's fermented breath. The odor of wine hung between them. "But he was on his way to Alliston's plantation with the others, was he not? The New Englander. And that was his cane."

"Yes."

Standing beside her, his shoulder touched hers as he inclined nearer. "I want his name."

"Sergeant Reid." Her voice cracked. "Sergeant Daniel Reid."

"And where is he now?"

She shifted her gaze to Colonel Banastre Tarleton, who now stood with several women. He smoothed a palm over the green wool of his uniform as a grin split his face. *Tarleton's Quarter.* She'd heard someone once say that the rebels referred to him as The Butcher, or Bloody Ban, but at the time she hadn't given it much thought. Men, and their wars. Now, however, after speaking with Daniel, she did not want the colonel or major anywhere near the storehouse. Sooner or later Lieutenant Mathews would probably reveal what he knew, but better to hope he waited until after the Colonel's departure in the morning.

Lydia swallowed past the constriction in her throat. "That is not important." She backed farther into the hall and waited for the major to join her. "All I need from you at this juncture is a horse."

"A horse?" The major cocked his head to look at her as he followed her away from curious glances. "So you can hand it over to one of Marion's men?"

"I could hardly give him one of ours. Mr. Selby would never agree to that. Besides, you are the reason Sergeant Reid lost his mount. Think of it as giving a messenger pigeon wings."

"You think you can control him?"

"He came to me when he needed help, did he not?"

Major Layton's mouth curved into a leer. "Indeed." He took her hand and laid a kiss to her knuckles. "And he cannot be blamed. Very well, Miss Reynolds, I shall give you a horse and leave him to your capable hands. But your time is limited to get Sergeant Reid to lead us to Marion, or deliver him to us."

"How long, exactly?" She wouldn't tell him that Daniel had a talent for question evasion.

"You give me something useful, and I give you time." The major released her. "But if you fail, you agree to hand Reid over to me?"

She had little choice. "Yes."

"Good. Then I shall get the information I want using more conventional methods." He made a slight bow and walked back to the gathering.

Lydia remained. She could not seem to move.

Footsteps approached from the kitchen. "I did like you said, Miss Lydia."

"Thank you, Eli. Remember not to mention anything of this to Mr. Selby. Or anyone."

"'Course not, Miss Lydia." But instead of turning, he stood there. As though waiting.

Lydia looked to the man and was struck for the first time that, in a way, Eli was all that remained of her childhood and youth. Him and Mother's Bible. "Do you believe in God?"

Lips pressed thin and eyes softening, he nodded. "That I do, Miss Lydia. And I'll be praying He leads you now."

"Thank you," she breathed. "I—I shall pray for

that as well." If only she believed He would lead her. As far as she could tell, God was as oblivious to her existence as she had been to His.

13

Daniel woke to darkness and reached to where the lamp had resided when he succumbed to sleep. A cough wracked his lungs and stopped him short as he attempted to smother it with his sleeve. He took up a wooden canteen Eli had brought and pressed his dry lips over the hole. The cold water sliced his raw throat like a blade but eased the need to cough.

After setting the canteen aside, Daniel lit the lamp and wiped the sleep from his eyes. Bound tight, the pain in his ankle was not as severe as the day before, and he tucked Wilsby's crutch under his arm so he could move to the door. The building had been well constructed, but the thin cracks outlining the door hinted at daylight.

Daniel stood only two feet from the entrance when the gentle plod of approaching footsteps encouraged him to the wall. The latch wiggled then opened with the wide swinging of the door, concealing him.

A feminine gasp drew a chuckle from his chest.

Lydia stepped around the door as she yanked it closed. "Why on earth are you hiding back there? You nearly frightened me to death."

He only smiled, struggling against another cough. He turned his head away to clear his throat. "Just stretching my legs. It's best I leave today."

Her eyebrows appeared to question his sanity.

"Of course, it will be much easier if I don't have to

walk."

"I think I have a horse for you, but…" she frowned at his foot, "today is out of the question."

Daniel hobbled back to his bed of grain sacks. The throb became more painful each minute he stood. Again seated with his foot propped up, he leaned his shoulder into the wall and worked his fingers through his hair. "I'll be fine as long as I have a horse. But I don't feel right about involving you. I don't suppose Tarleton left his mount nearby?"

Her hands dropped to her sides. "Colonel Tarleton's?"

Daniel couldn't contain another chuckle, though it did nothing for his throat. His voice rasped a little when he spoke. "I'm sure I saw him astride a quite becoming stallion when I first arrived in South Carolina. Though, if anyone owes me for the loss of my horse, your Major Layton may be the one to forfeit his mount. Do you think it a worthy creature?"

Lydia shook her head and strands of brunette fell loose against her cheeks. "I think you are daft."

"And I won't argue." He smiled, hoping to evoke one from her as well.

Her lips resisted compliance.

"I suppose you think your plan is better."

"I do."

Daniel settled back so he could look at her and folded his arms, relaxing them across his chest. "I shall leave it to you, then. And your most capable hands."

Her gaze froze.

"As long as you are careful. For your own sake." He wasn't comfortable with Lydia endangering herself for him, but few options remained. Daniel glanced to the satchel at her side, taking notice of it for the first time.

She also looked down. "Eli will be along shortly with breakfast and a few more items for your use, but I wanted to bring these." She folded open the leather flap and withdrew a quill, corked ink pot and folded parchment. "You said you wanted to write a letter." She set them on the top of the nearest molasses barrel.

"Yes, I did. Thank you." He could finally let his family know where he had strayed. But he tried to put them from his mind for a little longer. "What did Tarleton and Layton have to talk about last night?"

The light faded from Lydia's eyes. "Unfortunately, not much was said. A recent letter from General Cornwallis was mentioned, but with no detail." She stepped back. "I should go."

"Do you have to?" He coughed, hoping to clear the pleading from his voice. Lydia both warmed and lighted the small building with her presence, and he was bored of his own company. "We don't have to talk about Cornwallis, or Tarleton, or even Colonel Marion. But please stay a little longer."

Lydia glanced behind her at the closed door, letting the silence linger. Then she looked back to him and seated herself on the edge of a keg of ale. "Maybe a few more minutes."

~*~

Lydia entwined her fingers to keep her hands still on her lap. What was wrong with her? She should seize the opportunity to speak with Daniel at length with the purpose of extracting information about the Swamp Fox and his plans. Instead she sought an excuse to leave. As much as she needed Colonel

Marion's location, she could not afford to listen to the deep tones of Daniel's voice and wonder what he thought behind eyes so dark.

Yet here she sat.

The flame in the lamp flickered, and Daniel reached over to lengthen the wick. "What's your family like?" He glanced to her, apology in his eyes. "Not politically. But do you have sisters, or brothers? Are they older, younger than you?" His shoulder lifted a hapless shrug. "It's been a long time since I've been home."

Lydia focused on the shadows cast upon the walls. She didn't want to think about her family, or lack thereof. But excusing herself now would only make him suspicions. "One older sister." She sighed at the all too familiar ache rising within. "And two younger brothers."

"Like I said, I didn't have any brothers—not that lived past infancy. Stillborn. I have my sisters though. One's married and has a little boy." He brushed his hand over the stubble on his jaw. "'Course I didn't stick around long enough to see Fannie married. I was frantic to get away from there. Couldn't think of much else."

His words resonated. Lydia's own plight stared her in the face. "What were you running from?"

Daniel glanced away, looking momentarily sheepish.

"You now have my full attention."

A groan vibrated from his throat. "A girl."

"Pray tell me more." What sort of woman had sent this strapping man fleeing?

"I'd rather not elaborate."

Lydia wagged her finger at him, enjoying his

discomfort much more than she should—and far too curious for her own good. "You've come this far."

Daniel moaned again and leaned his head back against the wall to stare upwards. "Fine. It was a young woman I'd been planning to marry, and she married someone else."

Lydia gave herself a moment to collect her thoughts, which suddenly raced helter-skelter with...jealousy? Nonsense. She couldn't be jealous of the random girl who had jilted this man. There was no reason for it. She didn't even have any sort of attachment or attraction...at least she shouldn't be attracted to him. He was a reckless rebel whose life sat upon a precarious pinnacle, waiting to topple off. She refused to be attracted to him. And she refused to be jealous.

"So there you have it. The Continental Army kept me occupied for three whole years. And yet here I am. Still hiding, and ashamed to say it."

"Then you still love her?" Lydia tried to keep her voice even but for some reason it rose in pitch.

Daniel met her gaze, and she dared not look away. She couldn't. He would think she felt something for him that she didn't.

He shook his head. "No. No, I don't think I do. It's more the humiliation of what I did. I lost my temper and..." His breath released in a gust. "I would much rather talk about something else? Do you get along with your sister?"

Lydia frowned. She'd much rather pry about him than talk, or even think, about Margaret. Memories only hurt, and she was tired of hurting. She motioned to his scabbed knuckles. "Do you lose your temper often?"

Flattening the hand with which he'd pummeled the tree, he sighed. "I like to think I've gained some reserve over the last few years, but as you point out, obviously not enough. What about your brothers? How old are they? Have they been lucky enough to avoid the fighting?"

How could he turn it back on her so quickly? "No, they haven't had to fight." But only because they had lost their first battle as children. "How dreadful could you have been to warrant never returning home?"

"Dare I recount?" Daniel took a breath. "I attacked a man because he was with the woman I wanted, and then I gathered a mob and almost hanged him. Only the Good Lord's intervention saved me from facing the guilt of that for the rest of my life. But I still risked the lives of people I cared about, because of my own daft pride." He coughed against his shoulder. "You've probably always lived in a grand house with your servants and everything you wanted. I don't suppose you had to share much with your siblings."

Lydia gaped at him, still trying to process what he had just told her. She'd seen his temper flare but could not imagine him responsible for such violence. Then she registered Daniel's final statement and inwardly moaned. Why couldn't he let her family go? "We did not always live in a *grand* house. Before my father purchased the *Zephyr*, he was only a ship's captain, leaving us for weeks and months at a time in a drafty hovel. Three rooms. That is all we had."

His mouth twitched. "We only had two."

"And now we come to the real reason you do not want to return home?" She folded her arms. Pursing her lips was the only way to keep them from revealing the fun she was suddenly having.

A rumble started in his chest and broke free as a laugh. "Let the truth be known by all. Our cabin was too small to be cooped up with that many sisters."

Lydia's own insides warmed with a chuckle. Too warm. Gaining his trust was one thing, but this was beyond anything needful. The lamp's low flicker highlighted the angles of his face. She reached over to adjust the wick before standing. "I should go."

At the corners of his eyes, the creases that had marked his pleasure now smoothed. "I suppose you should."

She looked to the parchment and quill she had brought. Again she was walking away, no closer to giving the British what they wanted. "Who are you planning to write, if not Colonel Marion?" She picked up the small porcelain ink pot and turned it over in her hands, giving her a reason not to look at Daniel.

"My family. They don't know where I am. I got to thinking while wading up to my ears in that swamp, if anything happened to me, if I were killed, there is no record of my location. I've been released from the army." He tipped his head forward and shook it. "I don't want to leave them without answers."

At least he had someone who would feel his passing. People who loved him...and whom he loved. Lydia set the ink pot back in place and moved to the door. Staying longer, talking to him, had not been wise.

14

Almost three hours later, Lydia sat at the pianoforte, her hands on her lap, staring at the ivory keys. She couldn't say why she'd even sat down. She hadn't played in a year. Tomorrow would mark the date of Margaret's death—and her daughter's first birthday.

Lydia's attempt to avoid thoughts of the rebel hiding in the storehouse had taken her in a worse direction. She was in no mood for music, but she laid her hands to the keys and played a deep cord. The sound pressed against her, pushing her lower.

"Ah, there you are."

Instead of looking up to the bearer of the feminine voice, Lydia closed her eyes, picturing Margaret standing in the doorway. Her full skirts swept the floor as she passed to the pianoforte. *Why not play something merry for once?* Margaret had asked.

"I do not feel merry." Only broken and bleeding. Father's death still too fresh, and a reminder of other losses.

Margaret, on the other hand, hung to the hope of new life, her stomach already showing the growth of the child within her. She didn't know that the child would steal her life only months later.

"Mr. Selby thought you might be in the library, but I heard the pianoforte."

Lydia stood and straightened her skirts. "Ester, I

wasn't expecting you."

Their solicitor's daughter opened her reticule and withdrew a letter. "Father asked me to bring this to you since I was coming here anyway."

"Oh?" Lydia took the folded parchment.

"Mr. Selby did not tell you? He invited me and Father to join the celebration of Maggie's first year. Father has business elsewhere, but I am most anxious to see the little darling. She must be such a joy. Every time I look at her, I see more and more of your dear sister in her."

"But why today? Little Margaret was not born until the eighteenth." A day that, as far as Lydia was concerned, should not be celebrated.

"Mr. Selby said he had business that took him away from Georgetown tomorrow. To Charles Town, I think."

Another thing he had neglected to mention. Not that she minded Charles's absence.

Lydia turned away and unfolded the letter. Her gaze followed the severe slant of Mr. Hilliard's penmanship that inquired as to her intentions for her property in England. Would she like him to seek a buyer?

Of course not. She wanted to live there, not pawn it off, securing her forever under Charles's roof. Mr. Hilliard had already told her the cottage would bring little monetary increase because of its location.

"Would you be willing to deliver my reply to your father?"

Ester gave her usual pleasant smile. "So long as you have it prepared before I depart."

"Why not follow me to the library now? I would rather Charl—Mr. Selby, not be aware of this correspondence." Lydia held the other woman's gaze until she nodded. "Good."

Lydia led the way to the library, going directly to father's desk. She opened the drawer for a fresh sheet of parchment, but the ink pot was empty, and she'd left her remaining one with Daniel. Along with her father's quill.

"It seems I might have to delay my reply. If I have not given you a letter for him before you leave, tell him I shall call at his office tomorrow." Only, tomorrow she had no desire to go anywhere except the graveyard where dear Margaret lay only a stone's throw from Mother and the boys. It seemed she would be required to visit the storehouse much sooner than she had planned.

~*~

Daniel dropped the quill pen back to the parchment and lowered himself to the hard surface of the grain sacks. Lumpy and hard. He rotated to his side and buried his mouth in the nook of his elbow as his lungs heaved. Hopefully the walls muted what his sleeve could not.

As the cough subsided, he scowled at the door. Eli had visited him once today with food and new footwear, but it was impossible to determine how many hours had passed since then. With the lamp the only light in the tomb, days would easily fade into each other as the hours did. Enough to drive a man insane if not for the relief it was to lay and let his body heal. His mind knew no such luxury.

Instead it replayed the same images in tormenting procession: Captain Wyndham dangling from a noose.

Rachel Garnet's face aflame with anger as she slapped his face, awaking him to the reality of his actions. Dawn lighting the tears in her beautiful eyes as she stared at the Garnet barn, left in ash. The look on Mama's face when he'd said goodbye. Pa's words. Young Gabe Marion alive and joking moments before he'd been murdered. Lydia and the subtle curve of her genuine smile. He clung to the last. So much more pleasant than the others.

All the more reason to leave tonight. If he could get a horse. And put a boot on his foot.

Sitting up, Daniel eyed the pair of mid-calf riding boots Lydia had sent for him. They looked large enough, but he would have to straighten his foot to slide it in. He tested his ankle and pain spiked up his leg. It wouldn't be pleasant, but little choice remained. Not if he didn't want to draw attention to himself on the road north.

Thick leather and a new sole. The boot was as fine as any he'd owned. Finer. He pulled it onto his good foot, and then picked up the other, braced himself, and shoved. Daniel clenched his jaw against a cry of agony, but without full success. He dropped back and sucked a breath.

A key rattled in the door before it was shoved open.

"What happened?" Lydia hurried across the room.

Daniel didn't answer immediately, waiting until the pain subsided a little. He pushed up on one elbow. "I got the boot on."

"What?" She glanced to his feet. "Why would you—"

"I need to leave. Today. How soon can I have the horse?"

"But you are not well. What about your ankle?"

"It'll be fine now that it's in the boot." He shifted, lifting his foot back onto the makeshift bed. The throb ebbed slightly. "Just don't ask me to take this boot off anytime soon. I've thought about when would be the best time to leave. I should go before dark."

"Ride out in broad daylight?"

Daniel nodded. "There are too many sentinels at night, and I imagine the British are extra watchful with Colonel Marion so close. Only a couple redcoats know my face, so it should be easy enough to ride out of town with these clothes you've—" A cough broke off his speech.

"But you are ill."

Daniel cleared his throat. "I'm fine." His voice remained gravelly. He sat up and reached for his coat, thrust his arms in the sleeves and shrugged it on. "Besides, I have numbers for the Colonel. Only eighty regulars posted in Georgetown. He'll want to know that." Daniel looked at the door, again closed. Always closed. "And after a full day, I'm honestly going insane caged in here." He frowned. What would a British prison be like? He couldn't imagine a week, months, years, locked away. Like on those prison ships the British had anchored in the New York Harbor. He'd heard tales about the crowded holds, the stench...the death. All the more reason to leave Georgetown now.

"What about your letter?" Lydia dropped a small bundle on the barrel and snatched the blank parchment. "Have you written nothing?"

He sighed. "Alas, no."

Though hesitance showed in her movements, she seated herself. "I have need of the ink, and while my sister's husband keeps an abundance in his office...I will wait for you to finish."

Daniel picked up the quill. He ran the clean tip over his thumb. If he couldn't write the letter in the hours he'd had alone, her presence would not make the task any more possible. "Take it, then. It's doing me no good."

"I can wait."

"But for how long?" He shook his head. Mama hadn't said much when he'd left, but her disappointment in him for letting his temper hurt the Garnets had been palpable. Pa, on the other hand, though not given to rage, had laid some well-placed verbal lashes. They still stung. "What do you write the people you care for after such sorry neglect? No words seem sufficient."

"So you will leave them unsaid?"

That would be the easiest. But… "No. I'll write something." He again took up the quill and dipped the very tip in the pool of black. Now what?

D-E-A-R

He looked down at the hen scratching, each letter painstakingly printed.

"So you do know how to write." Lydia's voice was light and teasing, but it ripped the scab off an old wound.

Daniel straightened and whipped the parchment so she could see it, but not get a good look. "Obviously." Anger drained away along with his pride—some of his pride. "Just not very well. If I take my time I can write, or read, about anything. My parents did teach us, and my sisters took to books like foals to new pasture. I, however…" He braved a glance at her face. "I am not daft. Nor an idiot. If you tell me something, I will remember it. You give me a message to deliver by mouth, and I will recite it word for word. I just...I don't..." How could he explain his struggle to someone who was probably the model of accomplishment? The men of her acquaintance were, no doubt, educated far beyond his own rude training.

His heart thudded against his ribs, and his thoughts slowed, returning to the past. Maybe that was why Rachel never opened her heart to him. Her words rang in his head, speaking of her British captain, as learned a man as Daniel knew. *"At least he has book learning."*

"Nothing to be ashamed of." Lydia took the paper from Daniel's hand. "My father had almost no education. He was a sailor from his youth. When he gained his first command, it became important to him to learn to read and write, but in the end, even when he built his shipping company, he preferred others to act as scribe." She snatched the quill away. "I have written many a letter for him."

Daniel's gaze shifted from the quill to her face.

She straightened a barrel in front of her and smoothed the parchment over the top.

"Um..." He'd had enough trouble trying to decide what to write while he held the pen. Now, with large pools of blue focused on him, the task seemed impossible. "I'm not sure."

"Who do you want to address?"

"My mother...no, my whole family." Daniel looked to his hands in an attempt to take his mind off the woman sitting across from him. Not a complete success, but he had to get this letter right.

"My dear family?"

He nodded and rested his chin on his knuckles. Silence enveloped the room, adding pressure to his brain and volume to an imaginary pile of false starts sagging with rhetoric. None made it past his lips.

"You are thinking too hard." Lydia dipped the quill. "Stick to the simple facts for now."

"I am alive."

She wrote. At least it was a beginning.

"Though I have finished my time in the Continental Army, I now find myself in South Carolina, continuing this fight for freedom." Daniel clamped his eyes closed and saw them, his family, each in turn. Mama, gentle but strong. Pa…the man he wanted to be. Solid and steady in both his faith and his actions. "I'm sorry I didn't come home. It seems wrong for me to be so far from you when the Mohawk Valley is by no means exempt from this war. If anything were to happen to you while I…" And his sisters. Teasing, giggling, and youthful.

"Are you all right?"

Daniel didn't look up. "Perhaps the Mohawk Valley isn't one of the main focal points of the fighting, but the British have tried to use it as a spear through New England before, and the Tories, Joseph Brant and his warriors, constantly raid the settlements. What if they needed me? How will I live with myself if I return home to find it burnt to the ground, and Pa, or Mama and the girls…" *Dead.*

"What do you want me to write?"

Daniel glanced at Lydia who stared at the quill while drops of ink dripped, blotching the cream parchment. "I would never forgive myself," he said.

Her hand trembled as she set the tip of the quill to the page. "You might have to accept that you have no control over what happens to your family."

"Perhaps, but my duty is to protect them. That is

why I started fighting this war in the first place. Somehow I lost sight of that." All in an attempt to hide from his shame. "Honestly, I don't belong down here. While I want the British to go home as much as you, I have no loyalties to South Carolina. The people I care about are far away." Even as the last words left Daniel's tongue, they lost meaning.

Lydia sat in her cinched stays and flowery gown, born into a world removed from his. But the more she spoke of her father, of meagre beginnings, the more Daniel wondered if perhaps she didn't look down on him. Not that she'd ever willingly leave her grand home and genteel existence. He needed to return to the wild frontier of the Mohawk Valley—back-breaking work and few comforts.

Daniel was mad to let himself consider the possibility of an attachment. He couldn't afford to open his heart to her in the slightest degree only to be hurt again. And yet, even as he fortified his resolve, he realized it might be too late.

~*~

"Maybe I have no real control over what happens to my family, the Good Lord is the only one who has that, but I am no use to them down here."

The shaft of the quill bit into Lydia's fingers as her grip tightened.

"It must be nice to have your family safe, here with you."

Cold washed over her body. "I have little time. What else do you wish written?"

His gaze remained on her as moments passed.

Lydia wouldn't look at him. If she did, he might

see into her soul and all the demons she hid.

"I hope all is well with you."

Not even a little. But she scribbled the sentence across the page for him.

"I thank you for the letters you have sent, and especially for the ones that found me. I wish I could be home for Christmas or the New Year, but I am not certain this letter will even reach you by then. As soon as I am able, I promise to come home. I shall be there for planting this next spring."

As soon as Daniel signed the bottom of his letter, Lydia stood and plucked up the ink pot and quill. "If I stay any longer, I will be missed."

"I understand," he said, his voice still husky. He held too much passion for life, for people, and it would only continue to hurt him. "I hesitate to ask, but would you be able to send that for me?"

"Of course. I shall take it with me now."

As he gave her a name and location, Lydia made the mistake of meeting his gaze. It held her in place, a different kind of fire smoldering in the dark coals. What was he thinking? Or feeling? Did he...?

He couldn't.

And neither could she.

Lydia forced herself to walk to the front of the building. The steel door latch helped her ground herself in reality. "That is your dinner there on the barrel. I forgot to give it to you."

"Thank you."

"And I found you a horse."

"Oh." Daniel cleared his throat "When can I have it?"

She needed to hurry him on his way before she grew any more attached, but his ankle was far from healed, and his cough seemed to be moving deeper into his chest. Not that she should concern herself with his health, but…

Lydia turned back to him, compelling everything but logic from her mind. She would stand nothing to gain if this man died of pneumonia before he could help her. He was her most valuable asset right now. "You will return to Colonel Marion?"

"Yes."

"Where is he now?" That was all she needed to know, and she could be done with all this.

"That is a good question. After the loss near Allston's plantation, he won't make an attempt for Georgetown yet. He probably headed north."

"Does he have a favorite place to camp? How will you locate him?" *Give me that much, Daniel. Please, let this come to an end.*

"There are places I can look, people I can ask. It shouldn't be too difficult to find him again."

And yet that seemed quite impossible for her. Lydia tried to think of another tactic. Maybe if she followed Daniel, he would lead her to Marion's camp. "Give yourself a little more time to heal. One more day. I will have the horse for you tomorrow evening."

She stepped out into sunlight and closed the door before Daniel could make a reply. She glanced to the narrow gap between the larger storehouses at the scarlet sentry Lieutenant Mathews had posted to guard Daniel. She was the only thing keeping the British from hauling him away to who knew what fate.

The letter to his family seared both her hand and her conscience.

15

"Where have you been?"

Lydia paused on the stairwell to glance down at Charles near the parlor door. "I have a letter to write before Miss Hilliard leaves."

His blue eyes became thin slits. "Nothing to do with our last conversations, I trust."

She gave a tight smile. For once she could answer honestly. "Of course not."

"Good. Then come down and spend some time with our guests and your niece. I insist."

"Must you?"

He stepped nearer and took hold of the banister. "I do not understand you, Lydia." His words hissed with his breath, not quite a whisper. "You were so close to your sister. I know her passing has been difficult for you, as it has me, and this event, marking the day we lost her..." His voice thickened. "But do you not think she would have you love her daughter?"

No doubt, Margaret would have wanted that. But Lydia was not like her sister—not as strong. "I will come down in a little while, Charles. My head hurts, and as I said before, I have a letter to write before Miss Hilliard leaves."

He shoved away from the banister. "Fine," he boomed. "As you please. Heaven knows I have done what I can."

Yes, you have. And she would not be controlled by

him, despite his attempts to feed her guilt. She refused to be manipulated. Without honoring his outburst with a response, Lydia tugged her hem a little higher and hurried up the stairs into her bedchambers.

She sat at her dressing table and withdrew a piece of stationery from a drawer. No, she would not sell her property for the little Mr. Hilliard said it would bring her. She had full intentions of living in that cottage herself. Freedom. She would do anything to have it.

A tap at the door issued a groan from her throat. "What?"

"Pardon, Miss Lydia." Molly slipped into the room with a tray. "Master Selby asked me to bring up some tea and cake for you."

"Thank you, Molly. Set it there by the bed." Lydia looked at the tray after the girl left, Daniel stealing into her thoughts. A warm drink was probably what his throat needed to ease that cough. If he would drink the tea. She would send it down for him later along with the cake. She might as well force that into him too, as she was in no mood for celebration.

~*~

Daniel laid back and stared up at the heavy rafters above. His family would soon have the letter. And he would follow it to New York. Heaven permitting. "Lord…" He rolled to the ground beside the makeshift bed. His ankle objected, but he did his best to ignore the discomfort as his knees met the packed dirt. He clasped his hands and laid his forehead against his knuckles. "Dear Lord, I know I am a man with weaknesses aplenty, but for my family's sake, for Mama, help me make it home."

Mama wanted him. He didn't doubt that. And his sisters would be glad to see him as well. But Pa...

"I raised you better than this, Daniel. I thought you'd grow up to be a man I could be proud of, but what you did to the Garnets makes me ashamed to call you my son. You are rash, boy. You never think things through." Pa had looked to his bad leg and his head wagged back and forth. *"Just like when you ran under that tree. You are never the one hurt. Like always, everyone pays the price but you."*

Daniel pinched the bridge of his nose, but the burning made it as far as his eyes. He'd hoped giving up his cabin and land to Rachel and her new husband, and serving in the Continental Army would change his father's opinion of him, and Mama wrote that Pa was pleased. But the thought of facing him again... Sometimes Daniel wondered if it would be better to die for the cause. Like young Gabe Marion. Surely that was something his father could respect.

Emptying his lungs, Daniel swiped his wrists across his eyes. Though not finished with his prayer, he wasn't sure what was left to say. He knew what he needed to do. He had to get out of this storehouse and on a horse. He'd head to Snow Island and report to Colonel Marion. As soon as his ankle was mended, he'd go home.

The shuffle of feet at the door jolted Daniel upright. He glanced to the low lamp light. What if someone besides Lydia or Eli entered? If he snuffed out the flame and hid behind the larger barrels, he could avoid being seen unless the person moved toward the back. A closer proximity would give him a better chance of overpowering an intruder.

The door swung open, and Lydia's slave stepped in, a kettle in one hand and a plate draped with a napkin balanced on his arm.

A slave. After three years in the army, Daniel could imagine what it would be like to do the bidding of others and never his own. But he would soon go home and be his own master, not endure a lifetime of such servitude.

Eli set the plate and kettle on a barrel, while keeping an eye on Daniel.

"How long have you served Miss Reynolds and her family?"

"I have been with this family since before they came to South Carolina. Long before Miss Lydia was born." The man said it as though something to be proud of.

"You must care about Lydia—I mean, Miss Reynolds."

Eli's midnight gaze narrowed a degree. "I have no intention of letting her be hurt. By anyone."

Though edged like a threat, Eli's words eased some of the tension from Daniel's shoulders. The Negro might be a slave, but he was also a man Daniel could respect. "Good, then we agree on one thing," he said, peeking under the cloth at the meal beneath. And cake. When was the last time he'd eaten cake? Daniel dropped the corner of the napkin and refocused. "You know my presence here will not do her any favors."

Eli's granite expression answered.

"You know what horse she planned to lend me?"

A nod.

"Miss Reynolds is a generous woman, a saint really, but she puts herself in danger keeping me here."

"You want me to bring you the horse so you can leave tonight."

Daniel returned the nod. "If you can do so without

detriment to yourself. You can place the blame fully on me. Today is Saturday, is it not? I'll meet her one week from Sunday. If you tell her that much, she'll know where."

The wrinkles etched in the old man's face relaxed slightly.

"Please. For Miss Reynolds's sake."

"For her sake, I could lock that door and tell the British where to collect you."

Daniel searched the man's stare. "Would that be in Miss Lydia's best interest? Her involvement might be suspected."

Eli backed out of the reach of the lamp's glow, his dark form swallowed by shadow.

Daniel's muscles tensed with the urge to lunge, to force his way through the single exit. If he could overpower the old man, he would assure his freedom. He could find a horse on his own or make his way on foot. With Wilsby's crutch and new boots, he might make it as far as...the edge of the swamps.

"Be ready for when I return," Eli mumbled.

The door closed in his wake, and locked.

~*~

Lydia rolled over and buried her face in her pillow. If only there were a way to smother her restless thoughts without smothering herself. A moan reverberated deep in her chest. She'd sent more blankets down for Daniel, and even some tea. As much as she did not like the sound of his cough, surely he would be fine. Why did he have to become ill?

She turned onto her back and stared up at the heavy canopy over her bed. Nothing left her feeling more powerless, more helpless, than disease. Without warning, it struck, taking even the strongest person and withering them to nothing but a corpse.

Flickers of memory tormented. Mother trying to keep the little boys tucked in bed as their bodies burned. Baby Martin had been the first to succumb to the smallpox. Then Mother began complaining of a headache. Lydia had gotten sick that same day. David died the next afternoon, and his little body was wrapped in his blanket. Motionless. Lydia had been sure she would be next. So cold, and then so hot. Pain spiked down her back and folded her in half. Mother must have felt the same, but sat with her anyway. Gradually, Lydia began to improve. Mother did not.

She remembered calling for Mother, wanting water. Margaret had been the one to bring the drink. Lydia shouldn't recall it so well, she was young, but how could one forget the look of the empty shells of loved ones left behind to be buried.

But Daniel wasn't that sick…and even if he was, he should mean little to her.

Lydia pushed up and stepped into her simplest gown without bothering with her stays and the like. What was the use of trying to sleep when every time she closed her eyes she saw him, pale and still, as she'd found him against the broad base of the ancient oak.

Moonlight stretched shadows across the house. She gathered her cloak but didn't bother with a candle. Down the back stairs and out across the yard. Lydia walked toward the harbor until the storehouse came into sight. The British guard was not. Perhaps he'd been called elsewhere.

"Stop this." She turned away. With the hood up to conceal her face, she journeyed across town toward the small church cemetery. Past midnight, it was now November eighteenth. One year from the day she'd rushed the physician into her sister's room. The mewling of a new baby rang in her ears while blood drained the life from poor Margaret, the only person she'd had left.

Amidst solid, silent stones with nothing but names and dates etched into their faces, Lydia stood alone. No smiles. No embraces. Nothing remained of her family but memories.

16

Eyelids heavy from little sleep, Lydia didn't notice Charles's strategic positioning near the door to the dining parlor until he stepped out to intercept her.

"Please step into my study for a moment. Breakfast will hold."

That was the least of her concerns. "Charles—"

"Only for a minute, Lydia. I need to ride to Charles Town today." He held out his arm, indicating she lead the way.

Fine. As soon as her feet passed the threshold of the room, she pivoted to him. "Speak quickly."

He nodded and pushed the door closed. "I thought it only right that I inform you of my decision to withdraw my offer of marriage. I know it was premature and understandably not well received." He began to pace the short width of the doorway, hands clasped behind his back. "I admit I had seen such an arrangement as a way to fulfill my need of a mother for Maggie, and the promises I made to your father to see to your wants."

Relief met a strange twinge of regret and a measure of hope. "What I *want* is passage to England."

He squared his shoulders. "But alas, that is the one thing I cannot offer you."

She stared after Charles as he strode from the room, distancing himself from her in more than one way. Was it because of his suspicions concerning her "arrangement" with Major Layton, or because he realized she couldn't be controlled?

Collecting herself, Lydia moved to the dining room and took her seat while breakfast was served. She kept her focus on the egg as she cracked the edge of her spoon against it and peeled away the pale brown shell, the murmur of Major Layton and Charles's voices background to her muddled thoughts. The men probably discussed shipments, or politics, or the dangers of shipping between the continents now that the French had armed their navy against the British. She'd heard their talk before.

The morning sun brightened the room, but did nothing to dissipate the shadows laying over her. Despite the earliness of the hour, with how little she'd slept last night, the day already seemed to drag on.

A movement at the door made her look up. Eli stepped to Charles, inclining toward him, voice lowered.

Charles jolted from his seat and rushed the door.

"What is it?" Major Layton questioned.

"The *Americus*." The words were scarcely out of Charles's mouth before he was gone, Eli in his wake. A moment later the front door slammed.

Lydia looked to the major. "Perhaps the ship has finally come into port. The *Americus* is overdue, is she not?"

"Yes." He stood and straightened his coat. "There has been no word of her." He trailed the others.

Lydia stared after them. A hard knot formed in the pit of her stomach. She lifted her spoon to the egg then set it aside and pushed away from the table. A wave of nausea removed what meager appetite she'd had before. It should matter little to her if anything happened to the *Americus*, but anxiety pricked her skin as it had when news first arrived concerning her father. She'd sat in that very spot, Margaret beside her. Charles was called away and hadn't returned for hours. Finally, he'd summoned them into the parlor with the news that the *Magellan* had gone down, sunk by two of the new Continental Navy's frigates—the *Hancock* and *Boston*. Only a handful of the crew had survived. Father had not.

Lydia pushed up from the table and called for her cloak. She wouldn't wait here reliving that moment. She burst from the house and made her way toward the harbor. The ships' masts stood tall above the buildings, but what if the *Americus's* were not among them? Were two ships now forfeit, all of Father's hard work, his dreams, sinking away?

She detoured. Daniel needed to be convinced leaving today would be foolhardy. His cough was likely no better, and she was no closer to finding Colonel Marion's location.

The hinges moaned from the weight of the door but did not seem to disturb the inhabitant. The lamp had gone out, and all lay in silence. Lydia shoved the door wide and the light speared across the floor and over the pile of grain sacks.

"Daniel?" She hardly realized she had spoken his Christian name as she rushed across the dirt floor. The air clung to her lungs, heavy with humidity and dust. Everything had been rearranged, leaving no sign that he had ever been there. She returned back outside. The scarlet-clad guard was still missing. Had the British taken Daniel? Was this Major Layton's fault? Or Lieutenant Mathews's deed? She would find the latter. She trusted him more than Layton, and he wouldn't cloud the truth.

A cool breeze rose from the bay and drew her attention back to the stately masts. None seemed as tall as those on the *Americus*, but the ship might be anchored farther from the docks. Lydia hastened her steps in the opposite direction. The day was still new, perhaps she could find the lieutenant near the garrison.

More than an hour of crisscrossing town brought Lydia no answers except that Lieutenant Mathews had already ridden out of town with a patrol. Soles of her shoes dragging, she returned home, arriving to the sound of hooves approaching along the road from the harbor. She leaned against the wall near the door to wait.

Charles swung from his horse in front of the house and handed off the reins to the stable boy, who collected Major Layton's, as well. Both men mounted the stairs.

"What news?" Lydia met them halfway. "Is the *Americus* in port?"

Charles shook his head, the muscles in his jaw strung tight. "No. She is lost. The Continental Navy sunk her out from Norfolk, Virginia. Only three men escaped with their lives."

"Goodness." Lydia's knees threatened to buckle. She raised a trembling hand to her chest. But why should news of the *Americus* affect her so? The shipping company was Charles's, and he still had one ship, enough to provide sufficiently for little Margaret.

Charles took her arm. "Are you all right?"

She drew back. "Fine. I am fine."

He held her gaze a moment longer, nodded, and then pushed into the house.

Layton moved to follow.

"Major."

He paused. "Yes, Miss Reynolds?"

"About the rebel, I—"

The corners of Layton's mouth dove. "Yes, Lieutenant Mathews already told me you let our pigeon fly."

Lydia opened her mouth, but her tongue remained paralyzed. How had Daniel gotten the horse? The only other person who even knew about the arrangement was Eli, and he wouldn't have done anything without her knowledge. At least, she had thought that to be true before this moment.

"I have noted Mr. Selby's ignorance of our arrangement, and doubt he would be pleased to know all of what his sister-in-law has been involved in. So very scandalous for a young lady." His tone held a threat.

"I would prefer he not be enlightened, Major." She was still too dependent on Charles to completely alienate him.

"Of course not, Miss Reynolds, but do not think of trying to back out of our agreement. Now that I have a horse invested, if I do not get my information, or my spy, not only will your brother-in-law be informed of your actions, but..." He eyed her up and down, his upper lips curling. "I shall likely come up with something more I want."

~*~

Daniel's jaw ached from being clamped against the pain pulsating through his ankle. With every mile he rode from Georgetown, he wondered if maybe he had been too hasty in his departure. And not just because

135

of his foot.

As he waded the sorrel gelding through the swamps, he kept his gaze on the rippling surface and the reeds. So far he'd sighted two alligators, their eyes and nostrils clearly visible. He braced for his horse to unsuspectingly step on one of the scaly beasts, maybe stumble over a tail, but he did not wish to contemplate the outcome.

"Who goes there?"

Daniel raised his hands so they could be seen. "Sergeant Reid. Continental Army. I'm looking for Colonel Marion."

"Come on through."

Daniel nudged the gelding forward, out of the marsh onto Snow Island. A man stepped out from behind one of the thick cypress trunks and waved him over.

"The Colonel's not much farther up ahead. Turn right after that fallen tree and continue past."

"Thanks." Ahead of him, a couple of campfires appeared through the veil of bare branches. Though not more than a week, it seemed much longer since he'd left camp to ride into Georgetown. With dusk settling into the woods, he was glad he'd arrived.

The area appeared mostly abandoned, and Daniel reined his horse to where several others had been tied. A couple dozen men milled around—a fraction of the hundreds camped here before. Colonel Marion and three others approached, and Daniel slipped to the ground. A jolt of pain nearly dropped him to his knees, but he gripped the saddle.

"What happened to you, Sergeant?" Marion asked coming beside him. "You don't look good, but a sight better than the corpse I believed you to be when you never returned with the others."

"My horse caught a musket ball, and I didn't get my leg out of the way." Daniel gained his balance but hesitated to put any weight on the foot.

"And lost your cane, I see. Now that you actually need it."

He hadn't given the cane more than a second thought. "Hardly the worst loss that day. I'm sorry about your nephew."

Any mirth fell from the colonel's face. "You saw?"

Daniel nodded. "It was wrong what they did." But he didn't want to rehearse it to Marion. Not now. "I wish there was something I could have done."

Marion's lips pressed thin, and he momentarily glanced away, nostrils flaring with the emotion he struggled to contain. He clapped his hand to Daniel's shoulder and squeezed. "At least he gave his life for what he believed in, and with honor. But...it is regrettable to think of what he could have become." Marion filled his lungs and stepped back. "Come sit yourself down before you hurt your leg any more. Is it the ankle?"

"It is."

"Broke mine shortly before Charles Town was taken this spring. Better to let it heal well, before you use it too much." He stepped out of the way. "Johnson, help Sergeant Reid find a place to rest his foot."

They made their way to the main fire, and Daniel propped up his leg on a large stone in time to be handed a warm sweet potato. "Thanks."

Colonel Marion sat across from him. "Your ankle and horse explain why you did not meet up with us. Captain Melton said he thought he'd seen your mare go down, but where have you been hiding out since then?"

"Sneaked into Georgetown. A friend helped me."

"The friend you spoke of before?"

He nodded.

"I'm glad you made it back. We lost a lot of men."

But certainly not hundreds. "Where is everyone else?"

"Home. With the colder weather settling in, even the British are not as active any more. It's pointless for men to huddle around a campfire trying to stay warm with their homes only miles away. They'll come back when we need them." He tossed another log on the fire, stirring sparks. "Any news from Georgetown?"

"A little. I overheard that there are only eighty regulars stationed there right now. From what I saw, they don't have the town very fortified."

Marion crossed his arms. "Then why wait?"

"Sir?"

He cracked a smile. "Just musing, Sergeant, but you might as well know I have had my sights on Georgetown for a while now. And I don't want to wait until spring."

Daniel carved back the blackened skin of the potato. Georgetown seemed a logical and strategic target, but an attack there would bring the fighting onto Lydia's front door. Could he leave South Carolina, not knowing that she was safe?

17

Lydia waited until the trunk was lowered to the center of the library floor and Eli left before turning to her father's shelves of books. She wouldn't be able to take them all, but she did want a few for her cottage. Something to remember him by. *Gulliver's Travels, Robinson Crusoe, The Arabian Nights*—she made a neat pile at the bottom of the trunk. The action helped fortify her resolve to leave.

If the opportunity ever arose.

Two weeks had crept by since Daniel disappeared. When confronted, Eli informed her that Daniel demanded he help him get the horse, but with the understanding that the Patriot would return. A week ago Sunday. She had waited at the oak, determined she would do whatever she needed to convince Daniel to give her the locations of Colonel Marion's camps, but he had never come. Nor had he sent word.

A rapping at the door caused her to look up. Molly entered. "Miss Hilliard is here. Would you like me to show her in?"

Lydia sighed. "No. I shall come to the parlor. Bring some refreshments." As much as entertaining held no appeal, propriety left her little choice. Perhaps Ester brought another message from Mr. Hilliard.

After setting *The Vicar of Wakefield* on the growing stack, Lydia removed the apron, smoothed the violet fabric of her skirt and exited the library.

Ester stood by the pianoforte, her hand resting on the silky mahogany. "Oh, Lydia, I am so sorry to hear about the *Americus*. You must be devastated."

"Not wholly." So long as she reminded herself the loss was more Charles's than her own. Lydia lowered onto the settee. "I assume Mr. Selby has been to see your father?"

Ester's head inclined in a nod, and she sat across from Lydia on a padded chair. "Yes, he was there again this morning. They had some..." her voice lowered, "business to discuss."

"I imagine so." But why would Ester think such should be kept secret?

Her hands kneaded the dainty handkerchief she held, an action that would do the pink lace along the edging no favors. "Lydia."

"Yes?"

A pause. "I am sorry you felt unwell last time I called. You were missed."

Lydia doubted that. Little Margaret probably didn't even know she existed. And Charles—not much had passed between them since he withdrew his proposal, and the news of the *Americus* arrived.

"You must dearly love little Maggie."

Love her? The day she had been born, Lydia had promised herself not to let anyone close enough for such a feeling to develop, but truth be known...

Lydia stood and walked to the pianoforte, keeping her back to her friend. "She is a dear child." What else would be expected of her to say? Lydia had done everything in the past year to avoid the babe, now a little girl looking more like her mother every week.

"After your sister's passing, I believed you would be the best mother for her."

No. "I cannot be her mother." Lydia knew that much. Strange to think that someday Charles would replace Margaret with a new wife. He had already said he wished to provide his daughter with a new mother. Lydia compelled her lungs to expand. Life would continue for everyone…except her. She should be in that cemetery with the rest of her family. None of them had really survived. Except the infant Margaret left. *I cannot do this anymore.*

"My apologies, Lydia. I did not mean to upset you." Ester came behind her and laid a hand to her arm.

"Do not concern yourself. I am not upset." Perhaps the greatest lie she'd not only spoken but tried to believe. "If you will excuse me, though, I should see what became of our tea." Lydia swept from the room.

Molly already approached with a tray.

"Pause for a moment before taking that in," Lydia said, stepping out of the way. "And tell Miss Hilliard it appears I was detained. Give her my regrets."

"Yes, Miss."

She started for the stairs just as Charles stepped into the house. "Lydia, where's Miss Hilliard? Her father told me she had made plans to call."

"In the parlor. Molly is taking in some tea now. My head is quite sore today. Why don't you join her?" She continued up the stairs, no desire to hear his reply.

"Lydia?"

She silenced his call with the door and then sat rigid on the edge of her bed. Beside her sat Mother's Bible, untouched for days. On their own, her fingers found the textured cover and slowly drew it open. Maybe somewhere in this book, in God, she would find the ointment for the pain that still ripped at her heart.

~*~

A gust of breath showed in the chill evening air followed by the cough Daniel had battled the past two weeks. The heaviness in his chest had lifted and his throat no longer hurt, but the cough continued to plague him. Daniel inched the length of log he used as a chair closer to the fire and held his hands toward the flames.

Another day sitting on Snow Island alone while Marion and the handful of men that remained scouted the British's movements and caused what trouble they could. The colonel insisted Daniel rest his foot, and while he knew the order was wisdom, staying behind did nothing for the boredom. It was again Sunday, and he ached to mount up and ride to Georgetown.

Daniel huffed out another breath. What was taking Colonel Marion so long? The men had left at first morning light, which seemed an eternity ago—and yet nothing compared to the fifteen days he'd been away from Lydia Reynolds.

Her image evoked a smile, though Daniel fought it. The longer he sat out here alone with his thoughts, the more logic and reason was pushed aside by his desire to see her again. Unfortunately, even if he wanted to meet her tonight, he couldn't very well walk the distance, and he'd lent the gelding to one of the other men whose horse had been lame.

Daniel pushed to his feet as the murmur of voices announced a return. The small band merged through the trees. *Hallelujah.* Maybe company would keep him from going insane.

"Anything today, Colonel?" he asked as they dismounted and moved to join him at the fire.

"Word came that General Green is now in North Carolina. He should be meeting with General Gates in Charlotte." Marion cracked a smile. "Otherwise, nothing but a small group of Tories who now have a greater respect for our cause."

Daniel listened to the several versions of the story while he set the kettle into the coals. Along with a handful of sweet potatoes. If anything drove him mad—besides his long absence from Miss Reynolds—it would be eating nothing but a single vegetable for weeks on end. Only Marion didn't seem to mind, but while others grumbled, no one complained out loud.

"You seem your cheery self, Sergeant Reid." Colonel Peter Horry clapped him on the shoulder.

Daniel raised a brow, but said nothing. Usually he didn't mind bantering, but another long, solitary day had soured his mood like week-old milk.

"Ah, leave the lad alone," one of the other men said, seating himself across the fire. "He's still young and probably pining over that lady of his in Georgetown. And why shouldn't he? He's a good decade younger than you, Colonel."

Horry frowned. "Not quite a *decade*. He's not *that* young, and I'm not *that* old. If anyone is a confirmed old bachelor, it's Francis Marion."

Finished with his horse, Colonel Marion waved them down and joined them at the fire.

Reds and oranges swirled together, radiating heat that only warmed half of Daniel. His backside remained chilled, and his stomach continued to churn. He was done sitting there. His foot protested with an ache, but not enough to dissuade him.

He was halfway to his horse when Marion's voice reached him. "Where are you going, Sergeant?"

"On a ride." Daniel glanced over his shoulder. "With your permission, sir."

"Would it not be wiser to wait until tomorrow?"

"Yes." Daniel took his bridle and slid the bit back into the gelding's mouth before the man who'd borrowed him had time to remove the saddle.

Horry came to his feet, but Marion motioned him back down.

"I might not ride that far," Daniel offered. He winced as he brought his good foot up to the stirrup, leaving all his weight on his injured ankle. It had done a lot of healing in the past two weeks, but the joint remained stiff and sore.

"That far, as in Georgetown?"

Daniel grunted, but didn't look.

"Well, if you do make it as far as Georgetown, it would not hurt to take a look around and find out what our British friends are up to."

A low chuckle rose from Horry. "Give her a kiss, Reid. War is not the time to wait on propriety."

Daniel shook his head and swung into the saddle. He didn't need a kiss from Lydia. Just to look into those beautiful eyes would be sufficient...for now.

~*~

The coarse bark pressed into the back of Lydia's head causing an ache. She'd sat there a while on the low branch, leaning against the ancient oak. This was the second Sabbath she had waited, and nothing. For all she knew, Daniel Reid was dead. Or maybe he'd decided to return to his New England frontier. Or perhaps his foot was still too painful. Or he was too ill. Or...

She sighed and stood. All the answers seemed to equate that Daniel Reid would probably not return, a thought that both tugged at her heart and washed her with relief. Yet, if he didn't return, she would have to find a new way to reach England, and a way to pacify Major Layton. He would not be happy with the loss of his horse.

Darkness settled into the woods. She'd lingered far too long, but it was still hard to walk away. A strange sort of anxiety swooshed in her stomach. Disappointment, worry, relief—none of which made sense. "I'll find another way." She would have to. Cloak drawn around her, Lydia started toward town. A breeze rattled the bare branches above her. This was the last time. No more waiting hours for nothing. No more wondering what became of Daniel Reid.

A flame danced from a torch as the lamplighter strolled to the next pole and climbed onto his step. She lowered her head and hastened past. One block farther and she reached the house. Instead of going up the front, she darted around the back and through the kitchen. A couple of the servants sat at the table, but she didn't look at them as she passed. They would hopefully keep silent about her absence from the house.

Making a beeline up to her chambers, Lydia threw off her cloak and dropped onto the edge of the bed. She had to find a way to convince Major Layton to simply accept her failure. Perhaps she would also talk to Charles in the morning, one last attempt to make him see reason. The *Zephyr* would soon return to port.

Lydia flopped backwards and spread her arms

out on the mattress. The more she thought of securing passage across the ocean, the more hopeless her plight appeared. The past two weeks, since they'd lost the *Americus*, Charles had been in the most unusual, reclusive mood. He appeared for meals as always, and put forth the appearance that nothing had changed, yet she sensed that was only a pretense. His eyes brooded. Maybe he worried about the remaining ship and only means of supporting his daughter. The loss of the *Americus* had been a massive strike to him financially.

Of course, Major Layton and General Cornwallis in turn had been quite livid when they'd been appraised of their losses—guns and powder and even a number of cannons.

Lydia rolled off the bed and began to undress. Better to wait a little while longer to discuss anything with Charles. Maybe when the *Zephyr* was again safe in harbor. Down to her shift before Molly came in, Lydia sat in her bed to sip her tea and read her mother's Bible. Few of the words settled into her, thoughts continually stealing away to the fate of the rebel sergeant. Cursed man. The least he could have done was write her a note or something to inform her of his condition and why he had not returned, so she could rest her mind concerning him. It was the mystery she hated of his absence. Surely that was all.

The Bible brought her little peace tonight. Lydia blew out the lamp and settled into bed. Rest was what she needed, and then she would be able to put thoughts of *that man* from her.

Fitful as it was, sleep finally did come, followed all too readily by dawn.

She buried her face in her goose-down pillow as Molly drew the drapes and laid out her gown. Lydia's eyes burned, but she had an appearance to make at breakfast. Compelling herself from bed, she dressed and washed her face. Instead of looking in the mirror while Molly pinned up her hair, Lydia stared absently at the window and the light streaming in. It didn't matter so much how she looked, so long as she was present. "Thank you," she murmured on her way to the door.

A screeching cry met her in the hall. Little Margaret seemed beside herself this morning. She was soon hushed to a whimper, but even that dragged Lydia's steps.

"Miss Reynolds." Major Layton hurried down the stairs to come alongside her, his smile as artificial as his powdered wig. "I trust you slept well."

"Well enough." She could sense he had more inquiries on the tip of his tongue. How could he not after hearing nothing for two weeks? She would meet with him today and explain about Daniel. Perhaps the major would not be too angry. She had done some service for him, and she had a few items of jewelry father had bought her...

"Miss Lydia." Eli met them at the bottom of the stairs. He paused, watching Major Layton halt beside her.

"Major, will you give me a moment." Lydia motioned toward the dining parlor. "I shall join you and Mr. Selby presently."

He gave a dutiful nod and moved past, though he slowed as he reached the door to glance back.

As soon as the major was gone from sight, Eli opened his palm to a small square of parchment. She unfolded it to two words and her heart kicked against her ribs.

Meet me.

Eli cleared his throat and nodded toward the stairs as footsteps pounded down the steps behind her. Lydia crumpled the paper in her hand.

Charles touched her shoulder as he paused beside her. "What is that?"

"Nothing."

He held out his palm.

"It is nothing more than a note. From Miss Hilliard. I shall go directly after breakfast."

His eyes narrowed. "What does she wish to speak to you about?"

"I—I cannot say."

He made a strange humph in the back of his throat and turned his palm down, offering his arm instead, dressed in the dark brown woolen sleeve of his coat. "I have business with Mr. Hilliard. We shall go together."

He led her into the dining parlor where Major Layton waited, his own coat as scarlet as the blood surging through her. The morning sun spilled through the windows, creating a cross work of shadows across the room. Like a prison.

18

Hardly a word was spoken as the carriage conveyed them to the Hilliards' home.

Lydia kept her face passive though her insides knotted.

Charles suspected her falsehood.

He gave a tight-lipped smile while assisting her down from the coach. "Are you feeling well?"

"Quite." Lydia pulled her hand back and led the way to the house. As soon as their knock was answered, she pushed past the servant to where Ester appeared at the door to the parlor.

"Why, Charles, Lydia, what a supr—"

"I came as soon as I could after receiving your note." Lydia caught her arm and towed her inside the room and momentarily out of Charles earshot. "Please do not question me. Pretend you beckoned me here."

Ester's eyes widened. "Why? What has happened?"

"No time to explain right now. Only..." Lydia stepped back as Charles entered the room. "I am so very happy for you."

Charles's brow creased. "What has happened?" He looked to Ester. "I hope you do not mind me keeping you ladies company for a few minutes. Your father is meeting with someone and asked that I wait."

"Not at all. And nothing has happened." Ester's

head gave a quick shake. "Nothing that concerns you." Their gazes locked for a brief moment, before she glanced back to Lydia. "Just something inconsequential. We women like to have our secrets from time to time."

Silence settled between them, drawing taut the air they breathed.

"Would anyone like some tea?" Ester indicated the settee and chairs.

Charles nodded, and Lydia took a seat, searching for any pretext to excuse herself. Minutes passed as they waited for the tea to arrive.

Ester tried to make conversation, but neither Charles nor Lydia offered much in return. The same continued as they sipped the warm beverage.

As soon as the teacup settled empty to the saucer in front of her, Lydia stood and stepped away from her chair. "I feel terrible leaving so sudden, but I must stop at the milliners for a hat I have commissioned. Thank you for sharing your news." She kissed her friend on the cheek and shot a quick smile at Charles.

His voice followed her out. "What was that about?"

Hopefully he would never know.

Lydia left the carriage for Charles. She preferred to walk, the thought of sitting a moment longer unbearable. She walked as fast as she could without drawing attention to herself. Her legs itched to run when she breached the edge of the grove, but she held herself back, slowing her steps. She couldn't rush in without being prepared.

Nothing had changed. Major Layton had invested interest, and she would be unwise to underestimate what he was capable of if angered. He did not strike her as a man who made idle threats. Meanwhile, Daniel was still her best chance at gaining passage to England and her grandparents cottage—the life she wanted. She couldn't let her guard down. She had to rein in her racing heart.

Lydia saw the horse first, the gelding Major Layton had provided. And then Daniel's form rose from where she had sat the evening before against the massive trunk. Her lungs emptied. He was alive and well. Her legs momentarily forgot her bidding. Especially as a grin spread across his face.

"My message found you." He turned his head to the side and released a short cough, as though to clear his throat. A great improvement from the chesty hacking he'd left with.

"Yes, I saw your note. Why did you not come earlier?"

Though his smile had slipped away, his eyes remained bright. "You waited?"

"You told Eli Sunday last, but when you did not come, I…" She shrugged away any further explanation.

Daniel frowned. "I do hope you weren't angry with Eli for helping me. I convinced him it was in your best interest."

"I admit to being somewhat frustrated. He should have inquired with me first."

Daniel looked at her pointedly. "I suppose he usually begs your permission for everything he does." The edge of his voice sliced between his teeth. "Eli is a good, intelligent man who followed his conscience. In order to keep you safe, no less. Can you fault him for that? Perhaps if you saw him as a man, instead of an heirloom—"

"Of course I see him as a man."

"Do you?" Daniel's jaw relaxed, but he shook his head. "Did you know that Mr. Jefferson wanted to declare freedom for all men when he wrote our Declaration of Independence from Britain? No man should be enslaved, not by a king or his neighbor."

Lydia bit back the need to retort—to tell him there were some things he couldn't possibly understand. She cared deeply for Eli, and his life was with her family, as it always had been.

"Forgive me." Daniel groaned. "I did not come here with the intention of starting another war." His eyes took on a new intensity, but with no trace of anger. Quite the opposite. "I have no desire to oppose you, even with words."

"You—" Her voice cracked. She cleared it. "You still have not told me what kept you?"

Daniel smiled, looking just as eager to redirect their conversation. "Colonel Marion insisted I give my ankle time to mend. I guess he's had some experience in the past. But not coming near drove me mad." The side of his fist beat out a steady rhythm against his thigh. "Especially at the thought of you waiting."

"At least you are alive. How was I supposed to know what happened to you? Over two weeks and no word?" More frustration tightened around her voice than she'd intended.

He only smiled. Insufferable man.

"Your foot seems better."

"Much." Daniel took a step nearer, a limp apparent despite his obvious efforts to ignore his ankle. "Though quite sore after riding most of the night."

A tiny spark ignited somewhere in her chest. Lydia quickly doused it. She had to stay focused. The longer her absence from the house, the greater Charles would suspect she had lied to him, and there was only one reason for her meeting with Daniel. "Where were you? I need to know."

~*~

The look of pleading in those blue orbs flecked with green did something to Daniel's gut he hadn't experienced in a while. Even his chest felt a little strange, as if his heart was constricting, yet so full in the same instant. "North of here." Did she want directions? "Why?"

"You vanished for two whole weeks without a word. What if I had news—important news?"

"Do you have news? What are the British planning?"

"Nothing that I know of, but that could change all too quickly. I would feel better if I knew where you were."

Daniel could understand her desire, but how would she send him a message? He would have to find someone closer who could relay it to Marion's camp. Letting her ride through the swamps was not an option. "Let me think about it, and I'll come up with something. Meet me back here next Sunday evening. Every Sunday if I can make it." A perfect excuse to see her. "Until we make other arrangements, anything you find out, I'll pass to Colonel Marion." Daniel was not in a hurry to replace himself.

Lydia's hands jerked into the air. "Why can you not tell me where you will be?"

"I don't want you to risk yourself."

"Any risk I take is nothing to what you face." Her

voice gained a measure of control as her dark lashes lowered over her eyes. "I am...I am more worried about you."

"I see that, and I can't tell you what that means to me." Daniel extended his hand to her arm until his fingers hovered near her elbow. "Lydia..." He stopped himself. He'd made such a fool of himself with Rachel. All she'd wanted was a good neighbor, a friend. What if that was all Lydia felt for him as well? Friendship.

Completely sobered, Daniel withdrew. Silence hung between them, screaming the truth of it.

She would likely never love him any more than Rachel had.

"Mr. Reid."

He looked at her.

"Daniel."

Again silence. His ankle throbbed as he forced himself to reverse a step.

"Daniel...I want to know you are safe. When I hear about skirmishes over dinner, Major Layton and the other officers gloating, how will I know if you were there, if you are all right. If I knew where you were, your movements, I will not be left in the dark...worrying."

"But would it be safe?"

She looked at him, but only briefly. "Nothing about this war is safe."

Daniel fought the urge to wrap her in his arms. "I know. And I admire you for your bravery. Your strength. Your passion for our freedom from Britain. Not to mention...you are so beautiful." Heat coursed through him. What was he doing? Was he fool enough to give his heart so freely? The answer came easily as her blue eyes widened at him. He might die a fool, but he wouldn't die a coward.

~*~

Beautiful? The way he looked at her, open and honest, his dark irises ablaze with affection. And desire.

God, help me, please.

Daniel Reid, her rebel pawn, was falling in love with her. Lydia had seen the beginning of interest, attraction even, but she was unprepared for this. What sort of fool was this man? He had no thought of her higher station, all their other obvious differences, or even the short duration of their acquaintance. And yet, this was all her doing. She had led him to believe she cared. Behold, her success. She had no choice but to use his affections, or Major Layton would demand she betray Daniel to him. What would become of her rebel sergeant then?

Lydia pressed her palm against the firm ribbing bracing her midsection. Perhaps she had again cinched her stays too tight. Surely that explained her shortness of breath. "Daniel, I..." She needed to step back, to consider how to best to proceed. She also needed to arrive back at the house before Charles. Most of all, she needed Major Layton to give her more time. "I cannot stay longer, but I want you to promise me you will meet me again. Here. As soon as you can."

He nodded. "And if all else fails, next Sunday evening." Daniel's hand slipped to hers, callused, but warm, as he brought her knuckles to his lips, and pressed an even warmer kiss over them. A sheepish smile stretched across his face when he released her.

Her spine prickled with guilt. But she returned a

smile—at least her best attempt of one. "I should go." *What am I doing? What am I doing?* Lydia's mind raced faster than her feet back into town. She glimpsed the carriage arriving at the front of the house and darted through the back door to cast her cloak aside. She somehow managed to compose herself by the time she reached the main hall.

Charles entered moments later. "Ah, you are home." He removed his gloves. "I paused at the milliners in case you wanted a ride, but you had already left. I should like to see your new hat."

"It did not turn out the way I wanted. Hence my brief stay." More lies. It seemed what her life had been reduced to.

His stare burned. "How unfortunate."

"Rather. Now, if you will excuse me, this morning has been rather busy. I want to rest before dinner."

"Please." Charles motioned to the stairway. "Do not let me keep you."

As Lydia ascended, the affection and hope on Daniel's handsome face joined the image of Charles's suspicion. When she had first been told of her inheritance in England, it had seemed such a simple thing to leave and start a new life. How had she managed to weave such a tangled and binding web?

19

Though now December, Lydia climbed from the carriage into brilliant sunshine. As much as she longed to linger in the light, the day was spent, leaving her only a few minutes to go upstairs and make herself presentable for supper. She tightened her grip on the package containing her new hat, purchased for the sake of putting to rest Charles's suspicions, and quickened her steps.

Five days and no word from Daniel. Lydia did not look forward to confronting Major Layton, but she could no longer avoid him. She had to convince the major to grant her more time, though she had little to offer him.

Lydia entered the house, stopping short at the sight of Charles. He leaned against the wall, hands braced and ear cocked toward his office. She closed the front door and he jerked around, his Adam's apple dropping low, eyes widening.

"Char—?"

His hand hushed her as he lunged forward and caught her arm. Without a word, he dragged her to the dining room.

"What is going on, Charles?"

He released her to straighten his coat and cravat. "I did not want you to disturb Major Layton. He is meeting with his officers."

Lydia took a step back to eye him. "And you are

standing sentinel to keep everyone hushed?"

The short laugh sounded out of place on his lips. "I admit to some curiosity. This is our home, our community, and I like to know what to expect."

"And?" Though probably as simple as that, sneaking around in the woods in an attempt to glean information from a rebel made her search the shadows for conspiracy. "What should we expect?"

"Nothing. From what I hear, the focus of the war is moving to North Carolina. All is well in Georgetown. For now."

"For now?" The ominous tone of his last words seeped into her. "Why do you say that?"

"This war is far from over." His lips tightened. "And the Swamp Fox is not going anywhere."

"For now." Her conversations with Daniel spilled guilt through her. If only she could put this war, this colony, and that man behind her. "Do you know if Major Layton will be much longer?"

"I do not imagine so. But he has requested supper to be served a half hour late to accommodate him and his officers."

"Who will also be joining us?"

Charles nodded, and then glanced to the tote she held. "Is that...?"

"The hat I wanted." Lydia had more time than expected to prepare for the meal, but she had no desire to spend another minute of it with Charles. "I should hurry and dress." She hastened past him. She shut herself in her bedchamber and leaned into the door before noticing the bolt lock residing above the handle. It had not been there this morning.

Molly arrived a few minutes later with a fresh pitcher full of water and to help her with the ties of her gown. Lydia pushed aside thoughts of Charles's eavesdropping. She needed to decide how to approach Major Layton. If he didn't give her more time, and she kept her side of their agreement, she would have no choice but to tell the major where Daniel would be Sunday night and allow the major to set a trap. But then what would become of Daniel Reid?

The man was a fool, too eager to give his heart. Had he not learned his lesson from the woman he had told her of? Lydia swallowed back a wave of nausea. If Major Layton refused to give her more time, Daniel would likely end up in one of the British prisons he so feared, and if she succeeded in extending their agreement, would it not be her task to strip Daniel of his heart? To make him fear to trust? To fear love? Which would be worse? Was there another option? There had to be.

As Molly tightened the laces over Lydia's stomacher, Lydia looked back at the door bolt. "Do you know who ordered the lock placed on my door?"

"I don't, miss. Eli put it there, though."

Lydia arrived for dinner shortly after the officers.

Charles stood with them as she entered. He smiled and nodded as though to remind her to keep his secret.

The next hour passed as a haze of conversation. She barely took note of what was served, barely ate more than a bite or two.

Charles finished first and excused himself to see to business at the docks.

Lydia waited.

Finally, Major Layton emptied his glass of wine and stood. "We had best return to our discussions." He paused while the other six men in uniform set their napkins and drinks aside. He followed them out.

Lydia came behind him. She could wait no longer. "May I have a quick word with you, Major?"

He paused. "Where is my horse?"

"That is what I wish to discuss with you."

"I am glad to hear it." He waved the other officers into the study. "I shall join you in a minute."

They disappeared inside and closed the door.

"I was beginning to think I'd forfeited a horse to the enemy for no reason. I had even planned a rather unpleasant conversation with your brother-in-law." Layton folded his arms across his chest. "I need not remind you that you have agreed to turn the rebel over to me."

"I am aware of that, but I've hardly had a chance with him recovering in a swamp somewhere. I need more time."

"As much as I would love to accommodate my curiosity of what sort of information you would be able to get from him, if any, I no longer have that luxury." Urgency grated his tone. "The battlefield is moving to North Carolina and with it more men, leaving Georgetown vulnerable to Colonel Marion if he comes against us."

"I can get you that information, Major. I know I can."

"Three weeks and you give me nothing. I am afraid, Miss Reynolds, you have no other usefulness than to tell me where and when to find the rebel. I shall proceed with my own methods."

"Two more days. I cannot promise you the Swamp Fox himself, but if I have sufficient information about the rebels' camps and their movements, with a guarantee of more, you will give me a little more time. That is all I ask."

Layton ground his teeth, glancing to the door of the room where his men waited. "Sunday night, you bring me more than a whimsical fantasy or this conversation is over, and I shall begin ones with your brother-in-law and your rebel."

~*~

The next two days were torture. Lydia excused herself early from dinner Sunday, stole out the back door, and made a direct course toward the old oak.

There he sat, just as promised. Dusk gathered, but Daniel's face lighted upon seeing her. "I'm sorry I couldn't come earlier." He stood. "My ankle was slow to forgive the rigors of my last visit, and Colonel Marion is quite determined I let it heal."

"How is your foot now?"

His stride betrayed the remains of a limp, but he shrugged. "Better."

Good. But now to the reasons she had come. For both their sakes, she needed something to appease the British. "Major Layton said they have not seen as much of the Swamp Fox of late. Word is, only a few skirmishes. Has Colonel Marion settled in a more permanent camp for winter?"

A laugh broke from Daniel's throat. "In the middle of a swamp north of here. I hate alligators."

"Alligators?"

"Aye. Riding past them, wondering if there is one you don't see." He continued toward her. "I'd rather face a bear or wolf any day."

She'd rather avoid them all. "Which swamp area? In which parish?"

One last step landed him directly in front of her,

his broad chest only inches away.

Lydia couldn't very well back down with Daniel close to giving her information she needed, so she tried to ignore the way his dark gaze searched hers.

"One much too far from here," he said.

"How far?"

"If we were closer, I couldn't have stayed away so long."

Lydia turned away, refraining from wrapping her fingers around his neck and giving a good shake. She should have known the man incapable of providing a straight answer to any of her questions. He left her no options and that realization sank deep into her stomach, making her ill.

"I'm doing it again."

The mixture of both apology and frustration in Daniel's voice made her glance at him.

The muscles danced in his jaw as his eyes clouded. "I'm doing exactly what I did last time and with the same effect. Perhaps I am daft."

Lydia shook her head at him. "What are you talking about?"

~*~

Something in her expression triggered memories Daniel had thought long buried. The surprise. The guilt. The trapped look that Rachel had also worn when he'd asked to court her, and again when he'd proposed marriage. At the time, he'd tried to ignore it, tried to imagine her reaction had nothing to do with him. But then he had seen the way Rachel looked at her British captain.

Daniel could no longer claim ignorance.

Please, Lord, do not let me make those mistakes again. He focused on Lydia. "I need you to tell me that you don't care for me." Because if she said it, he'd be able to walk away without looking back, without any second-guessing.

"Daniel, I—I..." Lydia looked away. Did he need a clearer answer?

"It's fine. I know you helped me because you wanted to assist in pushing out from under Britain's thumb. You're a Patriot. And you'll be a boon to this state. I apologize for being presumptuous."

"No, Daniel. It is not..."

"Maybe it's best that we focus on the matters at hand." He moved back under the tree. His ankle burned with each step. The physical pain was a relief—anything to get his mind off the live coal planted in the center of his chest. How could he have let himself fall for her so quickly? He attempted to clear the thickness expanding in the back of his throat. "I tried to get a feel for what the British are up to in the area on my way here. I heard Cornwallis is in Winnsborough. Rumor had it he awaits recruits from Charles Town." He dislodged his hat to rake fingers through his hair. The tricorn did not fit as well as the one lost in the swamps, but he wasn't one to complain. "Have you heard anything?"

"Um..." Lydia walked parallel to him, keeping her distance as she approached an extended branch. She touched it and then turned.

Even knowing how she felt, it was hard not to appreciate how she looked with the setting sun glowing from her skin and eyes. His sister Fannie had a similar complexion. No wonder Joseph Garnet had been taken with her. Only, in Joseph's case the girl had been more than willing to be his and share his life.

Daniel had always thought it would be as easy. He'd find a woman he liked and they would marry and have children. Reality proved much more complicated and painful. He would do well to follow Francis Marion's example and remain a bachelor.

"I have not heard much." Lydia still did not look at him.

"I should get back to camp. Colonel Marion will want to know about recruits being moved."

"What do you think he will do? Will he ride against them?"

"Hard to say." Daniel started to the gelding. He'd make finding a new mount a priority, so he could return this one to her. "He usually doesn't pass on opportunities to nip at the enemy's heels and send them running. Most of the men have returned home though, so I doubt he'll do anything drastic without calling them back."

Lydia's full attention was now his. "Would you send me word? When he makes his plans. I'd like to know."

"Why?" Daniel frowned. She was too anxious.

The natural blush in her cheeks slipped away. Her shoulders lifted with a deep breath against the constraints of her corset. Then her murky blue irises centered on him. "Because—because I do care about you. Have I not already told you as much, Daniel?" She inched closer. "Hearing nothing from you for those two weeks, and then a full week, not knowing if something had happened, if I would ever see you again... I cannot live that way. I need to know when you face battle. I need to know where you are when you are not here. Please." Lydia touched the tips of her fingers to his sleeve. "Daniel. Find a way to send me word."

Pressure built where his brows pressed together. "But...do you speak the truth?"

Her lips curved. "I do. I do care for you. I admit that I fought it. What with my family and their loyalties and positions in this colony, I could not contrive a way for us to be together. But I hardly care anymore. My only concern is your safety—and with Major Layton reporting each battle, I need to know where you are. I need to know the Swamp Fox's plans."

At the moment, Daniel cared nothing for Colonel Marion's plans. Not with Lydia so near—her eyes bright and her lips full. The desire to lower his mouth to hers edged him closer. "I had hoped... I've been such a fool in the past and the thought of making those mistakes again..." His chest expanded as he let his hand cup her shoulder. "Even though you speak it, I dare not believe it."

Hesitancy showed in Lydia's movements as she leaned near and pushed up on her tiptoes. Her warm, sweet breath caressed his face as she paused, her lips just out of reach of his. Her fingers brushed across his ear sending a pleasant tingling through him. "Believe it, Daniel Reid," she whispered. Then pressed a kiss to his cheek. She left him paralyzed, her hands falling away as she stepped from him. "How far is Marion's camp from here?"

"Almost forty miles. I should be there well before morning."

"Good. Send me word, Daniel. I need to know where you are and when you plan to engage the British. Please."

"But would it be safe? To send you messages, I mean. If your family discovered—"

She pressed a finger to his lips. "As long as the letter is sealed and in my name. Address it from Ester Hilliard. No one will suspect."

He managed a nod, and then she was gone, turning and hurrying through the woods toward Georgetown. Daniel stood dumbfounded for a while longer as he stared after her. He walked back to his horse. He had information to deliver to Marion and a future to plan.

20

Though full dark by the time Lydia reached the house, the door to the library sat open. She stepped inside. *Please do not let this be a mistake.*

Major Layton glanced up from the book he held, then tossed it aside and stood. Like a scavenger bird, he circled her before closing the door. "Well?"

"Colonel Marion only has a handful of men with him." She followed him with her gaze until he again disappeared behind her. "The rest have gone home."

"And?"

She had no choice. "His camp is in the swampland about forty miles north of here."

"Some of the locals have suggested Snow Island. A hard place to reach, and easily defended." Layton stopped in front of her. "More."

"Sergeant Reid knows about the recruits traveling north from Charles Town."

His eyes became thin slits.

"And so does Colonel Marion. Or at least, he soon will."

"I am listening."

Lydia compelled her lungs to expand a little more. Her head already spun. "Reid has agreed to let me know more of their movements. As they happen. You must give me more time."

The creases at the corners of Layton's eyes lengthened toward his wig. "Pray you have something substantial for me soon, Miss Reynolds."

She nodded. Her freedom—and Daniel's too—depended upon her success.

Upstairs, she lay in bed for a long time. Sleep easily evaded her. Daniel's words, the tenderness in his expression, the hope in his eyes, all tormented her conscience. Mother's Bible sat beside the unlit candlestick, condemning her. *What would You have me do, God? What other option is left to me?* It was not as though she believed in God. He had never given her reason to.

But Mother had. And Eli did. Even Margaret had spoken of Divinity from time to time.

Lydia lit the candle and dragged the book onto her bed. The Gospel according to St Mark. She read about Christ's words and miracles until she could no longer force her eyes to remain open. One phrase echoed in the recess of her mind as consciousness slipped away.

Lord, I believe; help Thou mine unbelief.

~*~

By the time Daniel rode the miles back to Snow Island, he'd convinced himself the likelihood of Lydia leaving her comfortable life for a much ruder one was next to nil. Still, the memory of her lips warmed his cheek.

It was dark long before he reached the swamps. Daniel camped in the open rather than risk getting lost or tussling with an unsuspecting reptile. He waited until dawn, his head propped on his saddle as Lydia's words plowed furrows through his mind.

She cared. Not quite a profession of love, but sometimes, a softness touched her eyes when she looked at him, which made him believe that given time…

The colonel and his men still slept when Daniel dismounted the gelding and moved to the coals that remained from the night before. He waved his hand over the charred logs, still resonating heat. With a stick, he bared the heart of a log and flecks of life glowed in the early light that sifted through the high branches. Laying fresh kindling close, Daniel blew against the embers until a tiny flame took hold of cattail fluff and grew.

"How was your ride?" Marion asked. He rubbed his palms against the morning chill. His breath hung on the air momentarily before dissipating.

Daniel clamped his jaw to keep from grinning.

"Any news?"

"Yes." He snapped thin branches in his hands and set them over the flames. Lawrence Wilsby had provided what Lydia could not. "Cornwallis is still at Winnsborough. But I doubt he'll stay much longer. Colonel Balfour is sending him reinforcements from Charles Town."

Marion sat on the log beside him. "Route?"

"Nelson's Ferry and the Santee Road."

"No surprise there." Colonel Marion cupped his hands and blew into them, his gaze distant.

"What's happening?" Horry questioned as he joined them.

"Seems the British don't feel we're keeping them busy enough. They think they can spare to send men up North Carolina way."

"Shall we inform them they are mistaken, Colonel?"

Marion nodded. "We shall. Send up some birds,

signal the men to return."

Horry turned to go, but paused and clapped Daniel on the shoulder. "I take it you'll ride with us now that your foot is healed enough to scamper after a petticoat?"

Daniel inwardly flinched at the crudeness of the words, but nodded. His ankle didn't love him for his escapade, but it would fare. "I'll be with you." As Horry left, Daniel looked to Marion. "I was wondering, Colonel, if I could borrow some of your stationary later."

"Of course. Least I can do. We appreciate your help, Sergeant." He set a larger log over the growing fire. "The distance is starting to wear on you, isn't it? You're fighting a long way from home."

"It's not just the distance. The war is by no means kinder in my valley."

"So why are you here, then?"

Daniel stared at the tongues of flames as they lapped at the kindling. A month ago, South Carolina had been a place to escape to, to procrastinate going home. Now, dark waves and blue eyes held him in place. He did need to go home. Soon. But first he'd find out if he had to go alone.

The back of his mind nudged him with doubt. Lydia had been too eager for information. Especially the whereabouts of the Swamp Fox. Her questions always seemed to lead back to Marion's camp and movements. What if that was all she wanted? The question struck him, a boot to the gut. He would be careful what he told her from now on, but prayed it wasn't true.

~*~

170

"Is there anything else you need, Miss Lydia?"

Lydia opened the cover of the old ship's log and glanced over Father's faulty penmanship. No wonder he had used a scribe whenever possible. She closed the book before nostalgia took hold, and set it on the top of the pile Eli had brought down for her from the highest shelf. "No, that is all."

"Very well." The gray-haired Negro turned toward the door.

Perhaps if you saw him as a man, instead of an heirloom. Every time Eli came into a room, Daniel's words whispered in her ears. *No man should be enslaved, not by a king, or his neighbor.*

"Eli?"

He turned. "Yes, Miss Lydia?" Though that was all he said, his eyes asked deeper questions.

She had her own. *What would you do if you were free?* But she couldn't ask it. Maybe because she was afraid of the answer. What if he wanted to leave? What if he wasn't happy here? But why wouldn't he be? This was his home. They supplied all his needs. *But what of his wants?* "Nothing." She tried to smile at him.

The man knew her better than to be fooled. That, too, showed in his eyes.

"Actually, I was wondering, did Mr. Selby ask you to put the door bolt inside my chambers?"

"No, Miss."

"But then..."

Eli stiffened. "I hear how the officers carry on when the wine loosens their tongues."

He had done it on his own. "Thank you."

"See that you use it, Miss Lydia."

"I will."

With a nod, he left.

Lydia ran her fingers over the silky finish of her father's desk before grasping the brass handle and opening the drawer. The same one she had found the Bible in. She unloaded the few remaining items onto the desk and put her mother's book from her mind. The guilt was not so easily displaced. She had lied to almost everyone...including herself. Was she any better than a tavern maid, convincing Daniel Reid of her affections, toying with him? If only she did not feel so trapped. Lydia chose a penknife and blue sealing wax to pack into the corner of her crate. She didn't want to think of Daniel right now, either.

The door swooshed open and she jerked up.

"Charles." Her heart rate accelerated. "What do you want?"

He opened his mouth, and then closed it as he took in the full library, gaps missing on the shelves where she had taken books, the large trunk in the center of the floor. He waved a sealed envelope at the shelves. "What are you doing?"

Her gaze remained on the letter. "Is that for me?"

Charles glanced to his hand as though he'd forgotten what he held. "Yes, from Miss Hilliard. I was told you had come in here, but...what is the meaning of this, Lydia?"

She settled her shoulders back and stood. Her full skirts swished past him as she took the wax and penknife to the trunk. Only a matter of time before he found out anyway. "I will be leaving soon." *Please, God, let that be the truth.*

"But where?" Little more than the blacks of his eyes showed. "England? That cottage near Brighton? Is that what this is about?"

It seemed he remembered. "Quite. Since you will not help me, I am finding another way to secure my passage." She snatched the letter from his hands. It indeed bore Ester Hilliard's name, but was not her handwriting. "Now I must go find Major Layton."

He twisted after her as she hurried to the door. "What does Ester's letter have to do with Major Layton? Or...Oh, Lydia, please tell me he is not the one you are bargaining with." His tone degraded.

She hadn't meant to tell Charles as much, but the liberty of it rotated her back to him. "How dare you reprimand me? You have no right. Not when you have the power to send me to England. The *Zephyr* will be home soon."

"She docked this morning," he murmured.

"She has taken passengers before." An escape beckoned with the power to put her beyond the major's power. She wouldn't have to give him Daniel. "There is no reason—"

"No! I already told you that. I cannot help you." His eyes closed momentarily. "Even if I wanted."

"You simply do not want to. Even after everything my father did for you. This was all his. Well, you no longer have the right to voice your opinions. I will go to England, even if I have to strike a bargain with the devil himself." Lydia rushed from the room. Her eyes welled with frustration. What if such a bargain had already been made?

21

Despite the sun's attempts to breach the heavy clouds that darkened the sky, the air remained cold and pricked Lydia's skin, making her shiver. Or was that the thought of what she was about to do? She perched on one of the chairs set out on the veranda and stared down the street at a cart as it passed by, the man pulling it mostly hidden behind a gray woolen scarf. She told herself she had no choice, but such rhetoric did nothing for the cluster of knots binding her insides.

The door swung open and Layton stepped out flanked by Lieutenant Mathews and another of his officers.

Lydia stood. "May I have a brief word with you, Major?"

He paused, as did his men.

"Alone."

He motioned them past. "Do you have something for me?"

The letter trembled in the breeze as she extended it.

Major Layton took the paper from her hand and smoothed it. "Why is it wrinkled?"

Lydia didn't answer. He didn't need to know that the mere mention of smallpox by Daniel had clenched every muscle in her body. She didn't know why it affected her so this time. Even if she did care for him, it was not as though Daniel were a weak child, susceptible to succumb to the dreaded illness. He was a grown man and, now that his cough had improved, a strong, healthy one. According to his letter, he hadn't even set foot inside the house where the illness was. After an initial skirmish with the British, the Patriots had tried to set up an ambush for them by hiding in and around the Singleton mill and the surrounding outbuildings. Until it was discovered that the whole Singleton family had the smallpox.

Major Layton glanced down at Daniel's scrawled words—not elegant in the least, but all correctly written—and then looked to her. "This is well and good, but gives little information of any use to us."

"Perhaps," Daniel had only stated what had already taken place, "but it proves I am closer. And is it not also useful to note how quickly the Swamp Fox called his men? Almost seven hundred within a day."

"Yes, the same men who yesterday torched one of our boats near Nelson's Ferry after removing anything of military value." Layton thrust the paper back in her hands. "Your news is almost three days old. What good is it?"

Lydia folded the letter away. "I will get more."

The major pulled at his coat, and then thumbed one of the brass buttons adorning the front. "And I admit to losing patience." He turned thoughtful, and the corner of his mouth twisted upward. "I think it is time to put your rebel to use once again."

A chill touched her spine. "What do you mean?"

"You were successful at directing him and his friends into one successful ambush. Before your next meeting, I will instruct you exactly what to say to him. Perhaps this time we will trap that sly swamp fox himself."

Instead of just his nephew? The recollection of what Daniel had told her of young Gabe Marion, along with her role in the boy's murder made her ill. She could not play such a part again. "Major—"

Charles stepped out onto the veranda.

Lydia tucked the letter out of sight. There had to be a way to stop everything from unraveling.

"Are you ill, Lydia?"

"Hardly." She tried to subtly clear the tightness that strangled her words. "Where are you off to?"

"I have some business with the Hilliards."

The solicitor had seen a lot of Charles since the sinking of the *Americus*. Not surprising with a loss to the company so great. Only one ship remained.

But even it wouldn't help her.

"What were you discussing?" He pointed a look at Lydia. "Or need I ask?"

The blood returned to her face with a rush of heat.

"We were observing the difficulty of finding someone to trust in the colonies," Layton answered. "Loyalist or rebel. You all dress the same and wear the same hat, as it were."

Charles cocked a brow. "Perhaps with some it is difficult, but many are outspoken in their politics one way or the other."

For a brief moment both the major and Charles looked to her.

The major spoke. "Unless they have reason to hide it. I am sure there are those disloyal to the crown among us here in Georgetown who say nothing for either their own sakes or to garner information for the enemy."

"Such as?" Charles asked.

Major Layton tugged at his coat. "I am not so

concerned with those at the moment, but I am glad the rebels are more complacent with their trust." He tipped his head to Charles and then to Lydia. "Now, if you will excuse me, my men await."

Charles nodded and turned to Lydia. "What did you say to him?" he whispered.

"Nothing." Another blatant lie. She'd lost track of how many she'd told. "Nothing that concerns you."

He pointed a finger. "Do you have any idea...?" He pulled back and shook his head. "No. Heaven help us if you did." His boots echoed on the solid steps as he jogged down to where one of the stable hands waited with his sorrel stallion.

Lydia filled her lungs with the cool December air and then turned back inside the house. The bawl of a baby hastened her feet to the stairway. She knew the difference between little Margaret's hurt cries from her upset ones. And if anything had happened to her...

The child's wails faded to a whimper before Lydia reached the top of the stairs, but she couldn't help from being drawn to the nursery door and peering in at her young niece in the arms of the nursemaid. Tear streaks lined Maggie's full cheeks and her eyes still glistened. Lydia's arms ached, the sensation real and painful with the desire to hold the child, to be the one to kiss away those tears. But instead of giving in to her need, Lydia forced her feet to step away and closed the door.

~*~

Daniel encouraged the gelding to lengthen its stride. With all the action they had seen this week, he hadn't been sure if he'd get away today, but the Sabbath had come with a gentle peace about it—and a plunge in temperatures. Nothing compared with a mid-December day in New England, but cold enough that it paid to keep one's blood moving. Only his fingers and face felt any of the chill as he raced toward another rendezvous with Lydia.

The sun lowered in the west, and brilliant rays of light filtered through the branches, the lengthening shadows a sharp contrast. The broad angel oak stood with arms extended, stately and welcoming. Daniel dropped to the ground and fastened his reins to a branch. Then he moved to the large trunk and settled in to wait. That only lasted a minute or so. The temperature didn't compel him to pace, but the growing uncertainty of Lydia's loyalties badgered him on, nagging the back of his mind. He needed to be sure of her patriotism and affections before he could fully acknowledge the feelings mounting within him.

The rustle of footsteps over dried leaves pulled his gaze to the cloaked figure hurrying toward him. He had no power over the curve of his mouth or the acceleration of his pulse. He shortened the distance to her. "You're here."

"Why do you sound so surprised? *I* have been here every week." Her lips pursed with a hint of smugness.

"Not surprised. Just pleased." He braced both her shoulders and grinned. He probably appeared ridiculous, but he couldn't help it. "For the past week it's been hard to think of little else besides seeing you again. If a ball from a Brown Bess musket found me, it would have been almost entirely your fault."

Any blush faded from her cheeks.

"I'm sorry. I suppose that is not what you want to hear. I'm afraid I can be given to teasing. My sisters can testify to that. But growing up with four younger, how was a lad to help himself?" Daniel took her hand and led her to the base of the tree. "You told me you have three siblings?"

Her fingers slipped from his. "Had."

"Had?"

She tipped her face away from him. "I am not here to talk about my family."

"Why are you here?"

Hesitation gave way to a small smile. "To see you, of course."

"And I want to hear more about your family."

"But—but I have news. I—I overheard Major Layton speaking with his lower officers. They said Lord Cornwallis was—"

Daniel placed the tip of his finger over her lips. "There is time for that later. Tell me about your family."

She staggered back a step, again breaking contact. Her mouth opened, but hung silent as pain etched her face.

"Lydia?" Daniel pulled her into an embrace and her shoulders trembled. "What's wrong?"

"I do not have one." She pushed against him, shoving him back. "I cannot do this. Stay away from me." She tried to run, but he pulled her to a halt.

"Why? Lydia, please tell me what happened. Did they somehow discover what you are doing? Are they angry? Or are you just worried they will find out? Please help me understand what happened."

She twisted. "I wish they were angry. I wish they felt anything at all. But how can they? The dead cannot feel."

"Dead?" Tension built behind his temples. "I

thought..." He tried to recall everything she'd said about her family, but he remembered little other than their differences in loyalties. "What happened?"

"Small pox. Privateers. Childbirth." Lydia tried to shrug away, but he didn't release her. Her gaze rose to his face and then dropped to his boots. "Please let me go."

Something in her expression made him doubt that was what she really wanted. "Are you sure?"

"I—I..."

She leaned into him, and Daniel wrapped her in his arms, the need to shelter her overwhelming. He touched his mouth to her hair and breathed deeply of rose water. He tightened his hold. "I'm sorry."

"I do not need you to be sorry. I need..." She pulled away and started walking east, toward the bay.

He followed, no sign of a soul as they passed from the grove, and she made her way down to the shoreline. Across the neck of shimmering water Daniel could see the long length of island, and beyond, on the edge of the harbor, boats nestled against the docks.

"What do you need?" At that moment he might give her anything she asked.

"Freedom," she whispered.

"Freedom?" He understood the desire for freedom from the British, but... "You live in a fine house and your family's shipping company is at this time dependent upon what it hauls for the British."

"My father is dead. The shipping company means little to me anymore. The freedom I seek is from a shadow, a feeling so oppressive." Lydia shook her head and backed away another step. "Sometimes I feel as though I am suffocating."

"Having a redcoat in your home probably doesn't

help." Daniel's confidence grew. She spoke with such earnestness, he could not doubt her words. "But I don't suppose you want to leave Georgetown."

Her gaze flickered to his, a desperation lighting it. "But I do."

A surge of hope warded off the deeper chill gathering in the air as the sun continued to sink lower.

"There are too many memories. My mother, brothers and sister are buried not far from here. I have lost everything I care about." She sank down, her skirts billowing out as her knees met the ground. "Have you felt that pain?"

Daniel sat beside her. He knew loss well enough. "When I was a child I lost a brother, born dead. And I've lost many a friend to battle." The thought of young Gabe Marion still constricted his chest. Yet how many boys just as young had he watched breathe their last? Too many. Still, that wasn't the same pain she spoke of.

"You mentioned a woman once. You loved her?"

He nodded, though he did not like the direction of the conversation. "Yes."

"I cannot imagine why she would have wanted anyone else."

Daniel jerked his head to look at her.

Lydia blushed. "I only meant—"

"Thank you."

She pushed up and started south along the coast, her shoes leaving indentions. Lower on the shore, small waves lapped at the mix of sand and stone set in mud. The sun continued to sink, adding a pinkish hue to the blue-gray horizon. "What was her name?"

"Rachel." The word he had dreaded speaking. No longer did her name invoke the same emotions it once had. Regret perhaps, but not longing.

"And what did you love about this Rachel?"

He followed a pace behind. "Our families traveled up the Mohawk together. She was beautiful, intelligent, and a hard worker."

Lydia's head tipped down. "The last is no doubt an important trait for the wife of a New England planter."

Daniel scuffed the bottoms of his boots along the ground. This was not what he wanted to discuss, not with Lydia. Again he nodded, though she wouldn't see it.

"What happened? Who was the man who stole her from you?"

Strange that the sensation of jealousy, though not as strong, still remained at the memory of that day. "A British officer."

Lydia glanced back at him, brows arched.

Daniel chuckled. "I didn't take it so well at the time."

"I imagine not." She searched his face. "So *your* Rachel was a Loyalist, then?"

The use of both terms grated his nerves. "No. I would never let myself love someone who could not share my passion for our independence from Fat George. I have bled and watched friends die for our freedom. Not only do I find it impossible to understand those who turn against their own neighbors to keep their loyalties for a king who does not share their affection, but I hate them more than a soldier in scarlet." His passion heated him and his words, but he couldn't help it. "The war between neighbors in the Mohawk Valley has not been pleasant. One of the bloodiest battles I took part in was against the very people who had once worked alongside us to build our community." He tugged at his hat, fighting down the images of Oriskany. "They slaughtered us."

Lydia turned her sad eyes away from him. "I can understand your feelings." She started to walk again, this time slower.

"Lydia." He hurried to catch up, taking her arm. "I know this is not the best time or place, but if things were different, I would ask to visit your father."

She swung to him. "Why?"

"Because I would want to court you—like a proper gentleman." He let go so she wouldn't feel the tremble in his hand. "Would I have any hope, or do you think he would shoo me away? I am but a simple soldier and farmer."

Lydia's eyes softened. "Hardly simple."

Her words seeped through him with tendrils of pleasure and hope. "Thank you."

~*~

Lydia ducked her head, chastising herself for her words, and for the fire ignited in her heart. "I should go." She would think of some excuse to give Major Layton. It would be better to face his anger than let him harm one hair on Daniel's head. She should have stopped this long ago. Or never let this charade begin.

Daniel took hold of her shoulders, and she glanced to his face. Horrible mistake. Dark pupils merged into equally dark irises glowing with lighter tones of brown. They penetrated her, seeking. He glanced to her lips, but her gaze remained on his eyes as they neared and closed. Warmth touched her mouth, then withdrew, lingering a breath away.

His eyelids fluttered open. His voice rumbled in

her ears. "May I kiss you?"

Lydia shook her head as her body inclined toward him.

22

Lydia tipped her chin up at Daniel's touch, her lips parting as they met his. Her eyes closed, but not to darkness. A strange sort of light filled her, along with the scent of moss and earth, and something distinctly and wonderfully him. She deepened her breath as Daniel deepened the kiss, his fingers traveling across her back, drawing her against him.

Slow and needy, his mouth moved against hers. An ache welled within her, as though she were being ripped in half...and then a sudden release. Her defenses crumbled. Her hands slid with a will of their own to his face and the hair at the nape of his neck. She answered his silent plea with an equally silent *yes*.

Daniel's withdrawal was gradual, as though weaning her from his touch. He never completely let go, but gave a boyish grin that broke dimples in both cheeks and melted her reserves as surely as his kiss had. How could she deny any longer that she cared?

Lydia thought to step back, but her legs didn't respond to their cue. "I should go." She needed to tell him to leave and never return.

"Do you have to?" Daniel lifted a shoulder. "It might be awhile before I see you again."

"Oh?" She couldn't seem to break contact. "Does Colonel Marion have plans?"

His hands fell to his sides. "Nothing to speak of." He tapped his knuckles to his thigh and turned away.

His removal was so abrupt, she almost lost her balance. "Daniel?"

He looked back.

Lydia fought the dread welling up in her as more strings tightened around her heart. He would be so easy to truly love, but losing him was inevitable.

His lips pulled up, but his eyes did not brighten. "I want to believe this—believe you—so badly, but after everything, I fear to trust myself and my senses. I know our acquaintance hasn't been long and circumstances have been quite irregular, but I believe I love you, Lydia."

Love?

"I do care for you, Daniel. Very much so." Too much. She needed to distance herself from him before she cost him his freedom or life. But when she opened her mouth to tell him the truth, the words wouldn't come.

He stepped to her and kissed her again.

She lost herself in his touch for only a moment before she reclaimed her senses. Both hands pressed against his chest, she gasped for a breath. "No, Daniel. We cannot."

"Cannot what?"

"I will be missed. I must go." She had to clear her thoughts. Find a way, and the strength, to tell him to never come back, never meet her again, talk to her, hold her...kiss her.

"All right. I suppose we have gotten a little swept away." He grinned. "I forgot you wanted to tell me something about Cornwallis."

The wagonloads of ammunitions bound for North Carolina...and the hundreds of hidden soldiers waiting to pounce upon unsuspecting rebels. "He

hopes to bait the Swamp Fox. Don't take any chances."
As for Major Layton, she would tell him Sergeant Reid
had never come back. Gone forever. It would be the
truth all too soon. "Be safe."

Daniel smoothed his thumb over her cheek. "And
you." He stole one last kiss before saying goodbye.

Lydia waited until he vanished back into the
woods in the direction of his horse, before starting
north along the shore toward Georgetown. Her mind
still spun when she reached home, where Major Layton
waited on the veranda.

"How was your rebel friend?"

Lydia cradled her cape around her. "I never saw
him."

The major frowned. "Then I have sent my men out
for nothing."

"Your men?" Her heart took flight. "What do you
mean?"

He wagged a letter at her. "General Cornwallis has
rejected my plan, and I am weary of these games, Miss
Reynolds."

"But our agreement—"

"My patience was on the conditions that you
provide us something useful, and you have failed at
that, Miss Reynolds. I want my horse back."

No. If they caught or harmed Daniel it would be all
her fault. "But—"

Major Layton held up his hand, silencing her. "Do
not fret, Miss Reynolds. We still have plans to raid
Snow Island. If we find Colonel Marion, I will see you
find passage back to England as I promised. But if
not..." He crumpled the letter and turned back to the
house.

Lydia remained in place as the major disappeared

inside. She couldn't follow. *Dear God, do not let them find Daniel. Please let him get away.*

~*~

With the hazy blue of dusk draped over the woods, Daniel mounted the gelding and reined west. He'd ride a mile or so away from Georgetown before heading north. That would give him more time to get this ridiculous smirk off his face before he found Marion's camp. He couldn't help the upturn of his mouth with thoughts of Lydia. And their kisses.

A horse nickered up ahead, and the gelding stretched its neck to return the call. Daniel cranked the animal's head around, cutting the whinny short. "Whoa, boy." He listened. There was only the rush of the breeze through the naked branches overhead. But someone was there.

Daniel encouraged the gelding forward again, but this time turned him south with a slight curve toward the west so he wouldn't find himself pinned against the river. As he neared the edge of the woods, he slowed the gelding's gait and searched for any movement ahead. A flicker of red. A British uniform.

Regulating his breath, Daniel spun the horse north and applied his knees with a nudge. With a quicker pace, he worked his way through the trees. More redcoats sat astride their mounts, watching. As though they waited for him.

"Halt!"

The cry had the opposite effect. Daniel yanked the gelding's head to the east and spurred him. Dried leaves and dirt strayed from the animal's hooves as he dug over the littered ground. Daniel crouched low in the saddle. A musket ball whistled past him. Branches snatched at his clothes, and one whipped across his face, his dodge not sufficient. He veered toward Georgetown, hoping for a gap. Deep scarlet flashed between the trees, also headed in his direction. He was surrounded on every side but one. Trapped.

Daniel broke through to the shore, the rush of hooves following, closing in on him, and leaving him nowhere to run. He kicked the horse toward the bank.

The gelding only made it several rods toward the water when it balked, throwing its head, its hooves sinking into the sand and mud. Madam would have plowed through, but Daniel couldn't wait for the young horse. He leapt from its back and raced downwards, his boots bogging with each step as though the very elements plotted with the British for his demise.

Lord, help me!

One of his boots stuck deep and he stumbled to his knees as another ball sank into the mud in front of him. He yanked his foot free and scrambled forward, meeting the water's cold embrace with no resistance. He swung his arms to propel himself forward despite the burn already in his lungs. He had to reach the island.

~*~

Lydia touched the tips of her fingers to her mouth, her silent prayer not ceasing. Her lips still tingled from Daniel's kisses. Darkness spread over the small town. Surely Major Layton's men would soon return to report their failure. They had to fail.

"Oh, God, please."

The front door swung open, and she jerked as Charles's long strides carried him past her chair on the veranda.

"Where are you going?"

He pivoted. "Lydia? Evening is upon us. You should not be sitting in the cold."

"It is not that cold." As she spoke, a shiver worked its way through her. "But it is late. Where are you going?" He could not possibly have more to speak with Mr. Hilliard about.

"The docks. With the *Zephyr* being refitted for its next cargo…" His lips thinned. "I have much to discuss with Captain Hues."

"Tonight?"

"Yes, tonight." Charles continued toward the harbor.

From what Lydia had overheard, the *Zephyr* would be in port another two weeks, not leaving berth until the New Year. Not that it meant anything to her with Charles's refusal to even consider granting her passage. In many ways, she was as much a prisoner in Georgetown as Daniel would be if he was caught. Though how much less pleasant would it be for him in Major Layton's clutches? If the major wanted more names and locations of the Patriot forces, what would it take to induce them from a man like Daniel? *You are not supposed to care. You are not supposed to care.*

Her mantra flitted away with the touch of a breeze, replaced by the image of Daniel's dark eyes and boy-like smile. The deep resonance of his voice. The warmth of his hands. The brown waves tied at the nape of his neck.

"I cannot do this to myself. Not again." Lydia stood and turned to the door. Her hand gripped the latch and she glanced heavenward—to the underside of the terrace above. *I asked for Your healing, God. I asked for peace.* The pounding of hooves along the hard-packed road pivoted her.

Layton's men. Almost a score of them. No Daniel.

Major Layton must have been waiting, or having one of the servants watch for him, as he stepped out of the door before Lieutenant Mathews reached Lydia's position.

She stood out of the way with hopes they would ignore her presence.

"We have wasted our time, Lieutenant. He did not meet Miss Reynolds."

Lieutenant Mathews straightened, his eyebrows pushing low and together. "But the rebel—the New Englander—was there."

"What?" The major rotated to her.

Lydia shook her head, panic rising in her throat. What had become of Daniel? "He must have come after. It was too cold to wait long." And yet she still remained out of doors. Her lies wrapped her like stays cinched too tight.

Mathews continued his report. "We pursued him back through the wood, but he took to the bay. I have men going out in boats to search the island and others are scanning the shoreline, but for all we know he went down when we fired on him."

No. Lydia's fingernails bit into the tender flesh of her arms.

Mathews motioned behind him at one of the men holding the reins to a young sorrel. "We have reclaimed the gelding, though."

A harrumph sounded from the back of Major Layton's throat. "That might serve us better if the animal could talk, but he will not very well lead us to Marion." A string of curses spewed from his lips, and he glanced again to Lydia.

"Excuse me, sirs." She stole into the house, her whole body trembling. In her bedchambers, silence surrounded her along with thoughts of her Patriot and her lies. She needed something for her hands, but needlecrafts had never been her talent. Lydia abandoned her room and paused at the nursery. She paced by the door. More silence.

Maggie probably slept.

She went back downstairs. No sign of Major Layton. He appeared to have left with his men. And Charles would be gone for a while longer, as well. Lydia took one of the lamps from the hall into the parlor with her and set it on the edge of the pianoforte. Her fingers itched for occupation and her mind begged for relief from a bombardment of thoughts of Daniel. And fear.

Laying her fingers to the keys, a chord rang, echoing in the emptiness of the house. Though stiff from lack of use, her hands continued across the instrument. A simple tune, slow and sorrowful, dredged the feelings from her soul. She tried so hard not to form any sort of attachment, but evidently she had failed.

Dear God, keep Daniel safe.

23

Daniel crouched low as a flickering lantern continued farther along the shoreline. Water dripped into his eyes, and he blinked the sting away. His stay on the island had been short-lived, the British soon joining him with a couple of rowboats. He would have liked to relieve them of one, but the soldiers had been wise enough to post a guard, so he'd hid until it was dark enough to swim back to the main shore. If he avoided the redcoats long enough to find a horse, he would hopefully make it out of Georgetown once again.

Clothes clinging to him and water running in streams from his hair and shirt, he crept up the bank. His foot, sore from the swim and again without a boot, pinched with each step as he darted, half hobbled, across the narrow road and into the trees on the other side. Even in the dark, he recognized the proximity to the harbor and the two large storehouses. No stars were visible in the overcast sky, but several lamps lit the docks. He was on Georgetown's front porch. Daniel made his way to the smaller storehouse, cloaked in shadow.

The smooth planks of the back wall braced him up as he caught his breath. He would have to leave the settlement before dawn, which made his exit more difficult. The soldiers would probably be watchful for him. The question remained as to how they knew he was a Patriot and where he'd be? Had they been told, or had Lydia been discovered? Was she in danger?

A rattling at the front of the building put all other thoughts aside. Voices mumbled, and he strained to hear.

"Do you know what has the soldiers riled?"

"I have my suspicions. But as long as they are busy elsewhere…" The shuffle of feet entering the building drowned out the words.

Curious, Daniel inched around the side of the storehouse. A light glowed from the doorway, before being squelched by the closing door. Again, the voices became mumbles. He moved forward, and pressed his ear to a small crack extended between the hinges.

"Are we ready, then?"

"Almost. By the first of January we will be. *I* will be."

"And then this will all be over. What will you do, then?"

"As long as my family is…"

Daniel pulled away from the door as footsteps pounded from between the other two buildings. A dark form of a large man barreled toward him. Daniel grabbed for his knife and dodged back around the side of the smaller storehouse.

More rushing footsteps, the men inside the building joining the hunt. By the time he again reached the back wall, they had him flanked, one on either side, pistols in hand and aimed.

"Toss that blade down," the larger man ordered in a harsh whisper.

No other option presented itself.

As soon as the knife struck the ground, the second

man snatched it up, and grabbed Daniel's pistol from his side. "You will not need this, either." The tall, thin man also kept his voice hushed.

"Who are you?" Daniel asked. They obviously didn't want to draw attention to themselves any more than he did.

Instead of answering, the large man, and a third, shoved Daniel to the front of the storehouse and inside. A single lantern gave little illumination.

"Now, who are you, and why were you spying on us?" The larger man straightened his tricorn hat as he squared off with Daniel. Though only an inch or two taller, the middle-aged man probably weighed twice as much, and the huge coat that hung off his shoulders resembled that of a ship's captain.

"Where was he?" The second man stood near in gentry's attire.

"With his ear to the door, trying to listen in. For all we know he's a bloody Tory."

Relief strengthened Daniel's limbs. "I assure you, I am not."

The gentleman relaxed his hold on his pistol. "Then who are you?" He eyed Daniel's soaked clothing. "And what are you doing here looking like a piece of driftwood?"

"My being here is merely coincidence," Daniel answered. "With a little curiosity when I heard you talking. You seem distrusting of our red-clad visitors. Are you Patriots?"

The man glared. "You still have not said who you are, and with all the Kings' soldiers standing watch in this town, I suggest you hurry if they are the ones you wish to avoid."

There was only so long he could skirt their

questions. "Daniel Reid. And, yes, I would rather my presence in Georgetown remain unknown. Can you help me?"

The men looked at each other. The gentleman spoke. "We cannot very well leave him here, I have wagons emptying all this tomorrow. Do you think we can get him past the sentinel they left us, Captain Hues?"

Hues nodded. "None of the crew is aboard, so all we have to worry about is that guard Major Layton left for us."

"I can distract him while you come past."

Daniel wasn't sure whether to feel relieved or uneasy as they discussed their plans. "To take me where?"

"Safest place right now is onboard *the Zephyr*." The thin gentleman, obviously in charge, nodded to his men and started to the door. "I suggest we delay our discussions until after this matter is settled."

He left, and a few minutes later the others followed, Daniel between them. His one foot sloshed in the boot while the other felt every pebble freckling the path. South Carolina seemed to have cursed his ability to keep a pair of boots—or to stay dry, for that matter.

"Are you one of Sumter's men, or Marion's?" Hues asked as they skulked toward the ship. "Or did you escape from the British?"

"I've been with Colonel Marion, but the king's soldiers seem to have a vendetta against me today. But who is the tall gentleman?"

"Charles Selby owns the *Zephyr*." Hues paused in the shadows.

Selby approached the scarlet guard patrolling the dock. Their voices murmured, blending with the hush of the tide breaking against the bank.

Daniel tensed as a red-clad figure abruptly hurried down the dock and then in the opposite direction. He soon vanished from sight.

Hues shoved Daniel forward. "Let's go."

Selby waited for them near the plank stretched between the dock and ship.

"What did you say to the lobsterback?" Hues questioned.

"Told him I did not feel comfortable with him as a lone guard with half our cargo still aboard. I insisted I would watch things while he reports my suggestion of more men."

More soldiers guarding the ship did not sound like a good idea to Daniel. His pulse took on a different rhythm as they led him into a box of a room with a single cot. Selby hooked the lamp on the wall. "Rest yourself while we find you dry clothes, Mr. Reid."

Then they left, the door swinging closed behind, followed by the slide of a latch. British guards were on their way with him closed in this small room aboard the *Zephyr*. The name resonated in his head, so familiar to him. But from where?

Lydia.

One of her father's ships. The first. Now her brother-in-law's, who was a known Tory. Daniel stepped to the door and tried the handle. It didn't budge.

~*~

Lydia slipped into the nursery, the room abandoned but for the child lying asleep in her small bed. Dark hair crowned her face, fine against flushed skin. Lydia ran a finger across the silky hair and soft cheek. Little Margaret turned her head, but remained unconscious to her aunt's presence. Another baby appeared in Lydia's memories. Poor, darling Martin had only been a few months older than Maggie when he had passed from his life, cold, pale and stiff in the bed at Mother's side.

Lydia clamped a hand over her mouth to smother a sob. She had failed at locking her heart—protecting it. She loved Maggie despite all her efforts to keep her distance. Just as with Daniel. What an awful, torturous feeling. Especially knowing that she could keep neither of them.

Eyes stinging, Lydia hurried downstairs to the library. The trunk remained in the middle of the floor. She threw open the lid and grabbed handfuls of books from the shelves. She no longer cared where she went or how she got there. She would sell the cottage for the little money Hilliard thought it worth and move to a hovel in Charles Town if she had to. She had to leave this place. Distance herself.

The door opened, and Charles stepped in.

Lydia ignored him, glancing around the room one last time. She would not be back.

"What has upset you?"

She clamped her jaw tight and settled her shoulders back. He didn't need to know how utterly weak she was—wide open and as vulnerable as ever. That had always been her problem. It was too easy to care too deeply and that only brought pain. She couldn't fight it anymore—she could only run.

"Lydia, say something."

"You need to let me travel on the *Zephyr* when she returns to England. You have to, Charles. I will do anything."

He studied her for far too long, his brow creased. "How am I to understand this? I know the past year since your sister's passing has been most difficult for you, but before that you were happy. Your father built this house for his daughters. This is your home."

"How can it be a home without the people I care for? All I have are memories, and I cannot bear them anymore. I cannot bear being the only one left here, everyone else gone." She grasped his sleeve. "Please, Charles. Let, me go on the *Zephyr*. Please. I do not care if I have to sleep on deck—I need to leave this place."

He stiffened and shook his head. "I do wish I could help you, Lydia. I loved your sister and have tried to do everything in my power to make you happy and provide for you for her sake and your father's, but *that* is one thing I cannot do."

Lydia gritted her teeth as she released him. "Why? Why will you not help me? Charles, you are the only one who can. You own the ship. You can give me passage."

"Not this time." He averted his gaze. "I have already agreed with the British that I shan't take cargo this time. Not *real* cargo, I mean."

"Then what?"

"Prisoners. They want me to transport a shipload of prisoners." A small muscle in his jaw ticked. "They insist."

Prisoners, like Daniel may very well be...if he wasn't dead. Lydia tried to push the dread aside. "There are plenty of cabins on the *Zephyr*."

"Lydia, please accept that I cannot help you. You have a home here. I have made sure of that. So please, do not ask—"

"No, Charles, I will not accept it!"

"It is too dangerous. We have already lost the *Magellan* with your father, and the *Americus*. French fleets patrol the main routes, and even the Continental Navy has become formidable."

"I do not care. Leaving here is worth the risk. Many ships still make it through. I ask so little for my sister's sake. For my father's memory and all he left you. Give me passage to England."

"The ship is not going to England!" The words came sharp and chopped.

Lydia clamped her mouth closed.

Charles moaned and waved her to not speak. "Please, everything depends on your silence. No one can know." Face drawn, Charles sank to the nearest chair and massaged his temples. "If the British find out..."

"Find out what, Charles? Where is the *Zephyr* bound? You said you had agreed to ship their prisoners."

"And I shall." He took a breath and looked at her, then stabbed his finger in her direction. It trembled with his words. "If you care anything for Margaret's child—for Maggie—or have any consideration for myself or for Ester, you must keep your silence in this one thing." His hand fell open. "I beg you."

"Ester? Why would...?" The pieces began sliding into place. "You and Ester Hilliard? You plan to marry her." She would be Maggie's new mother.

"Yes."

"Why the secrecy?"

"These are strange, dangerous times. I wanted everything in order. Everything in readiness, before..." He let the sentence die with a sigh.

Lydia leaned into the corner of the desk briefly, and then she pushed away. "I need to go." She rotated toward the door. She needed air. She needed to clear her mind enough to process what was happening—and what was about to happen.

24

A half laugh, half grunt pushed from Daniel's chest as he pulled new boots on.

"What?" Captain Hues questioned, pausing at the door.

"I left home with a good pair of boots and wore them for three years. *Three years.* I arrived in South Carolina not two months ago, and this is already my third pair of boots."

The ship's captain chuckled and again reached for the latch.

"Why are you helping me?" Daniel asked before Hues had a chance to leave again. "Or is that what you're doing?" Who knew what would happen when Mr. Selby returned. "Is this a game of sorts?"

Hues turned. "A game?"

"I know who Charles Selby is." At least Daniel was quite sure the man was Lydia's brother-in-law. "And he's a Tory."

A smile forced up the corners of the large man's beard. "So they say."

"Are you trying to tell me he's a Patriot?" Daniel shoved his arms in his now dry coat and stood.

"One of the truest."

"Then why does he ship weapons, ammunitions, and supplies for the British?"

Hues folded his thick arms across the breadth of his chest, making Daniel hope he would never come to blows with the man. "He inherited the arrangement from old Mr. Reynolds. Reynolds was a Tory as true and blue as they come. When he went down with the *Magellan*, Mr. Selby had no choice but continue on to support his wife and then his child. But he has not been sitting idle. Slowly he's been switching out the crew with them who are Patriots, myself included. The *Americus* was the first. He arranged for her to join the Continental Navy along with a hold full of supplies not three weeks ago. And soon the *Zephyr* will follow, but with men—prisoners meant to be shipped away from their homeland." He swore.

Daniel braced his hand against the wall behind him. "Then?"

"Mr. Selby has been biding his time. Now his personal affairs are nearly in order, and he will be ready to leave Georgetown when the time comes."

"But...does not his family know what his plans are?"

Hues shook his head. "Maybe his wife." Another chuckle rattled in his chest. "At least, she soon will be Mrs. Selby. But he couldn't trust any others with a secret like this."

All Daniel could think of was how relieved Lydia would be when she knew that she wasn't alone in that house, the only one true to the cause. If she was safe. Unless she was the one playing a game. He shook the thought from his head, her reply to his kiss too fervent to be pretend. Still he wondered. "Why are you telling me?"

"Because if you're one of the Swamp Fox's men, you know how to get a message to him."

~*~

Lydia watched the clouds of breath billow from her lungs as she moved through the grove in the early morning light. She followed the hoof scratches toward the shore line. One set of hoof prints deepened and then dug up an area, clods of mud marking where the gelding had stalled and turned. Footprints led to the water's edge. One still held Daniel's boot—the one she had given him. A gull cried and swooped to the water's surface. Sunlight glistened. The air warmed. But even a summer's day could not thaw what felt like a solid piece of ice wedged in her core. "God?" Her voice resounded in her ears, hollow and raw. Moisture touched her cheeks and she looked heavenward. A brilliant blue sky. No rain. "Help Thou mine unbelief."

"Miss Lydia?"

She swiped at her tears and spun to where Eli stood. "What are you doing here?"

"Mr. Selby was asking for you. Sent me to find you, and I'd seen you coming in this way." His black eyes regarded her without expression. "Are you all right, Miss Lydia?"

Another blatant lie formed on her tongue. "Yes. I am fine." But no doubt Eli could see past her pretexts. He had known her since her birth. What must the man think of her—his master through inheritance?

Perhaps if you saw him as a man, instead of an heirloom.

She had never considered it before Daniel had said those words, and she had tried not to contemplate it since, but she could no longer help herself. This was Eli's life, but did he like being a slave? Could anyone *like* such an existence?

No man should be enslaved, not by king, or his

neighbor.

Daniel's words pricked her with the thought of her Patriot in chains—still possibly his fate. Bondage. When his whole reason for fighting was freedom.

"Is there anything you need?" Eli's voice held concern.

Need? The answer was yes, but she didn't know what she lacked. She glanced down to Mother's Bible cradled in her arms. Could the answer possibly be within? "You said you believe in God."

"I do. Your mother shared that with me. She was a good woman with a strong faith."

Lydia hugged the book to her chest, wishing she could do the same with the one who had given her life. "I want to believe too. Will you help me?"

His mouth pressed into a frown, but his eyes seemed to smile as he nodded. "I would like that, Miss Lydia."

Walking with him to the ancient oak, Lydia sat on the large branch that formed the perfect seat against the wide base and opened her mother's Bible onto her lap.

Eli leaned nearby. "Open to the Psalms—the heart of the book. That is where your mother used to read the most. Maybe you will find more than God within those pages." He looked as if he wanted to say something more, but shook his head and started away.

"Where are you going?" He was supposed to help her.

"I think what you need right now, Miss Lydia, is time. Sit and read awhile. I'll tell Mr. Selby you'll see him after dinner."

Eli walked until his retreating form vanished through the trees as though a messenger from the heavens.

Had God sent him? She'd tried escaping the hurt without success, and she could no longer bear such a burden alone. If there was a God, she had to find Him. Opening to the very center of the Bible, Lydia began to read. With real intent. Hope. Desire to believe. She read and prayed, and prayed and read. And gradually a gentle balm smoothed over her heart. "'He only is the rock of my salvation: He is my defense.'" A rock. A defense. That was what she wanted. But what she needed… "'My *refuge* is in God.'"

Lydia had thought a cottage on the other side of the ocean would be that for her. She had been ready to give everything for *that*.

"'Trust in Him at all times; ye people, pour out your heart before Him: God is a refuge…'"

Lydia slipped from the branch to the cushioned ground. The Book remained open before her though she no longer saw the words. She didn't have to. They recited over and over in her mind in a voice not her own, yet so familiar. Margaret's? Mother's? Lydia wasn't sure.

"Help me, God." She flattened her palms against her moist cheeks. "Give me refuge, please. Heal my broken heart. Teach me to trust."

When her tears were finally spent and her face dried, Lydia sat back and closed the Bible. Her soul felt more complete, and she no longer doubted God heard her prayers. But now what? England was again out of her grasp. Charles was in the process of committing treason, and forming himself a new family in which she had no place. And Daniel was gone—perhaps forever. With nothing left but to return home, Lydia hurried through the back and up the stairs. Her niece's laughter drew her to the nursery.

The nursemaid sat in a rocking chair, Maggie on her knee.

Lydia took a breath and stepped into the room. "Will you please leave us for a few minutes?"

The woman looked up in surprise. "Pardon me?"

"Set Maggie on the rug and leave us."

Though hesitant, the woman did as ordered. "I'll be right outside in the hall."

Lydia waited for the door to close before she stepped to the baby and lowered herself to the woven rug. The child stared at her with wide eyes as though she were a stranger, which in many ways she was. Lydia traced a finger down Maggie's arm, skin so smooth and fair. Maggie wrapped her small hand around the finger, gripping it, and then tried to pull herself up. Giving her a second finger, Lydia helped her stand. Maggie smiled, and Lydia tried to do the same, but pain distorted her lips. Again, her vision swam.

"Look at you. Already such a little lady." She blinked to clear her vision and tears cascaded down her cheeks. "Your mama was a fine one. So beautiful, and strong…" Lydia suppressed a sob, her breath jagged. "Be like her. Not like your aunt."

Maggie stared, eyes wide and curious, appearing happy just to be on her feet.

The last of Lydia's resolve crumbled, and she pulled the baby to her. She rocked, holding Maggie as images and memories filled her, displacing the pain she had clutched for the past year. It leaked from her, again running with the tears from her eyes. Until every last one was spent and peace settled into her heart.

A tapping at the door forced Lydia to compose

herself, and she set Maggie back on the rug. She let the nursemaid in to care for her charge. Excusing herself, Lydia moved toward her own chambers. The mumble of voices pulled her short, and she stepped to the stairwell. Below, Charles stood, a letter in hand.

Ester leaned near. "I cannot begin to imagine who would use my name. You say this is not the first you have seen? It is not even my penmanship."

"I had not considered that." Charles turned the envelope in his hands and ripped the edge.

Lydia rushed down the stairs. "No! Charles, you mustn't."

She tried to grab the letter away, but he snatched it out of her reach. "Who is the letter really from, Lydia?"

"None of your affair." She lunged and ripped the envelope from his hold. "It is in my name."

"But what is my name doing there?" Ester asked.

Not a question Lydia wanted to answer. She darted back up the stairway, Charles on her heels. She slapped her chamber door in his face and jammed the bolt to lock it.

His fist hammered the solid wood. "Lydia!"

"This is none of your affair, Charles. It has nothing to do with you. Either of you."

He muttered something, and his boots pounded back down the stairs.

The thundering in her chest drowned out any further conversation between Charles and Ester as Lydia tore the envelope and freed the note. Daniel's halting penmanship marked the pale page with glorious streaks of black.

Dearest Lydia,

The weather was tempestuous yesterday outside of Georgetown, and the horizon was painted in scarlet. I pray you are well, but fear I will not be able to visit you as planned. Forgive me.

What was that supposed to mean?

She took a jagged breath. Foremost, it meant Daniel was alive. He probably swam to safety and hid. He would not be coming to her, and she wasn't to expect him for their usual meeting.

At least he was alive and out of Major Layton's grasp. For now.

25

Far from Georgetown, on a horse supplied by Charles Selby, Daniel rested his hands on the pommel of the saddle and closed his eyes. The black mare stirred under him as the rushing water of the Santee River sounded close by. Not an identical sound to the Mohawk, but it still tugged at him, reminding him of home.

Christmas Eve. In most ways Christmas had been much like any other day of the year back home, but his mother had always tried to make something a little special, something sweet. In the evening they had sat around the fireplace and told stories, read the Christmas story together, and even sang hymns when his sisters had their way.

More than ever since he'd left home, a lonely sort of melancholy pressed over him. He wanted to go home and be with his family…and he wanted to ride back to Georgetown. Thoughts of family were drowned out by the memory of Lydia's lips against his and the feel of her in his arms. Her eyes. Her smile. The stubborn determination he often saw on her pretty face.

"It's been a quiet week," Colonel Horry said, pulling his horse alongside Daniel's. "Do you think the King's soldiers are celebrating Christmas?"

Daniel straightened, shifting his weight. The saddle leather squeaked. "Colonel Marion must not think so, else why would he have us out here patrolling?"

"Probably just wants us to keep warm." Horry winked. "Though, your restlessness is keeping you from chilling, isn't it? Explains why your horse is always pointed toward Georgetown."

Daniel looked to the northeast. It would be foolhardy to return after his last meeting with the British. It wasn't as though he could meet her under that oak again. Had she understood his note, or would she be left waiting for him? And if he did go to town, where could they safely meet? The thought of waiting even another day to see her was misery. Maybe he'd figure something out during the ride. Fully aware that he was indeed insane, Daniel looked to his superior. "Do you think I'd be missed for a few hours?"

"Probably not. It has been quiet." Horry smirked. "We won't miss you, that is. Can't say the same for that lass you're dreaming about if you don't show up tonight. If Colonel Marion asks where you went, I'll tell him you rode out to get some more information from Georgetown. Might as well, seeing we aren't getting much riding this river."

Daniel needed no more encouragement, though the mare needed some. The beat of her hooves on the ground matched that of his heart as anticipation rushed through him. He might be risking his freedom, and even life, but that seemed to matter little at the thought of being with Lydia again.

He could only hope that she hadn't been the one to betray him. He hadn't felt confident enough in Charles Selby to risk asking him about his sister-in-law, or even informing him of their acquaintance. He had no proof of Selby's or Captain Hues's loyalties other than their word, and the fact they'd helped him. Not knowing the contents of the message he'd conveyed to Colonel Marion, made it difficult to judge. He raced his mount toward Georgetown, with the very real possibility he would ride into another trap.

~*~

Lydia glanced to Eli as he shifted her chair closer to the dinner table for her. "Thank you."

The wrinkles on his face deepened with the slight upturn of his mouth. He gave a nod.

She had never sensed his pleasure before. But since they met together in Father's library to study the Bible, he'd been approving. Though Eli couldn't read, he was her guide as they pored over verses that reinforced what she had read in the grove. God was her refuge. Eli had also prayed with her, and for her, with such fervency that even now her vision moistened at the sincerity of it.

Lydia forced her attention to the meal that was being served. Already, she had garnered Charles's gaze. Major Layton did not seem so perceptive. Did Charles sense the change taking place in her over the past week? He was so busy with preparations on board the *Zephyr*. Prisoners, brought in from the surrounding area, were being loaded into the hold. One more week and the ship would sail to Charles Town for more "cargo".

And then the prisoners would be surrendered to the Continental Army to assist in the fight against Britain.

Eli stepped out of the room, and voices mumbled through the half open door. Then he returned, walking to the far end of the table to whisper something to Charles.

Charles touched his napkin to his mouth before dropping it, and shoved away from the table to stand. "Excuse me." He disappeared after Eli. The door closed.

Lydia looked to her fork hovering over her food. Her appetite dulled. What if something went wrong with Charles's plan? The penalty for such a betrayal would be extreme. And what of his family. What of Maggie? Or Ester?

"Any word from your rebel friend?"

Lydia's fork clanked against her plate as Major Layton's voice startled her from her spiraling thoughts. She glanced to make sure Charles wasn't returning. "Do you really expect him to contact me again after you cornered him? He has probably taken that as full evidence of my loyalties." Though the single note since the incidence suggested otherwise. No matter what his suspicions, it would be safer for Daniel if he did keep a wide berth of her. His safety was most important.

"What I expected was to catch him." Major Layton gave a thin smile. "But do not worry. I think we have not seen the last of your Sergeant Reid. When he attempts to contact you again, I shall be waiting. And you shall help me." His tone carried a threat.

"Of course. Though, I do wonder if you ever had intentions of finding me passage even if I handed you the Swamp Fox on a gold platter."

A glance away seemed to be the only answer she'd get, but it was answer enough.

"It's too late for that now," he said. "Besides, when my men searched Snow Island all they found were cold fire pits and horse droppings. Little of what you've given us has been worth anything."

Except for sending a group of Patriots into an ambush. "I have been a fool, but this time I think you are mistaken. Sergeant Reid shan't return. He is an intelligent man, and I am sure he no longer trusts me."

Major Layton stood and moved to where she sat. "Just as I no longer trust you?" He placed a hand on the table and leaned over her. "I am beginning to suspect the rebel is breaking your loyalties, Miss Reynolds. Your eyes betray you."

Despite the strength abandoning her legs, she pushed to her feet. "You are mistaken, sir."

"Am I? I hope so. But in either case, I am not concerned. You shall turn him over to me."

Or what? The thought made her tremble inside. Lives were at stake. Lives that mattered to her. Maggie would lose her father and the chance of having a mother who loved her if Charles's treason was discovered. And dear Ester, who had always been a friend, appeared to care for her fiancé. Lydia wouldn't subject them to her own reality. She could not betray Daniel, either. It took every ounce of control to walk gracefully from the room and upstairs.

Maggie's happy chatter spilled out of the nursery door.

"Miss Lydia." Eli's voice turned her. He crossed the floor and pressed a small scrap of paper into her palm.

She unfolded it to the scrawl of Daniel's writing.

The scent of molasses and honey reminds me of you.

"Thank you, Eli." She stole a glance over the banister.

Major Layton stood observing.

"Be careful, Miss Lydia," Eli whispered, before

turning away.

She touched his arm. "Please see that the carriage is prepared." She looked once more to the major. "Miss Hilliard has asked me to call."

Eli hesitated before nodding. "Yes, Miss Lydia."

She turned to her bedchamber and quickly burned the note in the small fireplace. The paper withered and fell to ash. But was that enough? Major Layton would be watching her every move. Cloak donned, she paced her room until the carriage was ready. Lydia barely made a step out of the front door.

Lieutenant Mathews jerked from one of the veranda's chairs.

"Miss Reynolds." He folded a letter he had been reading and inclined in a brisk bow.

"Is something the matter, Lieutenant?"

"No..." He sighed, his gaze following hers to the letter. "It is from my wife. She is unwell."

"I am sorry to hear it." But she was more surprised to learn that the man was married, though she did not know why. In his forties, there was no reason the war had kept him from matrimony.

"Her mother is there to help her, but with five children to mind and only room for them to play out of doors..." Mathews folded the letter into a pocket of his uniform. "My apologies, Miss Reynolds, it is hard to be so far away from my family. But I see your carriage is waiting."

"Yes." All she could think about right now was meeting Daniel. "I do hope Mrs. Mathews feels better soon."

At the Hilliard's, Ester greeted her with surprise. "I did not expect a visit today, Lydia. Is all well?" She seemed apprehensive as she glanced behind her to the closed parlor door.

"Of course. Am I interrupting something?"

"No. Not at all." Still, she did not move to invite her in.

Lydia decided to ignore her behavior. Her own was peculiar enough. "I was wondering if you could help me."

"Help you? What's happened?"

Instead of acknowledging Ester's question, Lydia stepped past her into the house. "Please, if anyone follows me here, you must tell them I felt unwell and laid down upstairs."

"Are you unwell?"

She was, but shook her head. "I need to borrow a cloak. An old one, preferably. Something a little tattered. Perhaps your servants have one suitable." She glanced around. "Where are your servants?" It was unusual for Ester to answer the door.

She waved away Lydia's question. "Never mind that." Ester grabbed Lydia's arm and pressed a hand to her brow. "You do feel very warm. And moist. You're perspiring. Are you feverish?"

"No." At least she hoped not. "Please, Ester. Find me the cloak. I must leave forthwith. My carriage shall remain outside."

Her friend glanced back at the parlor. "Perhaps it would be best if I summon Charles for you. You worry me, Lydia."

The parlor. The closed door. Ester's striking gown. "He is here?"

"I was not to say anything." Ester spoke quickly but kept her voice hushed. "Not yet. I am so sorry. I did not want to keep it from you. You are my friend, but—"

"It no longer matters." Lydia pulled her toward the back of the house. "Do not tell Charles I was here and my mouth shall remain closed on the matter."

"All right. I will find you a cloak."

Ester was only gone for a moment before returning with the requested garment.

The exchange was made, and Lydia hurried out the door at the back. She ducked through a hedge of trees and then started north, walking a moderate pace as to not draw attention. One block. Two. Each grated her nerves—Daniel waited in the opposite direction. But she took her time, making a wide circle, watchful for any sign of someone following.

The day was warm and the old cloak overheated her by the time she reached the door of the small storehouse. Still locked. She scanned the immediate area, but there was no sign of Daniel. Had she misunderstood his note? Or maybe her journey across town and back had taken too long and he had already departed.

She unlocked the door and stepped inside…to emptiness. Her feet seemed the weight of kegs of powder as she walked to the center of the barren storehouse. Nothing remained but the scent of molasses and wheat still clinging to the musty air. She pushed the cloak away from her arms and pulled at the ties binding around her throat. Perspiration gathered at the back of her neck. When had Charles emptied the storehouse?

The room darkened, the sunlight blocked as a form filled the doorway. "You did understand my letter."

Lydia spun. *Daniel.* She blinked back a sudden wave of emotion at seeing him standing there. "Yes. I was afraid it took me too long to come and you'd already left."

"No. Just waiting, watching, making sure you'd come alone." He stepped in and closed the door, plunging them into darkness.

Her breath hitched. "Of course. That's why it took me so long. I wanted to be certain Major Layton did not have me followed."

"Is that what happened last time?" He took the lamp from the wall and lit it. The flame flickered as he adjusted the wick, lighting the angles of his face.

For a moment she forgot his question.

He returned the lamp to its hook and took a step nearer. "Did the soldiers follow you to the grove? Does the major suspect you? If it's no longer safe for you here, maybe—"

"I am safe enough," she answered quickly. *For now.* Either way, she didn't want to lie to him anymore. All the ones she'd already told formed a tangled net waiting to ensnare her. "Major Layton suspects, but he won't try anything. Not with the position my sister's husband holds in this community, and in the good graces of the British Army."

Daniel's hand brushed her sleeve and then dropped back to his side. He glanced down. "But what will happen if Mr. Selby loses those good graces?"

He knew about Charles? Maybe it shouldn't surprise her that much. Charles would have had to be working with someone to make arrangements with the Continental Navy. But how much did Daniel know? Had he spoken to Charles in person? Would Charles have said anything about her arrangement with Major Layton? No. Daniel wouldn't have come if he suspected her of trying to use him for information or betraying him to the King's men.

"I'm sorry." Daniel's hand again returned to her shoulder. "I didn't mean to frighten you." His gaze swooped to her mouth, and Lydia was helpless as he moved nearer and cupped her other shoulder. He looked into her eyes and grinned. His dark eyes asked a question.

No! Kissing him again would not help her let him go, as she must. She needed to tell him to leave South Carolina and go home to his sisters and his parents. She should be the one to explain what she'd done to him, and where her true loyalties had lain. But instead she nodded.

Daniel's lips sank against hers, smoothing over them as he drew her in. It was as though she stood in a thunderstorm and lightning danced in the sky around her, sending a charge through her. Lydia slid her hands to his face and the bristly stubble on his jaw line. Strange she couldn't feel it against her face. Or maybe she just wasn't paying enough attention. Otherwise she might have heard the hooves thundering toward them, halting along the road beside the storehouse.

Daniel broke away, eyes wide. "I trusted you."

26

A single exit and nowhere to hide. Nowhere the soldiers wouldn't find him. Lydia must have led them directly here. How else would they have located him? Daniel palmed his pistol. He'd left his sword with his horse in the nearby grove and a single shot would do him little good against the group gathered. Their horses snorted for breath, winded.

Lydia's fingers closed around his arm. "They must have followed me. I swear I did not lead them here."

"Quiet." Daniel moved to the door and laid his ear against the warm wood. No one had rushed the building yet. And from the murmur of voices, it sounded as though the horses weren't the only ones out of breath.

Lydia's arm brushed his, and he glanced at her and the fear in her eyes. It seemed he'd spoken too soon. Her mouth opened to speak, but he shook his head and reached for the latch. It wasn't as though he could keep them out if they set their minds on getting in.

He eased the door open a crack. Green woolen coats. Not the local guard. Not Major Layton and his men. Daniel's head still pounded with his heart, but some of the tension left him. The Queen's Rangers. And not even Tarleton's Dragoons. It appeared to be a new bunch. Twenty of them, or thereabouts. And it didn't look as though they'd made it to Georgetown unscathed.

"I am sure he is dead," one man panted. "He did not move after the second horse went down."

"Whether dead or alive, we cannot leave Cornet Merritt out there, and no doubt the rebels have withdrawn as well."

None of the men looked anxious to go, but all remounted. Several reloaded pistols as they rode away.

"Thank Thee, God," Lydia said with a released gust of breath.

Daniel pressed the door closed. "I'm sorry."

Her eyes clouded and she stepped away. "You owe me no apology. It is difficult to know who to trust."

"Yes, but..." He took up her hand, entwining his fingers with hers. "You have never given me a reason not to trust you." Daniel searched her eyes, and then tipped his forehead to hers. He let the remainder of the tension bleed from his shoulders and arms. "I can be a fool at times. Most times."

Lydia's grip on his hand tightened. "You are hardly a fool, Daniel Reid." She planted a quick kiss to his cheek, and then pulled away.

He didn't let her. Instead he hauled her back into his arms and gave her the kiss he'd been dreaming about. When he finally released her, she wouldn't meet his gaze, and he fought the reflex to apologize. Not this time. He wasn't at all sorry for kissing her.

"Daniel...there is something I need to tell you."

The hesitance sharpened his fear. Something was wrong and it would tear her from him. "Is there someone else you care for more?" He could remember too easily the burning sensation of seeing Rachel in Captain Wyndham's arms. Daniel refused to react this time. He would simply walk away.

She shook her head. "No one." But she continued to study the dirt floor.

"Then you do love me?"

Her mouth opened…and remained open, not a word emerging.

"All I want is the truth, Lydia." No more false hopes. And he would start by being truthful to her. "I know we haven't been acquainted so very long, and the circumstances have been…unusual. But I have found it hard to think of anything else since I met you. Maybe at the beginning it was because you were like a piece of home, a memory of my family. You are so much more now. I…" *Love* came to mind and clung there. "I want to go home, back to the Mohawk Valley, but—"

"I think that is for the best."

"What?"

Lydia pressed her hands to her abdomen. "I do not think you should come back to Georgetown. That is what I came here to tell you. I—I do not want you to try to contact me again."

Daniel stared at her. *You can't mean this.* For him to leave. And never look back? His lungs hurt as though he'd come off a horse and fallen flat on his back. More winded than any of the Rangers' horses had been.

"I must go." She brushed past him, but paused at the door.

He waited. What more would she say? Retract what she'd said about him not being a fool? Explain why he wasn't to return?

But nothing was said.

After a moment, Lydia stepped out of the building.

He followed.

She closed the door and locked it.

Daniel took several steps and stared out over the river, an island nestled in the center. The same one that had given him a rest from the current a week earlier. A different current swept at him now. Hurt, frustration, anger. Why had she let him kiss her—kissed him in return—if she felt nothing and wanted nothing to do with him?

He wasn't being fair. Rachel's rejection still clouded his judgment. Lydia must have felt something. He'd seen it in her eyes and felt it on her lips. Maybe she was only concerned for him with the British breathing down his neck. Or perhaps she feared going against her family. Mr. Selby had made the secrecy of his loyalties clear. She probably didn't know that he was also a Patriot, but maybe if she did…

Daniel turned. He couldn't walk away yet. "Give me a reason. Tell me why you want me gone."

~*~

Lydia leaned against the locked door, bracing herself. Daniel desired the truth. The whole truth. More than she could give him. He would hate her. "You do not belong here," she told him. "South Carolina is not your home and this is not your battleground. Go back to your family. I am sure they love you, just as you love them."

Uncertainty flickered in his eyes. "I plan on going home. I guess what I should have asked, is why you won't come with me?"

With him? Her chest seemed to expand on its own, as did her heart. She hadn't considered leaving with him as an option. How could she? Everything he believed of her was a lie. She had used him and endangered him. And if she went with him, she would have to open her heart even more, letting him in wholly. Lydia wasn't sure she could do that. If she loved him any more than she already did and something happened to him... Lydia blinked, first in realization, and second to clear her blurred vision. She loved him. And she *would* lose him just as she'd lost everyone else. Better now, on her own terms, than later when he saturated her very existence. "I cannot go with you."

"But you still haven't told me why. Is it because of your family, your brother-in-law? You needn't worry about him any longer. He's a Patriot. And now he's to be married, I don't believe he would stand in your way."

Every muscle in Lydia's body tensed. "How do you know so much about Charles?"

"I met him a week ago." Daniel's eyes narrowed slightly, probably trying to understand her reaction.

She was helpless to subdue it. Perhaps Charles hadn't mentioned her yet, but it was only a matter of time before he revealed her collaboration with Major Layton. Unless she convinced Daniel to leave South Carolina. The only way to make sure he left immediately was if she went with him...and lived a lie. He would never need to know. But oh, what a tangled mess. Her reasons for not going paled in comparison to keeping him, and her secret, safe. "Tomorrow night."

Daniel looked confused. "What?"

"I will leave with you tomorrow night." That would give her today, Christmas Day, to prepare. "Meet me here on the twenty-sixth, and I will go with you."

A grin broke across his face. "When you say you'll go with me, you mean to New England, to the Mohawk Valley, my home, as my wife?"

"Yes." That single word ricocheted through her, ringing with a strange sort of keenness. Excitement, even. A new life. Not the freedom she had been convinced she'd wanted, but perhaps this is what God had planned for her when He'd first brought Daniel Reid into her life. She had to learn to trust Him with her heart—and find refuge.

27

Lydia took a direct route home and stashed away the old cloak in a closet near the kitchen before moving to the front of the house. Her heart raced. She was finally leaving this place and the memories that made her want to weep. But instead of burying herself in an English cottage, she would build new memories. *Oh, please let them be happy.* Most importantly, she would take control and keep Daniel safe. First, she had goodbyes to say. Through the house toward the stair leading to the second floor, the nursery and the babbling of a young child beckoned.

"How sure are you of this?"

Lydia skidded to a stop and withdrew a step.

The voice was lowered, but recognizable as Major Layton's. Someone stood just inside Charles's office, door slightly ajar.

"Completely sure," a second man rasped. "Might have hesitated if I weren't. Isn't it peculiar Mr. Selby traded out captains handpicked by Mr. Reynolds when he was alive? Well, Selby's handpicked his own, I reckon. Rebels the both of them." He harrumphed. "The *Americus* wasn't lost to the Continentals. She was handed over on a platter."

Legs of a chair squawked against the floor, and Lydia drew out of sight of the door. She strained to hear what was said.

A rapping on the top of the desk suggested the

Major's knuckles or an object he held. "But is there any proof?"

Curses spewed from the man's mouth and the crack in the door. "Selby's not a fool. Been covering his tracks well. But I've overheard Captain Hues and him speaking when they thought none were about. I swear it's the truth."

"Fine, then."

Footsteps approached the door, and Lydia slipped into the parlor, closing the door enough to conceal herself.

Major Layton's hushed mumble accompanied the two men into the hall. "Speak of this to no one. I will see to this matter myself. Immediately."

Lydia hugged herself. She had to somehow warn Charles before the major slapped him in irons and shipped him to England with the other prisoners. Margaret was gone, but he was still her family. As was Little Maggie. She couldn't allow that precious child to lose her father too. But what could she do?

Major Layton would probably have Charles arrested as soon as he stepped through those front doors. If he made it that far. There had to be a way to provide him more time.

Shoulders squared, Lydia crossed the room to the pianoforte and seated herself. Raw fear filled her, but her fingers, stiff from a year of neglecting the instrument, still managed to move across the keys and create a merry tune. Maybe if she lost herself in the music enough, she could manage to play one last charade. As she finished the song, clapping resounded off the high ceiling.

"Well played, Miss Reynolds. I had not realized you were so accomplished." Major Layton moved deeper into the room. "Is there an occasion?"

"Yes." She laid her hands on her lap. *God, help me be convincing. Give me the words to save the ones I care for.* Her focus steadfast on Major Layton's, she let go of all emotion. She'd had enough practice. "I'm ready to make one last bargain with you. I know you were suspicious of the message I received this morning and your instincts were correct. It was indeed from Sergeant Reid. He asked to meet with me and I received some most interesting information about the rebel's movements in the area and a certain man of our acquaintance who…" She compelled her mouth to relax as she smiled at him. "But I shall come to that in a minute. First, you shall do *me* a favor."

He eyed her. "What, exactly?"

"I have fed the rebels information, and I all but handed you the location of one of their camps. It is not my fault you found nothing but cold ash and horse waste. I want you to give me what I have always wanted."

Layton settled back and smiled. "If I'm impressed by what you have for me, I will make the arrangements as soon as I leave here. Though, in the middle of a war, I cannot guarantee you a pleasant voyage, madam."

"I assure you, none of this has been pleasant, sir." Lydia walked to the doorway. "And this time I want our agreement in writing. I believe there is stationery and ink in Charles's desk, and our conversation involves him."

The major's eyes widened with interest, and he followed her into the office. She placed the paper and quill before him and waited. Hopefully the focus on what she wanted from him would keep him from doubting what she told him next.

He wrote what she asked but left the bottom unsigned. "Now, tell me what you know and I'll add my signature."

Lydia made him wait, studying the agreement instead. "Very well. It seems a certain relative of mine has been misleading about his loyalties and will soon be able to lead you straight to that sly fox that has been eluding you the past year." She paused, letting the major ingest the information. "Tomorrow night. Reid said he would rendezvous with Mr. Selby and take him to Colonel Marion for a meeting."

Major Layton's gaze threatened to light her on fire, but she could see his mind working, no doubt wondering if such an opportunity were actual. "Where?"

A very good question. "Somewhere near Shepherd's Ferry, but I do not have an exact location. You will have to follow Mr. Selby."

Please, let this work. She just needed Major Layton to leave Charles alone long enough for him to get away. If all went well, he could send for Maggie and Ester later.

A trill of excitement passed through her. Her plan would work, and as long as the major took his men and the Queen's Rangers with him to Shepherd's Ferry, Daniel would have no difficulty coming for her.

"You seem pleased with yourself, Miss Reynolds," Layton said.

"Should I not be? If all goes well, we shall both have everything we want."

He nodded and then signed the agreement. "Perhaps I misjudged you after all." He dropped the quill back to the desk and made a bow. "I will see about your passage, though it may require you to travel to Charles Town."

"Hardly an inconvenience." Lydia stood and followed the major from the room. There would be little time to freshen up before dinner. Charles had told her there would be company for their Christmas feast.

The major paused, eyes on Charles as he led Ester across the threshold.

Charles looked from Lydia to the British officer and back again, silent questions ridging his forehead.

Major Layton gave a nod, and then stepped aside so Lydia could properly greet their guest—the soon-to-be mistress of the estate.

"I'm so glad you could come, Miss Hilliard." Lydia took her hand and prayed Ester would have the frame of mind to remain silent about their earlier exchange.

"She is no longer Miss Hilliard." Charles placed Ester's hand back on his arm. "As of this morning, she is Mrs. Selby." He seemed to study Lydia for a reaction.

She smiled, this one much easier to muster than the one she had given the Major. "This morning?"

Ester nodded. "I am sorry I kept it from you."

Lydia's eyes misted and she blinked to keep them clear. A secret wedding. That explained the closed parlor door at the Hilliards. Had they not even trusted their servants to be present? She wanted nothing more than to embrace Ester—and Charles, for that matter—and tell them how pleased she was for them. And Maggie. Ester would be the mother the child needed so badly. A mother who would love and cherish her.

But Major Layton continued to watch.

Lydia stiffened both her spine and her smile. "No matter. I must excuse myself to prepare for dinner, but shall return shortly." She turned, giving Layton a slight nod as she moved past. *God, please help us.*

~*~

"What are you grinning about?"

Daniel reined his horse in, too pleased to be put off by Colonel Horry's tone. "You're a little closer to Georgetown than I left you."

Horry shrugged. "Been playing with the Queen's Rangers. A bashful group if I've ever seen one."

"I wondered what had them running scared. Though, with a dozen more men than them, perhaps it's understandable."

"You saw them, then?"

"Yes. And there being more of them than of me, I admit they had me ready to run as well." Daniel looked past the colonel to his men. "You have two companies? Where is Colonel Marion?"

"He rode up toward Indiantown. Why?"

"I've spoken with him about returning to New England soon." He momentarily reined in his smile. "I think it's time."

"A shame." Horry frowned. "We had all sorts of plans for Georgetown in the next few weeks."

"As much as I have enjoyed riding with you, I think it best I take my wife as far as possible from you crazy swamp runners." Daniel nudged his horse past.

"Your wife?" Horry twisted in his saddle.

Daniel's cheeks ached from the force of his grin. "That's the other reason I need to speak with Colonel Marion. I want his blessing on my wedding."

Horry laughed out loud. "Isn't right, Reid, a New Englander coming down to steal one of our belles."

Daniel slowed the horse long enough to shout back a reply. "When you're ready for a wife, come up our way and we'll repay the favor."

Laughter followed him as he encouraged the mare to quicken her pace. He had a few things to get in order before tomorrow night.

~*~

Her room dark but for a single candle on the nearby dressing table, Lydia sat by her window, listening as a handful of the King's soldiers had their ears filled with something quite displaced from Christmas cheer.

Charles Selby was missing. Nowhere to be found. He'd gotten away. For now, he was safe.

The shouting downstairs only grew louder, demanding every resident of the house make an appearance. Lydia fortified herself with a breath and a prayer, before she pushed up from her perch and moved to the door.

Ester stepped out at almost the same time from the nursery, Maggie's cries following her. There had been no time for Charles to take his little family with him. Not yet. He'd slipped away shortly after dinner. As soon as Eli had informed him of the betrayal.

"Stay with the baby," Lydia whispered, nodding Ester back to the nursery.

"No, the nursemaid is with her." A sharpness clipped her words. "I shall come see what the major wants." Her shoulders squared and chin raised, Ester led the way.

Lydia followed with wonder at her friend's confidence. If only she could manage the same, but an overabundance of "what if's" buzzed in her head and no answers for any of them. Only fear. She couldn't help the familiar sensation of dread feeding upon her. But though peace had fled, she clung to hope. Hope in a higher power, that perhaps God maintained control of everything that spiraled out of her grasp, that He was a loving Father as Eli had described him. Her one true refuge.

"Mrs. Selby, Miss Reynolds," Major Layton bellowed. "Down here now!"

The blush Ester had worn hours earlier as a new bride had faded, but little else suggested distress at her husband's speedy departure. "Yes, Major?"

"Do you have any knowledge of Mr. Selby's whereabouts, or who might have aided him? For your own sake, and for his, I suggest you be honest with me, madam."

"I know nothing." She maintained the major's gaze, a nonchalance in her tone. "He did not so much as tell me he planned to depart. And I cannot imagine where he has gone."

Lydia prayed she was as successful at keeping her face passive.

Major Layton palmed the hilt of his sword as he turned away. "You may return to your chambers, Mrs. Selby. You will be confined to this house under guard until your husband returns. Miss Reynolds, come with me."

As Ester turned back to the stairs, her eyes narrowed.

Lydia fell back a step under the condemnation that sparked in her friend's gaze. She had no choice but to let Ester go and trail the major into Charles's office.

He closed the door behind her and circled to the

desk. "Pray tell, how are we supposed to follow Mr. Selby to Marion if he has already stolen away?"

"You still have Shepard's Ferry." She held her voice even. "Lay in wait for Sergeant Reid and compel him to lead you." That would get them away from the town, giving her a chance to meet Daniel.

Major Layton folded his arms, his face lined with a scowl. "Very well. But you will come and provide a familiar face for your rebel. I am sure we can make him much more cooperative with your help."

28

Daniel pulled the cinch against his horse's belly and tightened the leather strap before tying off the remaining length. He had thirty-five miles to ride and wanted plenty of time to sneak into Georgetown to meet Lydia. Then they would ride back to Indiantown together to be married. It was hard not to grin like a fool.

"Reid!" The holler came from the small frame house where Colonel Marion and his officers discussed their plans. The plantation owner had been generous to let the troops camp on his property.

Daniel headed in that direction, curious. He had already taken leave of Marion. Unless there was a message or something they wanted him to deliver to Georgetown.

The Colonel met him outside. "Sergeant..." Marion frowned. "Daniel...there's something you need to know before you go." He took the reins from Daniel and handed them off to one of his men. "Come inside."

Daniel stepped into the low-lit room, his eyes needing a moment to adjust.

A group of Marion's officers stood in a cluster.

One man sat at the table, refilling a glass with water. Charles Selby. He looked at Daniel, eyes widening, then pushed to his feet and extended his hand. "Good to see you again, Reid. And thank you for passing that letter on to Colonel Marion. I wanted him to be aware of who I was and my allegiances in case I needed help. It has proved most fortuitous, though premature."

"What happened?"

"Major Layton found out about the *Americus* and my plans for the *Zephyr*. I did not even have time to bring my family. If one of my slaves had not warned me, I would probably be joining those prisoners aboard my own ship."

Daniel nodded, steadying himself against the edge of the table. Lydia was in danger. He couldn't delay. "Do you know who betrayed you? I thought only Captain Hues and a handful of the crew knew."

Charles sank back into his chair. He took the tricorn hat from his head and lowered it to the table with a *thunk*. The glass vibrated. "One other person. I hoped, prayed, and begged for her silence, but my late wife's sister, Lydia Reynolds, is thoroughly loyal to the crown and obsessed with the idea of returning to England. She has been bargaining with Major Layton for months now, feeding him information."

"A spy?" Daniel couldn't muster more than a whisper as the tiny nagging voice he'd been trying so hard to bury with his doubts about Lydia rose with a shout.

"As I understand from snatches of conversations I've overheard, she found some Patriot and deceived him into believing she shared his loyalties. The poor fool. Though I guess I was an equal fool."

Daniel's teeth began to ache. He wanted to protest that it couldn't be, that Lydia was a Patriot, and she loved him. But the truth of Charles's words only gave context to every conversation they'd had, her constant questioning and digging. No. It couldn't be. She was planning to marry him. Yet this wasn't the first time he'd been wrong about a woman's affections. If he had been honest with himself from the start, he probably would have seen through Lydia's pretenses, but he'd wanted to believe her. He could no longer refute reality. "Fool indeed."

Marion came behind him and braced his shoulder. "I'm sorry, Daniel."

For some reason the words didn't help him breath any easier. If Lydia had been working with the British, then the information she'd given him about Allston's Plantation had been inaccurate. Bait. And he'd taken it and led Gabe to his death. Daniel shoved away from the table and plowed through the door. The crisp, late December air did nothing to cool him as he stalked to where his horse had been tied to the top rail of a fence.

Someone jogged up behind him. "You were the one?" Charles questioned. "I suppose I should have guessed as much when we found you that night in Georgetown, and I had my suspicions, but—"

"Yes. I was the fool. More so than you can imagine." Daniel tugged at the stirrup. "Not that I gave her anything. Not much, leastwise. I had suspicions from time to time. I didn't give her information that mattered." He froze. "Until yesterday. I told her about you. This is all my fault."

His fist balled. Heat coursed through him, hazing his thoughts.

He'd ride to Georgetown as he'd planned. He'd find Lydia and...and he wasn't sure what he would do, but he had to do something. He hadn't felt so angry, so betrayed since...*Rachel.* When he'd rounded up a mob and almost seen an innocent man hanged. Daniel suddenly felt rather cold. He wiped his palms down his face. His vision swam. He wasn't that man anymore. *Lord, help me.*

Charles's voice penetrated his consciousness. "She already knew about the ship and about my plans. I am sure she was just biding her time, waiting until the information served her best."

"I still shouldn't have said anything. I was so sure..." That she loved him? That she would marry him? Lydia had played her part well.

"I'm sorry," Charles mumbled. He turned back to the house. "I know how it feels."

Daniel leaned into his horse's shoulder. The less the other man knew about how strong he'd allowed his feelings for Lydia Reynolds to grow, the better. If only he could trust everyone else in camp to keep it a secret. Not likely.

The retreating footsteps paused. Charles stood, again facing him. "I am attempting to convince Colonel Marion to help me remove my wife and daughter from Georgetown. It might help if he knew I already had a man willing to assist."

With the possibility of seeing Lydia again? When Daniel needed to get on this horse and point it north? He dropped his head forward with a nod. "You can tell him I'll go."

~*~

Darkness settled over them, all silently waiting.

Lydia sat stiff on her mount despite the fact that nobody would come. No one but a couple dozen or so of the Queen's Rangers and Major Layton. Daniel would be far from here. And safe. All that mattered.

"We've been patrolling the area for hours," the

major grumbled after a time. "Selby has probably already found Marion's camp and your rebel friend. Coming out here was a waste of time."

But no lives were lost. She had distracted Layton enough for Charles to get away. Even if she couldn't.

The major shot her a glare and gave the order to return to town. It was easy to look as disappointed as he did. All Lydia had to do was think of what this night could have meant. Had Daniel even come for her? Did he wait there still? Or had word of Charles's betrayal already reached his ears? Did Charles suspect her of informing the British? Was that what he would tell Daniel? Questions continued to ignite in her mind, one after another.

The troops made their way back to the grand house. It seemed a hollow shell of a building now.

Taking leave of a livid British major, Lydia climbed the stairs. She peeked in the nursery first. Ester sat in the rocking chair next to Maggie's crib, her head back, eyes closed. Lydia's eyes watered. It was too easy to picture her dear sister in that very spot, watching over her own child. But Margaret was dead. Father was dead. Mother and little David and Martin were dead. Only Lydia had survived.

In her chambers, Lydia waited until silence embraced the house. Then she stole down the back stairs through the kitchen to collect the old hooded cloak from where she had stashed it. She cracked the door open and listened.

A guard was posted at the front of the house and two more patrolled the perimeter. Their footsteps led away.

Darting across the yard, Lydia didn't breathe until she'd plunged into the deep shadows of the surrounding hedges. She glanced back. No one appeared to have seen her.

With her skirts lifted enough to allow her to run, Lydia stayed off the open streets and hastened toward the docks to the storehouses. She was out of breath by the time she circled around to the front of the one where she had promised to meet Daniel. She laid her hand against the corner while she fought to fill her lungs. The shadows remained still.

Daniel had either given up waiting or never come at all.

Leaning against the wall, Lydia sank to the ground, hugging herself against the wintery air. She could only imagine how it would be in New England this time of year. Snow piled high. Icicles hanging from the roofs. How would life have been in a small cabin in the wilderness? One room. Maybe more.

Daniel would have seen to it that they had plenty of firewood, and a blazing fire would have kept their home warm no matter how cold the wind blew in New York. And they would have been together. Building a life. A family. Everything she had begun to hope for again.

Hope.

Lydia closed her eyes as a shiver passed through her. Hope had been a foreign concept for well over a year and she could continue to get along without it if she had to. In all but one thing. She hoped Daniel found his way home safely...even if she wasn't at his side.

29

The odor of horse sweat saturated each breath as they slowed their mounts and directed them off the road. They rode several yards into the forests, then stopped and waited. The sound of hooves gradually grew and a company of green-clad rangers trotted past.

Daniel glanced to Charles and the moisture beading on his brow. Two and a half weeks of waiting to return for his family had been torture, and Daniel could well understand it. The last thing they needed was the British alerted to their presence and their wait prolonged.

Over two weeks. He could not blame Marion for waiting, with Major Layton watching for them and Georgetown significantly reinforced with upwards of three hundred King's soldiers and Queen's Rangers, two galleys and three nine-pounder cannons. But understanding the pause did not make it any easier. Daniel should have taken his leave as originally planned. He would have almost been home by now. Unfortunately, he'd always been a fool.

The Rangers passed, and the three men breathed a collective sigh. Only one more mile to town. A town whose guard was hopefully spread thin. Earlier in the day, Marion had sent Colonel Horry with four companies to hinder some Loyalists butchering cattle just north of Georgetown. The skirmish had become quite the tumult throughout the day and more men were drawn out of town to meet the Patriots, making the perfect opportunity to slip into the community at the southeast edge. They wouldn't have far to go.

Keeping to the trees, the small band skirted around the edge of town within a block of Charles's house.

"We should leave the horses here," Daniel said, dismounting. "It will be easier to sneak in on foot." He glanced at Charles. "The quieter the better, right?"

Charles nodded, obviously nervous about smuggling not only a woman, but a baby, out from under the noses of the British.

Daniel wasn't sure if his own anxiety came from getting Charles's family out, or the possibility of seeing Lydia. Or not seeing her. He wasn't sure which he wanted. A gust of wind off the bay encouraged Daniel to press his hat lower on his brow and tug his collar higher. The half-moon cast a low light over the town. He would have preferred it to be darker.

They sat in the shadows and watched the house for a time.

A guard stood near the front door, leaning against one of the thick columns. There was no sign of any others.

"See that window with the faint glow," Charles whispered, pointing to the second story of the house. "It appears Lydia still has a candle lit in her chambers. We'll have to remain quiet. As far as I can see, no lamps are lit. And Major Layton's quarters are dark."

Daniel's gaze snagged on the first window indicated and the soft light showing. Like a beacon. What he wouldn't give to face that little Loyalist, look her in the eyes and let her see the contempt he held for the games she'd played. Had she felt anything for him? Or would Miss Reynolds take pleasure in the pain he tried so hard to conceal under the layer of distain? Better to avoid her altogether.

"Follow me." Charles broke toward the back entrance.

As they stole through the door, legs of a chair vibrated against the floor and a shadow rose from a small table, a glow of red in a low lamp.

Daniel leapt past Charles, shouldering him aside as he slammed his body into the British soldier. The chair clattered over as both men hit the ground with a thud. The redcoat already had his pistol in hand, but Daniel wrestled the weapon from him and struck him over the head. His body fell limp.

Silence settled into the room, and Daniel's breath bated. Had anyone else heard the tussle?

"Smith." Daniel pushed to his feet and handed the pistol to the man who had volunteered to assist them. More had been willing, but they hadn't come for a fight. "You stay here and bind this guard. Make sure we can come back out this way."

He didn't wait for the man's response, or acknowledge the return of a familiar ache in his ankle as he motioned for Charles to lead the way through the grand house. Even buried in darkness, the elegance and magnificence slapped him across the face. Miss Reynolds had probably laughed after his proposal, offering her a life in the wilderness, away from all this luxury and wealth. Well, she could have it. And her King on his throne in England.

Daniel waited outside the door, sword in hand, as Charles slipped into one of the bedchambers. The sigh of a woman's voice followed. And then Charles's muffled reply. Surprisingly quickly they joined him, the woman already dressed and with a bag in hand.

Charles toted a baby bundled in blankets. "Let's go." He again led the way.

Daniel brought up the rear. His feet hesitated in front of what he reckoned to be Lydia's bedroom. "Good riddance," he whispered.

~*~

The light from the candle flickered over the page of her mother's Bible. Lydia lay across her bed on her stomach reading the small printed words as best she could. Her eyes ached, but she did not want to stop. Not until she could no longer keep her eyelids open. Only then would sleep come, carrying some of the peace she had gleaned from the pages.

The wind whistled at the window panes while a door tapped shut. Footsteps shuffled past her door. The only thing she could think was that Major Layton, or Colonel Campbell, who had also taken up residence in their home, had returned.

Ester had the crib moved into Charles's bedroom shortly after she'd arrived, wanting the baby close. She also left her luggage packed. Lydia had seen the bags and suspected they also contained articles for Maggie, ready for when Charles came for her. Lydia knew as well as Ester that he would return when the time was right.

Lydia sat up and listened. Definitely someone on the stairs. But leading downwards, not up. If not Layton or Campbell... Rolling from the bed, Lydia snatched a robe from the foot of the bed, slipped the bolt, and opened the door a crack.

Three shadows had just reached the bottom of the stairs. Two men and a woman. Packs and bundles. Charles had finally come. And now they were leaving. Without her. Alone with the king's officers. The last of her family ripped from her. Lydia stepped out, panic rising within. "Charles."

She hadn't spoken loudly, but the last man looked back. There was not enough light to make out his face, but his height and physique was very familiar. He shooed the others faster and then turned back as she rushed to the stairs.

"Daniel?"

He froze.

A horse whinnied at the front of the house and the heavy trod of weary feet approached the door. The officers.

Daniel's head swung from looking at her, to Charles, and back again. He mumbled something to the others and then lunged for the banister, taking the steps three at a time. The door opened below as he took hold of her arm. His palm clapped over her mouth and spun with Lydia into her bedchambers. He only released her arm to ease the door closed behind them and slide the bolt back into place.

With her head captured against his chest, Lydia was unable to hear anything beyond the thundering within. She couldn't tell whose heart beat the loudest.

"I won't let you betray them again," Daniel whispered in her ear, his breath hot.

Much like the heat building behind her eyes. If only he would let her speak, tell him what had really happened, who was really at fault, but his palm remained clasped over her mouth.

Men's voices echoed through the grand house,

neither Layton nor Campbell giving any thought to the lateness of the hour or whom they might disturb. Not that they would disturb anyone. Charles and Ester had made their escape with Maggie. By morning they would be well beyond the Major's reach.

Lydia clamped her eyes closed. *Dear God, please keep them safe, and speed their way.* A tear rolled from the corner of her eye. She could tell when the droplet met Daniel's hand as his grip loosened slightly.

He shifted his position, his chest expanding. His head ducked next to hers. Warmth touched her ear, and then his mouth clamped shut. He probably didn't believe she deserved a word from him.

Maybe she didn't.

"I won't hurt you so long as you make no sound," he breathed. "Just stay silent."

A tremble worked its way through her body and another tear claimed freedom. He thought so little of her as to believe she was only concerned for her own safety.

Daniel leaned low and blew out her candle. Then he dragged her to the window and peered down. Some of the tension ebbed from him.

She wrenched to look out in time to see three shadowed forms vanish into the hedges. They had made it. Soon they would be far from Georgetown with Maggie. Only God knew if Lydia would ever see her niece again, and the uncertainty sent more moisture to her cheeks—and Daniel's hand.

His grip slackened even more. "It's almost over," he said.

It was impossible to tell whether his words were meant for her or himself. They brought her no comfort. Soon he would also be gone. *Soon.* She had a little while yet in his arms. Lydia relaxed against him and memorized the rhythm of his heart. The strength in his arms. The earthy scent of his clothes. Memories were all she had left of her family—nothing could take them from her. Not disease, not privateers, and not death. Not goodbye.

~*~

Daniel stiffened as Lydia's body eased against his, almost as though she were falling asleep in his arms, but she remained steady on her feet.

The voices continued downstairs, not more than a word or two intelligible.

He wished they would hurry and retire so he could make his escape. If he waited long enough, he could go out the way they came in. Unless that guard at the back was discovered missing or regained consciousness. Had Smith had the time or the presence of mind to tie him?

The window spilled blocks of moonlight onto the floor and offered a second option. But what was he supposed to do with Lydia? He couldn't let her go. One scream and the British army would come running. He wouldn't be the only one they found. Charles and his family needed more time to get away. But Daniel didn't want to hold her any longer. He hauled her to the bed and threw off the heavy cover with the hand not required for keeping her silent. Something thudded on the floor and he glanced at the offending object. A book.

There was no break in the conversation downstairs.

Taking the linen sheet, Daniel bit the corner and

began to rip away a strip, slowly and quietly.

Lydia gripped his hand across her mouth, tugging at it.

"If you try to scream, so help me, I'll knock you unconscious." Even as he said it, Daniel questioned his ability to carry through. He hated her, despised her, but wouldn't be able to raise a hand against her to save his life.

Her head gave a little shake, and he drew his hand away ever so slightly, braced to slap it back at the first squeak from her throat.

"I swear I will not make a sound." Her words were conveyed on a breath, her eyes wide as she rotated to face him. "I want to help you."

He glared at her and finished ripping the sheet. "Like you helped your brother-in-law and his new bride? On their wedding day. Like you helped me by telling the British everything I ever said, and where I'd be."

"Daniel, you must believe me, I never—"

"That's the problem right there. I don't believe you." As much as he still wanted to. "I won't be your dupe anymore." The fact that he'd fallen for her lies still boiled his blood. If she wasn't so scared right now, she'd likely laugh in his face. He grabbed her hands and bound them together.

"Please, Daniel, I did not want to hurt you, or deceive you. Maybe when I first met you, all I could think about was finding a way to go to England, but that—"

Daniel yanked her back to him, clamping his palm over her mouth to hush her ever increasing volume. He'd be wise to gag her, but at least he finally had his confession.

Lydia looked up at him with apology-filled eyes, but she'd fooled him before. Daniel had been so sure he'd seen love in those eyes once. How had he been so mistaken? He let her go again only so he could tear another strip of linen.

She stood, obediently silent.

With two strips in hand, Daniel motioned her to the bed. She sat and he knelt at her feet. Heat burned across his neck at the sight of her bare toes and ankles peeking from under the white linen of her nightgown. He pushed past the sensation, and focused on binding them tight. Then he scooped her feet up onto the bed. The floor was cool and there was no reason to let her fall ill. He pulled the blankets over her and tucked them around her pretty throat, and the smooth skin of her neck. He let his fingers linger a little too long.

"Daniel."

He met her gaze and the anger fell away, leaving charred emptiness in its place. And an incredible loneliness.

"I am sorry."

He almost believed her. But perhaps that only proved him more the fool.

~*~

At the hurt in Daniel's eyes, Lydia ached to throw her arms around his neck and hang on until he believed her and agreed to take her with him, but the linen binding her wrists held all the security of shackles. And speaking only endangered his life.

Major Layton and Colonel Campbell's conversation had lapsed and they were probably headed to their beds. Any sound could draw them this way.

She had no choice but to let him go.

The last torn sections of her sheet were gripped in Daniel's hand as he leaned over her. His gaze lowered to her lips. His mouth followed, brushing over hers.

Don't leave me. Lydia brought her head off her pillow in an attempt to deepen the kiss, but he pulled away and the bland taste of cloth replaced his sweetness.

He stuffed her mouth and then wrapped the linen around her head and tied it over her ear. Hurrying to the window, he drew it open and leaned out. He glanced back one last time before he jumped. A muffled grunt split the night air as his boots thudded against ground. Then came the sound of loose pebbles on the path under hard soles, and the cry of warning from one of the King's soldiers.

30

A bolt of fiery pain lit up Daniel's leg from his foot as it met the ground, his momentum carrying him into a roll. He jammed a knuckle into his mouth and clamped down in an attempt to smother the cry halfway up his throat. With only partial success.

One of the redcoats rounded the side of the house, and Daniel scrambled to his feet. His ankle screamed at him with renewed agony and gave way.

"Intruder! Halt!"

The boom of a musket echoed in Daniel's ears as rocks again met his knees. He dove for the ground and rolled back toward the brick wall, though the spindly bushes, now bereft of any leaves, would give him no cover as he grabbed his pistol and...tossed it aside. Little choice remained with the barrel of a second guard's musket glaring down at him. Daniel held his hands away from his body. Not that surrender would make any difference. Three weeks earlier a whole company of Marion's men had been shot after being offered quarter and yielding their weapons.

Daniel gritted his teeth against the torture of his ankle—the same Madam had crushed almost two months earlier. It had never completely healed, but he hadn't considered that when choosing to jump from the second story window. How could he have with Lydia so close? This was simply another victory to her. Maybe he'd be better off with a lead ball through his brain.

An officer, no doubt Lydia's Major Layton, came around the corner of the house, hands working to button his uniform.

Three more soldiers flanked him, one with a lantern in hand.

The major secured the last button of his red coat and lowered his hand to the hilt of his sword. He glanced up at Lydia's window, and then back. "Sergeant Reid, if I'm not mistaken. One of you men check on Miss Reynolds. Hurry."

"She's fine." Daniel laid his head back to the ground. A wave of nausea washed through him, swelling with the pain, and then both slowly ebbed. "We merely talked."

"Very well." The major motioned to his men. "Bring him." He turned back to Daniel. "It is time you and I do the same."

After relieving Daniel of his sword, two of the soldiers pulled him up. With their help, he avoided pressure on his sore ankle as they hauled him to the front and inside of the house, even grander now the halls were lit. In a smaller room, they deposited him on a chair, and Major Layton seated himself on the edge of a large desk.

"Why were you here?" The major's eyes widened as though something occurred to him. "Someone, check Mrs. Selby immediately, make sure she is still—"

"Major, I am sure it is not necessary to disturb Mrs. Selby," Lydia said, stepping into the room rubbing her wrists. Her tresses, dark and tousled, hung about her shoulders, and she'd replaced her nightgown with a simple day dress. "I heard the baby fussing until late. I am sure they are both quite exhausted. Or, if someone must look in on them, let me. Anything else would be quite inappropriate."

The major straightened to his full height. "Miss Reynolds, my men will follow through on my orders and—"

"No, they will not, sir! This is my home and I am done with the improprieties I have already endured here tonight. Pray tell, how did your men fail to stop this man from forcing his way into my chambers?" Her eyes flashed with something strangely familiar, making it all the harder to understand her charade. "If you had not come when you did, I can only imagine what this brute," her voice quivered, "may have done."

The major settled into a chair. "Did he harm you?"

Lydia stiffened. "No. The rogue woke me, gagged me, tied my hands and feet, and then regaled me with his grievances. For some reason, he had many, now wise to my part in all of this. But coming here alone like this, I see he is every bit the fool we believed him to be."

Daniel flinched at her words, though they couldn't all be true. She had to have seen both Charles and Ester with him. Was it possible that Lydia now protected the very ones she had at first betrayed? Or was this only another layer of her twisted scheme?

The pain radiating up Daniel's leg did not help him make sense of the woman, but as he caught her gaze, he saw something that hadn't been present when he'd bound her in her chambers. Fear. He was daft enough to wonder if it was for him.

~*~

Four hours passed before dawn broke on the

horizon and the major ordered one of the slaves to wake Mrs. Selby.

Lydia had managed some semblance of shock at Ester's absence, but her thoughts lingered far from keeping up pretenses.

Daniel had already been taken to the *Zephyr*, now anchored in the bay while awaiting a new captain and crew. The British did not trust anyone close to Charles and his treason.

She had probably lost the last of Major Layton's trust, as well—especially since Ester's disappearance— but he knew she was no threat to them. Lydia closed the door to her chambers and examined the splintered wood and twisted metal remaining of her lock. The bolt remained attached, but the soldiers had ripped the keeper from the wall when forcing themselves in. She frowned and moved to pick up the Bible from where it had fallen the night before.

The guard had been taken from the house. With Charles long gone with his family, no one seemed to have illusions that he, or anyone, would come back for her. Why would they?

She was truly alone. Lydia hugged the Bible to her chest. What was the point of faith and trust in a God who did not care? She had tried. She had allowed her heart to open, but now it would break all over again. Maggie was gone, safe with her new mother, and her neglectful aunt would quickly be forgotten. And Daniel. Who could say what would become of him? Where was her Refuge now?

The pain of two more losses mingled with the ones of her past, unbearable. Lydia sank onto the bed and rolled onto her side, knees pulled up, and elbow tucked under her head. She lay in place, listening as life went on everywhere else. The streets hummed with townspeople going about their business like any other day, while the servants were busy about the house.

The Bible sat only inches from her face. She stared at it and the weathered pages Mother had once treasured. In quiet moments, the book had spoken to Lydia's soul...or God had. "Please, God." *I want for this to be real. I want faith. Help Thou my unbelief.*

Lydia opened the Bible and propped it with a pillow. She turned the pages, reading a passage here and there while letting her thoughts wander. Then a sentence focused her mind, and she pushed up on her elbow to read it again. *What doth it profit, my brethren, though a man say he hath faith, and have not works?* She stared at the black markings, and then read further about doing for others, service, and sacrifice. *So faith, if it hath not works, is dead, being alone.* Sitting up in bed, Lydia set the Bible aside. What had her works been?

"Oh God, forgive me. For all the lies. All the deceit. All my wrongs." *Make me pure...and teach me what to do.* She needed to be more like Ester, who had known Charles to be in the midst of committing treason against the Crown, yet she had not shrunk away from danger.

Lydia hurried to dress by herself, a difficult task though it was. Then she dropped to her knees at her bedside. "God, my attempts to save Daniel may fail. But mustn't I try?" Minutes later, she slipped through the front entrance and down the road. As she suspected, she was of no consequence to anyone. Though confident she would not be followed, Lydia wound her way to the opposite side of town and glanced behind her once more before turning up the short walkway to the humble cottage. She rapped a single knuckle against the solid wood and then waited.

The door opened to an old woman with mobcap and pinched stare.

"Is Mr. Wilsby at home?"

~*~

Daniel tried to wiggle his toes but wasn't sure of his success. He couldn't really feel them past the pain. His boot seemed to swell along with the foot, but only so far. Hence his concern. He'd known of men who lost their toes due to lack of blood flow to them. But there was no way to get his boot off without having it cut off, and the British hadn't seen fit to leave him with his knife. There was also the possibility that the thick leather worked as a splint if he'd broken the bone this time, and removing the boot would only make the injury worse. Not that he had a choice one way or another.

To distract himself from the pain and his lack of options, Daniel again examined his cell. Four walls and a door—a small room identical to, if not the same as, the one Captain Hues and Charles had hidden him in. Daniel had been taken to the ship but not put in the hold with the other prisoners. Although, the lobsterbacks had given him a good look down at what his future held. Stench, hunger, dark—a slow death aboard a prison ship. That is what the *Zephyr* had become without a captain or crew. Only guards and their victims.

The ship rocked, adding to the doom settling over him. Anchored in the bay, the *Zephyr* might as well be any of the prison barges the British had bobbing in New York's Wallabout Bay. They were deathtraps.

Daniel had heard about the bodies, dozens a day, tossed overboard or buried in shallow graves along the beach.

Maybe they would bury him in that mud he'd almost sunk in trying to get to the river when the British had cornered him a month ago. Or maybe he'd survive this and somehow make it home. Daniel dropped his head forward and clasped his hands. "Lord, I don't know what is in store, but whatever happens..." He pinched the bridge of his nose as his eyes watered. The little sleep he'd managed in the last two days left him on the brink of losing control, and the torturous throb of his foot did no favors. Daniel took a breath and continued. "Whatever happens, keep my family safe and help Mama not to fret too much if I...if I don't ever make it back. Lord, forgive me the mistakes I've made."

A symphony of hard soles approached.

Daniel quickly swiped his hands across his eyes.

The major, wig and all, was the first to enter the room, followed by four scarlet-clad soldiers, who also wore white pants and black shoes.

Daniel caught the hint of a smile on the major's face before a brown sack obscured his vision and he was yanked to his feet—foot. There was no way he'd put pressure on the injured one. He hopped along as best he could, as he was part led, part hauled over the side of the ship and directed onto a boat. His stay on the *Zephyr* would be shorter than expected. The sack over his head concerned him the most. Why was it there? Unless they didn't want him to know where he was going—unlikely—or they wanted him to fear. The hair bristled on his arms.

"Stop the boat here," the major ordered after too

short a time.

The small vessel bobbed on the waves, and Daniel braced against the edge. "What's going on?" He tried to keep his voice steady, but he couldn't help the slight waver.

"I thought it would be nice to pause here and have a little chat. Miss Reynolds was not very successful at getting information out of you, and honestly, I do not believe you have much to offer. But you helped Charles Selby slip through my fingers, and that has put me in a rather foul mood. It is up to you to lighten my spirits."

The boat rocked as someone grabbed Daniel's hands, binding them securely behind him. A second rope was looped around a shoulder and under the other arm before being tied tight.

"I want names, Reid. Names and locations. Every plantation and every shack that has housed you in South Carolina. Every man or family who has purposefully aided the Swamp Fox." He grabbed the front of Daniel's coat, giving a jerk. "And I want to know where Charles Selby is hiding." Major Layton released Daniel's collar while someone else dragged him up.

The boat pitched and swayed.

"You have a couple of minutes to put some thought into what I want, Reid."

Daniel gasped for one last breath as a hard shove thrust him over the side of the boat and into the cold embrace of Winyah Bay.

31

The rain started falling shortly after midnight and the trail clung to the horses' hooves. Lydia's woolen cloak had soaked through as had her gown, right down to her shift, but she hadn't let Mr. Wilsby stop at the last farm, either.

Apparently, the older man knew nothing—not Marion's location, nor what the Patriots planned—but he did know people who were better informed.

Before too long they were headed the right direction. At least, she hoped this was the right direction.

"We'll spend the night at the Perry plantation up ahead." Wilsby twisted in his saddle and gave her a pointed look. "Whether or not we find who you are looking for."

She nodded, though he probably didn't see it as he shifted to look forward again.

"No use catching your death out here. We can always ride farther tomorrow—right out to Snow Island if that's what it takes."

"Is Colonel Marion camped there again?"

"I don't know, and don't know that I would tell you if I did." He gave a low grumble. "I am still not sure how you convinced me to help you in the first place. Especially on such an unholy night."

It had indeed taken quite a bit of coaxing, but he knew Daniel and had hoped he was doing the right thing—or so he had mumbled under his breath.

If not for Lawrence Wilsby, Lydia would have ridden right past the small homestead, no light at all in the windows. As they approached the cabin, a faint glow, probably from the fireplace, became visible in the gaps of heavy curtains. Otherwise, it appeared all had retired. Not surprising for the earliest hours of the morning.

Wilsby dismounted and then turned to offer her a hand, but she was already on the soppy ground behind him. "Come along then, lass."

Their knock was answered by the cracking open of the door enough to wedge the barrel of a musket through. "Speak your name and business here," a man demanded. "Is that a woman with you?" His voice lost some of its strength. "What are you doing out in this weather in the middle of the night?"

Lydia pushed in front of Wilsby. "I am looking for my sister's husband, Charles Selby. Or Colonel Marion. Or anyone who can help us."

The man eased the door open. "All right, get yourselves out of the rain." He lowered the musket but kept it in hand. "*General* Marion won't be here until morning, but I reckon there are a few people here you might know. Including your sister."

As Lydia stepped into the large room with its crackling fire, she could see Ester up on one elbow, Maggie asleep beside her on a thick quilt by the fireplace. Lydia would not correct the man's assumption. She would leave that for Charles if he saw fit. He stood in nothing more than his linen shirt and breeches, the shock on his face merging with anger.

"What are you doing here, Lydia?" His voice held more panic than rage. "How did you find us? Are they with you? Did you bring the whole army down on us?"

"No, Charles, I would never—I was not the one who told the major about the ships. It was one of your crew."

He opened his mouth to say something more, but Lydia overrode him. "I overheard the man at the house speaking with Major Layton. The major would have arrested you that day had I not bought you time and sent Eli to warn you. Please believe me. Even last night, I did not give you away. When Daniel—"

"What happened to him?"

Lydia's shivering steadied.

Wilsby pulled at her cloak. "Best get your wet clothes off and set yourself by the fire."

Though the least of her concern at the moment, Lydia did as directed. She draped her cloak over the back of a chair. "Daniel is the reason I am here. He hurt his ankle again trying to escape. Badly, I think. He could not walk on it. The major had him taken to the *Zephyr*. There has to be a way to help him."

Charles considered her for a moment before looking to Wilsby. "And who are you?"

"A friend. A friend of Marion's." He pulled his boots off and sat at the long table. "When did they finally get around to promoting him?"

Shoulders slumping, Charles moved to one of the other chairs. There were nine of them, suggesting a large family. "First of the year, he received the commission from Governor Rutledge making him a Brigadier General." Charles raked his fingers through his already disheveled hair and pivoted back to Lydia. "Swear to me the redcoats do not follow you."

She hugged herself, the cold of the long ride still

holding her. "I swear, Charles. I was wrong to deceive Daniel and help the British, but he is the only reason I am here now. I want to right my wrongs." She pressed her lips together to keep them from quivering. Not that it did any good with her whole body shivering and her strength gone. And her thoughts on Daniel's arms holding her fast. His last kiss. "I want him safe."

~*~

The Swamp Fox didn't arrive until halfway through the morning with four companies and a carriage for transporting the small family the rest of the way out of South Carolina.

As Ester prepared Maggie for the journey, Charles took Lydia aside. "I promised both your father and your sister I would take care of you," he said. "Come with us."

"Charles, I…" Lydia looked at Maggie. The little cherub stood beside a chair and patted the seat with her chubby hands. When Ester handed her some bread, the child pinched the fragment with two fingers and studied it for a moment before shoving it in her mouth.

Lydia wanted to be near her niece, but there was something she wanted more. "Perhaps soon I shall come." If Daniel did not forgive her, she would have nowhere else to go. Except that ridiculous cottage across the ocean. "But not until I see Daniel safe. I must stay and assist in every way I can."

Charles shook his head, casting a glance to where Francis Marion stood with Lawrence Wilsby and the planter. "You may as well come now. I already spoke to the general and he does not want your help." A different truth lowered his gaze from hers.

"You told him I could not be trusted."

Even under the beard that had appeared on his jaw, she could see the muscles tighten. "Can you fault me for that?"

"No." Not in the slightest.

"Why should we believe you have changed your allegiances so fully that you would now risk yourself for a man you are barely acquainted with, one you as good as handed over to the British?"

Lydia swallowed back the hurt. "If you believe I am not to be trusted, why would you ask me to come with you?"

Charles stiffened. "I told you already. I promised Margaret. Besides, you are friends with Ester, and we will be out of reach of the British." He really didn't trust her.

Lydia picked up her cloak from where it draped over the back of the chair. It still held some moisture. Much like her eyes. She'd cried more in the past weeks than the whole year preceding. "I tried not to care, Charles." She whispered the words, not sure she wanted him to hear them. "After Margaret died. I did not want to hurt like that again. I was not strong enough to face losing someone else. But I do care. I care about you, about Ester. Maggie has wrapped herself around my heart without even trying. And Daniel Reid..." She raised her gaze to her brother-in-law's though her vision remained flooded. "I love him."

"Lydia—"

"I refuse to be the one left behind this time, Charles. My parents, my little brothers, my sister— everyone left me behind. Not again. Never again." Her voice rose with her conviction, her need. "I do not care what the cost. I *will* save Daniel." Or she would die trying. "I will not be left behind."

~*~

Lydia kept her head low, hood up despite the warmth of the day as the red-clad troop strode past her. She fought a yawn and lost, but she refused to return home until she'd been apprised of Daniel's wellbeing. Mr. Hilliard had seen her message delivered. Now she could do nothing but wait. And pray.

"You wanted to see me?"

Startling at the voice behind her, Lydia spun to Lieutenant Mathews. "Yes."

He motioned her to step farther behind the hedge, and then folded his arms across his barrel-like chest. "Perhaps you have news of your brother-in-law for us? Your absence the past day has not gone unnoticed."

"I am not here to talk about my family."

"Then why are you here?" The corners of his eyes pulled down. "The rebel?"

"We can discuss him forthwith, but first tell me about *your* family."

The lieutenant cocked his head at her. "My family?"

"Yes. Your wife. Your five children. Tell me of your home."

~*~

Daniel tugged the single, threadbare blanket snugger around his throat, hoping the extra warmth would ease the pain each swallow evoked. Either he was becoming ill again, or coughing and gasping on muddy water had scratched his throat raw. He crossed his arms over his good knee and lowered his head onto his forearms. At least the agony of his foot had again subsided to a deep throb that matched the rhythm of his heart. Most likely that was a result of the cold water numbing it. Or the fact that his head hurt a hundred times worse.

The door creaked open, but he didn't bother looking.

It felt too good to have his eyes closed.

"Mr. Reid?"

Daniel's head snapped up at the sound of Lydia's voice. "What…" He turned his head aside to clear his throat. Speaking felt as good as gargling sand. "What are you doing here?"

Lydia stepped in and pressed the door closed behind her, blocking his view of the stocky British officer behind her. She crouched low and whispered, "I came to help you."

He would have laughed if it didn't hurt so much. "You mean, *help them*, don't you?"

"No, Daniel." Her face screwed up as the tips of her fingers brushed over a hole in the blanket where his damp coat showed through. Even a full day hadn't dried it. "What did they do to you?"

"Tried to drown me." Even saying the words sped his pulse with the memory of struggling in vain against the water, only to be brought up with the wet sack clinging to his face, making it feel as though he hadn't really come above the surface. Gasping. Suffocating.

Someone gripped his shoulder. "Daniel?"

He blinked, focusing on her momentarily before dropping his head forward again. "Did they send you to interrogate me further? It's no good. I know nothing." It didn't matter what he'd told them, nothing would keep them from killing him in the end, and he wouldn't die with innocent lives on his conscience. Especially those families who had sheltered them and given them food. He wouldn't send the British to burn their homes and barns or slaughter their livestock.

"Daniel, I swear." Lydia's voice lowered to a whisper as she leaned in close. Her breath tickled his ear. "I swear I am here to save you. Please forgive me." She touched her head into his temple, and it was hard not to lean into the warmth.

He shifted away. No matter what she said or how she said it, there was no way he would ever be able to believe her. "Leave me alone."

Lydia withdrew, but only slightly. "Oh, Daniel. I cannot do that."

"Because it would disappoint the major if you failed again?"

"Because I love you."

Daniel looked into her lake-blue eyes. Unfortunately, he couldn't believe them either, and her games left him wanting air almost as much as the major's. Daniel gasped a breath. "Why would they let you in here then, if you weren't helping them *again*?"

She stood, bent over, and began digging through layers of petticoat until she bared her boot. "I arranged for a certain lieutenant to move his family into a fine country cottage in England." She slid a small dagger from the top of her boot and passed it to him. "I am here to help you, Daniel Reid, whether you believe me or not. Hide this and wait. I only have a moment, but we shall come soon."

"We?"

She straightened and smoothed her skirts. "A certain fox and his men." Lydia gave a tap on the door, and a moment later she was gone, as though an apparition of his exhausted mind.

He ripped a strip from the blanket and wrapped the dagger's blade. Then he slid it inside his boot. He startled as the door opened once more.

Another familiar face appeared, but one not as becoming. "Sit tight, Sergeant Reid," Lieutenant Mathews smirked. "It shan't be long before you wear out your usefulness." He dropped a rolled blanket near Daniel's foot. "Stay warm."

32

Lydia went directly to the library. She knelt by the large chest and opened the lid. With the haste in which she had thrown the last items into the chest, it took several minutes to find her father's quill pen and two novels. *Gulliver's Travels* and *Robinson Crusoe.* His favorites.

With the books tucked under her arm and pen in hand, she hurried to Charles's office for stationery and ink. Pulling a chair up to the desk, she set the books aside, drew a paper in front of her and dipped the sharp, angled tip of the quill. Her heart ached as she scratched the pen across the smooth, pale surface. Only the sound of someone approaching quickened her hand.

"Miss Reynolds," Major Layton boomed as he shoved the door wide and stepped into the room. "You have been missed these past two days. Pray tell, where have you been?"

"To secure new accommodations, sir." She flipped the paper over. "I am a young, unmarried woman. Perhaps it was acceptable to remain under this roof while my brother-in-law, or his wife were present, but they have gone. With Colonel Campbell and yourself in residence, it is impossible for me to stay here without tarnishing my reputation. I have only returned for a few of my belongings and then I shall leave."

"To go where, exactly?"

She lifted her books. "Mr. Hilliard has been kind enough to give me his daughter's quarters. He's most generous and I hope to repay him by offering some comfort. Mrs. Selby's sudden departure has been quite distressing to him."

"I imagine it has." The major did not look at all sympathetic. Only suspicious.

Eli stepped into the room behind him. "You sent for me, Miss Lydia?"

She hadn't yet, but his timing could not have been more inspired. "Yes, I would like you to help me with my things. I will be moving to the Hilliards." Lydia squared a look at the major and gave an apologetic smile. "You will excuse us?"

He frowned but offered a stiff bow. "Of course."

Major Layton's departure echoed toward the front door, and Lydia relaxed into the chair. "Thank you, Eli."

He nodded, but the worry lines around his eyes deepened. "Where have you been, Miss Lydia? Are you all right?"

"I am. But I do need your help." She turned the paper and pushed it across the desk.

"What is it?"

Tears welled before she managed to speak. "Your freedom, Eli."

The pendulum on the clock behind him swung in steady rhythm, a hushed tock the only sound in the large house.

"Mr. Hilliard has agreed to witness the document and make certain everything is in order." Lydia wiped at her cheek. "But the important thing is you'll be free."

The old man's chin wrinkled as his lips pressed tight. "Miss Lydia, with your Mama's help, Jesus already set me free. At least as it matters most."

The document remained on the desk. "I do not understand. I thought you would want this."

"I did too. When I was younger. There was a time I wanted nothing more." He brushed his long, thin fingers over the paper, his frown deepening. "But I'm an old man now. Where am I to go? What will I do? I was raised in your grandparents' house there in England. All I had was my Mama, and I'm sure she's passed years since. So, what is left me but what I know?"

Nothing. Because her family had taken everything else from him. "I am so sorry."

Eli picked up the sheet. "Though, maybe it will feel good, just to know that I am my own man." He passed it to her. "Go on ahead and have Mr. Hilliard make it legal, like you said. It might be nice to be owned only by the Lord Himself."

Lydia nodded. "Let me do that for you." *Though I owe you so much more.* She folded the document into the cover of *Robinson Crusoe* and gathered her things off the desk.

"Whatever became of your New Englander?" Eli asked. When her head snapped up, he chuckled. "Mr. Reid had something to do with this, didn't he? You've been pining for him for weeks now. Ever since I met you down on the shore and you turned your heart to Jesus."

"Longer." Lydia moved around the desk and toward the door. "I just feared to admit as much to myself."

"And now?"

She looked back at the man who had been her family's property spanning three generations. As though an heirloom. "Every man deserves his freedom. I will stop at nothing to give Mr. Reid his." Even though he'd made it very clear neither forgiveness, nor trust would ever be hers.

~*~

Daniel clamped his jaw as the physician cut through the boot and peeled the thick leather away from his swollen foot. What man went through three pairs of boots in barely as many months? Daniel would have laughed if his ankle didn't hurt so much.

The cold water had eased the initial swelling, but only enough as to not fully constrict circulation. Countless times, he'd considered using the dagger Lydia had brought him to cut the boot, but was not prepared to explain to the guards how he'd come by a blade. And he definitely hadn't wanted to give up his only weapon.

Thankfully, a Mr. Hilliard was brought aboard the ship last night.

Lieutenant Mathews had been rather silent as to the reason for the man's visit, but Hilliard had asked plenty of questions regarding Daniel's health and care. He'd been the one to encourage the Lieutenant to see after the injured ankle. And the lieutenant heeded—though waited until nightfall.

Was this Lydia's doing?

If so, why? Despite what she'd told him, or what he wanted to believe, he wouldn't be deceived again. First Rachel, then Lydia. Maybe he would be better off rotting on this ship. Daniel flinched, his ankle protesting the physician's prodding's.

"Bone seems to be intact as far as I can tell." The

weed of a man fished bandages out of his satchel. "But there may be a crack I cannot detect through the swelling. I have some ointment that might help."

Lieutenant Mathews didn't bat an eye. His arms remained folded as he leaned against the door. "Just leave him what he needs," Mathews growled. "He can wrap it himself. I need to get you back to shore. And remember what I said. No one is to know you were here."

"I remember." The older man set the strips of cloths and a tiny jar in Daniel's hands. "Firm, but not too tight."

Daniel glanced down at his swollen ankle and the black-fringed yellow bruises. Broken or not, he'd definitely done damage. "Thank you, sir."

A blast of misty air and the two men were gone.

Daniel dribbled the smelly ointment into his palm and rubbed it over his foot and halfway to the knee. The relief of having the boot removed countered the sharper pain stabbing through his ankle. Hopefully that would pass once he'd wrapped it. Daniel settled back and began the task, eyeing the single boot that remained him. He thought of the dagger now tucked away in the back of his waistline. As much as he wanted off this vessel, he wouldn't make it very far on his own.

~*~

"What is taking so long? It's been a full week. Seven days!" Lydia slapped her hands against the table in frustration, though what she really felt was probably more akin to panic. "How much longer before the British find their new captain and crew for the

Zephyr?"

Once that ship reached open water, the chances of a successful rescue became abysmal.

Charles waved her down. She wasn't sure why he remained while Ester and Maggie were now safely beyond the reach of the British. "We cannot simply walk into Georgetown and demand Daniel Reid be released," he said. "And what of those men in the hold? We must give General Marion time to plan."

"But a whole week?" If each day was torturous for her, how did Daniel fare?

"I have no doubt Lieutenant Mathews is keeping his end of the bargain knowing Mr. Hilliard will not give him the signed deed until the end of two weeks. Daniel will be cared for well enough."

If only she had as much confidence. Or enough faith.

God, keep Daniel, and help General Marion hurry and finish planning with his officers. Please…

Eli had spoken of God as a kind father who cared for His children. She tried to picture Him as such. Not a cold, aloft deity, but as a loving Father who cared for both her and Daniel.

Please do not let them delay further.

She glanced out the small window toward the thickly treed north-east, where Marion discussed plans with Colonel Henry Lee of Virginia. Lee had passed through yesterday on his way to Snow Island with his legion. Maybe she should feel grateful more men were available, but with their coming she also felt any control of the situation slip from her grasp. All she cared about was getting Daniel Reid safely away from the British, but he was of little importance to Marion, and now Lee. They lost men every day. War victories and stratagem were what concerned them most. Not a single New Englander. If they didn't hurry, she would find a way to rescue him on her own. She'd thought about little else the past week.

Lydia stopped pacing as their hostess and her ten-year-old daughter entered the house with a bowl of eggs and pail of milk.

"Get my large skillet down," the middle-aged woman directed her child. "The others will be done with their chores soon, and we'll want to have breakfast waiting."

Guilt pricked Lydia. It wasn't right for her to stand idly by, even if she would prove more of a hindrance than help. Over a decade had passed since she'd needed to cook or keep house. How would she survive and keep a husband in the wilderness Daniel had told her about? Not that he would ever renew his proposal—or even forgive her if they saved him in time.

In an attempt to control the despair and franticness binding her insides, Lydia moved to where the woman cracked eggs into the skillet. "Is there anything I can do?"

"You can strain the milk there if you have the mind."

"Of course." Lydia hefted the pail onto the table and then gathered the pitcher and a cloth as she had seen them do the evening before. She listened to the steady dribble of milk as it seeped through the cloth. A pool gathered at the top, rising. She slowed the flow, but the cloth still sank. One corner gave way abruptly, and the unstrained milk spilled, taking flecks of straw with it.

The woman clicked her tongue. "You will have to

start afresh."

Lydia nodded and pulled the cloth out of the milk. It dribbled across the table and on the floor before she got it over the pail. She tried to hold it in place with one hand while the other poured the pitcher's contents back. Too quick. Some sloshed over the brim. Lydia dropped the pitcher and cloth on the table and stepped away. "I cannot do this."

"Nonsense, 'tis easy, and you are learning."

She continued her retreat. "No. I do not know how to do anything anymore." Even if Daniel still wanted her, she couldn't allow him to chattel himself to such a worthless creature. Maybe it was a good thing he'd never forgive her. Or maybe he was already dead. She broke for the door. "I cannot wait any longer for General Marion to decide to help."

Charles bolted from his chair by the fire and grabbed her arms. "Do not be foolish."

"Foolish was waiting this long. Foolish was you staying in South Carolina. You should be safe with your family."

"You are my family too. I will leave as soon as this is resolved."

Lydia jerked away and reached for the latch. "Then I will resolve this now."

"How exactly?" Charles followed her out into the yard.

She wished he had not asked that question, but at least he had not questioned how she would make it the thirty-five miles to Georgetown without so much as her cloak. The exposure to the morning air was a welcome relief, but that would not last long.

A lone rider loped toward them on the trail leading to the small plantation. One of Marion's men.

She hurried to shorten the distance while she braced for another excuse and delays. "What news?"

"Tomorrow. Colonel Lee's already sent men in flatboats down to wait along the Pee Tee River, but we have one more we're trying to man." The Continental soldier looked at Charles as he approached. "Colonel Mari...er, *General* Marion is hoping Mr. Selby would be willing to involve himself in some subterfuge."

"Subterfuge?" Lydia and Charles spoke together.

"We have a few British uniforms lying about, but they would let us up on that ship of yours more willingly if we had a *prisoner* they wanted." He nodded to Charles. "The general believes your cooperation will save the most lives. Including your friend's."

"I want to come too," Lydia said quickly. She wouldn't be left behind while the men risked their lives.

"The General wants you to stay here, Miss Reynolds. He said to tell you that's an order. He thanks you for your help and the numbers and whereabouts of Georgetown's defenses that you brought back, and says he'll do everything he can to bring Sergeant Reid out of there."

"But..." Lydia frowned. "Is the general only sending the one boat, and the rest will be Colonel Lee's men?"

"No, no, of course not. He's sending guides for the other boats. Colonel Lee's men don't know the area." The soldier smiled. "Meanwhile, he'll go by land. So in essence we'll have the Brits and Tories surrounded. He says it's past time we pay Georgetown a visit."

With a full-out battle.

Lydia hugged herself. This was what she wanted, everyone to rush to Daniel's rescue, but what of the resistance? Men would be killed, and neither Daniel nor Charles was immune to that.

"Lydia." Charles pulled her around to face him. He sighed. "To think, not long ago I discouraged you from Major Layton because he was not good enough. I listed his place, or lack of it, in society and his family's equal lack of wealth. Those were not the real reasons for my concern, dear sister. But his character." Charles took both her shoulders. "Daniel Reid is a good man, he risked his life to help me, and I know how greatly you care for him. I will do everything in my power to bring him back to you." An indent in his cheek cracked with the suggestion of a smile. "I shall even try to convince him to forgive you."

Lydia slipped her arms under his, wrapping his torso in an embrace as a glint of hope swelled within her. "Thank you, Charles."

He kissed her head and then slowly withdrew and turned to the general's messenger. "I shall saddle my horse and ride back with you." He hurried toward the corrals.

Lydia followed. "Do be careful, Charles. Your family needs you."

"And I plan on joining them soon. If we are successful at taking the ship, I might try to sail her out of the bay and northward." The corners of his mouth turned down as he took his bridle. "I wonder how many men now prisoners aboard the *Zephyr* know anything about a ship's rigging or how to set sails. I'll need sailors." He opened the gate to the corral and hurried through.

Lydia remained in place. "What about someone who can teach the men what to do?"

He turned. "What are you thinking?"

"Eli sailed with my father. He knows ships. He knows the *Zephyr*."

"That was years ago."

"But maybe that is something he would want. Let me ask him. If he sailed north, he could stay with the family. What he knows. And you would pay him fairly. Wouldn't you?"

A gust of breath left Charles, but he nodded. "Fine. Ask him. If he can help me get the *Zephyr* out of Winyah Bay, I shall see that he is well rewarded and…that he is treated as a free man."

"Thank you."

He caught his horse and pressed the bit into its mouth, before rotating back to Lydia. "But how will you send word? General Marion ordered you to stay here."

She stood resolute. "I am not one of the General's men. I do not see how I am under any obligation to obey his orders."

33

"It's not safe for you here, Miss Reynolds." Hilliard hurried down the stairs in his robe, nightcap in place. "You should not have returned."

"I'm only sorry to have awakened you, sir." The single lamp the servant held did nothing to light the heavy shadows of night.

"Do you bring news of Ester? Have you heard from them?"

"Yes. They are safe." She and Maggie, at least. Lydia still worried for Charles. "Do you have anything for me? Have you seen him?"

"The lieutenant, or your Mr. Reid?" He took her arm and led her toward the parlor. He probably wouldn't let her leave again if he had any say. "Reid looks well enough. His foot appeared to still distress him, but Lieutenant Mathews assured me he would have a physician examine him forthwith."

"Good." She allowed her shoulders to relax from some of the worry that had built upon them since she'd seen Daniel a week earlier. "No matter what happens tonight then, you will send the deed of the cottage to the lieutenant's family."

"What is going to happen tonight?"

Lydia looked from him to the darkened window. General Marion and his brigade couldn't be very far behind her. "I cannot be sure, but—"

The muffled boom of a musket sounded near the

harbor.

"But I think we shall soon know."

~*~

Daniel relaxed into the wall and the gentle rocking of the ship. A yawn watered his eyes and he closed them. Sleep was what he needed now, but the murmur of voices on deck made him pause. Probably just new guards relieving their weary counterparts, but the timing struck Daniel as off. By hours. Or maybe he had lost track of time in this little room.

A shout rang, followed by the distinct clang of steel on steel. Daniel sat up and drew his dagger. A musket discharged. He shook off the strip of cloth binding the blade as he heaved to his good foot and hopped to the door. He laid his ear to the aged wood only to have it jerked away. The door swung open. His weight followed, and he stumbled into the man standing just outside. He grabbed Charles's shoulders. "Selby?"

Charles grinned. "I did not expect such a warm greeting." He glanced to Daniel's blade flat against his torso. "Or were you trying to stab me?"

Daniel righted himself, looking past to the cluster of redcoats circled by...more redcoats?

"Those are our men," Charles said, as though reading his thoughts. "General Marion decided to call on Georgetown. Some of us came down the river in flatboats while he strikes by land. We knew you would not want to be left out."

Daniel frowned at his foot and slipped Lydia's dagger into his belt. "Not that I'll be much help."

"Lydia told me you hurt your ankle again. Can

you walk?"

"With help. I do not think I'll be much use to you tonight." Not that they needed his assistance. They'd opened the door to the hold and the prisoners climbed out, looking worse for wear after a month aboard but more able-bodied than him. "Wait, when did you see Lydia—I mean, Miss Reynolds? You've been back to Georgetown?"

"No, she came and found us. Told us you'd been captured and asked for help."

"Help?"

Charles patted his arm. "It seems my sister-in-law is quite taken with you."

The doorframe supported Daniel. "But you were the one who told me..." She was a Loyalist. She had toyed with his affections. Lied to him.

"I do not think she is playing games anymore, my friend. I believe she is quite genuine in her affections."

Daniel watched as their British prisoners were forced down into the hold. He was too tired to think about Lydia right now. He'd untangle that web another day. "What are your plans with the ship?"

"We shall see if these men know of anything but plows, and then prepare her to sail. I want to have her ready to weigh anchor as soon as possible, but not until dawn, in case General Marion requires assistance. Then we shall sail out of this bay and north to join with the Continental Navy. And my family."

North. Daniel could stay aboard this ship and he would soon be on his way home. Finally.

He pushed from the wall. "What would you like me to do, *Captain*?"

Charles chuckled. "Do you have any experience as a sailor?"

"None."

"Then sit down and let that ankle of yours heal once and for all."

Not able to argue, Daniel found a seat on a crate out of the way.

The last of the scarlet coats disappeared below deck.

Across the bay, the darkened town was barely visible—too dark to tell what was happening there. Only the occasional popping of gunfire indicated that a battle had begun.

Daniel glanced back to the hold. He didn't remember seeing if Lieutenant Mathews was still aboard.

~*~

The town seemed much too quiet for one under attack. Lydia even dozed for a couple of hours on the settee in the parlor. Mr. Hilliard remained in his chair the whole night and listened with her. The world beyond the walls remained a mystery. Finally, a first hint of dawn glowed blue in the windows, and Lydia moved to the door.

Hilliard followed. "Where are you going? It won't be safe out there. We do not know what is happening."

"And sitting here will not enlighten us. I need to find Eli and get him to the docks. And I need to know what happened onboard the *Zephyr*." She set her hand to the latch, but her gaze moved to the walking cane Ester's father used on his strolls. It was propped against the small table hosting a lamp. "May I take that with me?"

"What?" He looked to the cane and grunted with

understanding. "Very well, but—"

She snatched up the cane and hurried out before he had time to say anything more. The streets seemed abandoned, not a soul in sight, but with windows shuttered and doors barricaded as though the town braced for a large storm.

Cane tucked under her arm, Lydia hurried the few blocks to the grand house her father had built for his daughters—now left to the British to do with as they saw fit. She searched the shrinking shadows as she went, all her senses alert. The shuffle of boots. The scrape of an opening door. The nicker of a horse. Lydia darted and dropped behind a hedge.

Two dozen partisans on horseback cantered around a corner and across to the next road leading out of town. General Marion's men.

As their hoof beats faded, she bolted across the street and cut through a yard. Home. The house appeared abandoned, and she dashed up the steps and inside. Shadows laid over the stillness. No one moved. No one spoke. Perhaps no one lived here anymore, but what had become of the slaves? Her boots sounded out each step to the back of the house. A gasp broke from her throat as she rounded a corner where someone stood.

"Miss Lydia?"

"What are you doing here, Molly?" And with a skillet in hand as though she were ready to attack. Two other women stood behind her, similarly armed.

"The officers left in the night. Rebels are in the town."

"Where is everybody else? Where is Eli?"

Molly glanced at the back door. "Went to help keep the horses, lest someone tries to make away with them." She followed Lydia across the hall. "Don't you be going out there!"

Lydia hurried through the door and ran across the yard and down the narrow lane to the stables. The barrel of a gun swung toward her as she burst inside.

Two men stood masked in shadows, their skin blending with the dark.

Eli lowered the weapon.

"What are you doing back here, Miss Lydia?"

"I came for you." She stepped back out into the sunlight and waited for him to follow. "Charles needs your help on board the *Zephyr*. It is your choice, but if you wish, you can sail north with him and have a home and employment in his house."

"How did Master Charles get aboard the Zephyr?" His eyes lighted. "That's where your rebel, Mr. Reid, is?"

"He is hardly *my* Mr. Reid." As much as she wished it.

"But my assistance aboard the *Zephyr* may keep him safer."

And take him home to his family. "I believe it will."

Eli's gaze grew tender. "Then I will go."

She stood in place, wanting to embrace him, but unsure. "Thank you."

He squeezed her arm, and she crumbled against him, letting the cane fall. "Thank you, Eli."

He gave her back a light pat. "Now, Miss Lydia. No time for this. I'm needed on the *Zephyr*."

Despite his insistence that she remain behind, Lydia took the cane and followed him east past the storehouses to the bay. The *Zephyr* sat in place, but she could hear shouts as the sails were hauled up the great masts. The ship was preparing to leave.

The harbor, like much of Georgetown, appeared abandoned, but she hurried with Eli to the end of one of the docks and one of the smaller rowboats belonging to the shipping company.

"If they were successful, Charles will be watching for you. But be careful." She passed the walking cane to him. "And give this to Mr. Reid."

"I wondered if that's who it was for." Eli climbed into the boat and yanked the towline free. He crouched and took up the oars. "Best be getting back to the Hilliards' where you'll be safe."

She nodded but didn't move as she searched the decks of the ship for the red of the king's soldiers. It was not to be seen. Most of the men wore earth tones with highlights of blues and maroons. Charles must have been successful. Daniel would be free now...but if only she could be sure. If only she could see him, even from this distance, and know that he would soon be on his way home to New England and his beautiful Mohawk Valley.

~*~

Daniel glanced to the east as the tip of the sun touched the horizon with its golden light. Timber groaned under the weight of booms being raised, fittings squawking against the strain. Sails swooshed with release and then billowed as a gust of wind rose on the bay.

"You look ready to go," Charles said, coming beside him.

Not nearly as ready as he should be. Daniel made sure his throat was clear before speaking. "That boat—

news from the General?" He'd seen the small row boat approaching.

"Yes. Marion and the rest of Lee's men are on their way out of Georgetown. They took Colonel Campbell and several other British officers. They will head down toward the Santee River. He suggests we also take our leave."

Soon South Carolina would be no more than a memory. "Did they say why the night was so quiet?"

"It seems the British did not put up much of a fight, and the Loyalists barricaded themselves in their homes. Only lost a couple of men. General Marion figures they have left enough of a mark as not to risk any more lives." Charles moved toward the bow, probably intent on one last look at his town. Leaning over the side, he squinted at the docks. "I swear. If that is..." He darted away and returned a moment later with a telescope. After a glance, he thrust it to Daniel. "I should have known she would come."

A cry went up that another rowboat approached.

"That will be Eli." Charles hurried to where men gathered along the portside.

Daniel's knuckles whitened from clasping the telescope as he brought it to his eye and peered through the magnifier at the lone figure standing on the docks.

Her arms folded across her abdomen, she looked directly at him in return. She pulled the hood from her hair and several dark tresses fell from where they had once been gathered on the back of her head.

Lydia.

The mumble of voices grew to a roar as men approached Daniel from behind. A hand clasped his shoulder.

"That woman does not know what is good for her," Charles said. "With Eli here now, we will soon be on our way."

"What about...?" Daniel lowered the telescope, but not his gaze.

"She loves you," Eli said from the other side of him.

Daniel stole a glance at the gray-haired Negro, and then looked back to where Lydia stood. Dared he believe it? As much as he wanted to...

"Told me to give you this." Eli held out a simple wood cane.

A shout rose as a larger rowboat pushed away from the ship.

Daniel leaned over. "You didn't say they were going back."

"Yes." Charles withdrew. "Several of the men who were prisoners are not anxious to go north. Their families are in this and neighboring parishes. They will take the flatboat as well and catch up with Marion and Lee."

"I should go too." Daniel said the words before they had time to register in his consciousness. His ankle still hurt, and Marion's brigade was withdrawing. It would be too easy to end up back in the clutches of the British. Or dead.

"If you are sure. As much as I hoped this would be your decision, perhaps it is unwise considering the state of your ankle."

Daniel took the cane from Eli. Charles was right, but Pa had never let his bad leg stop him from settling in the wilderness and supplying for the needs of his family...from following his heart.

But what if he was mistaken again?

34

"You want to get out of the boat here? Are you sure, Sergeant?"

Daniel wasn't, but he answered in the affirmative. "After you've found horses, I'd be obliged if you left one just southwest of town. There's a grove and an oak so old...you'll know it when you see it."

One of the men in the boat nodded. "I am familiar with the one. We will find you a mount if there is one to be had."

"Thank you. I'll try to catch up with you shortly." Daniel hobbled up the rocky bank very close to where he had swum ashore after being cornered by the redcoats. He dearly hoped his recklessness would not lead him to any more swimming.

Lydia had been headed past the storehouses.

Daniel hurried, with the hopes of meeting her. Though he still wasn't sure what he'd say. Or how to get the truth out of her. Or if he would even believe what she said. He slowed at the sound of Lydia's voice.

A man answered.

Daniel stopped dead. Major Layton's throaty growl had visited his nightmares more than once since his watery interrogation. Daniel stepped against the wall of the building and inched closer.

Lydia came into sight first, faced away.

Layton was more visible and appeared to have not had the most pleasant of nights. Too bad Marion hadn't hauled him away with Colonel Campbell and the others.

With Lydia turned from him, Daniel couldn't make out most of her words, just her tone—fresh churned butter on a warm day.

Layton's hand brushed up her arm and then held her shoulder.

Her fingers appeared over his.

Daniel leaned back out of sight to catch his breath. This couldn't be right. Not after what Eli and Charles had both said. She loved him. She'd even told him so. But now he didn't know what to believe. Or feel. Better to hobble away now and not risk himself again. Not for the likes of a Loyalist.

~*~

"You know where Selby is, don't you?"

Lydia shoved Major Layton's hand off her shoulder and tried to widen the gap between them, but he grabbed her wrist and snapped her back to him.

"You have been helping them this whole time, haven't you? As much a rebel as the rest of your family."

She started to shake her head, it really was not true...or, at least, it hadn't been. She had always wanted this war to be over, but now she wanted the British gone. Especially Major Layton. Lydia attempted to jerk away, but with no effect on his grip. "Let me go."

The crack of his palm stung her cheek and watered her left eye. His fingers bit into both her shoulders as he shook her. "Where is Selby now?"

Lydia wasn't sure if he had the ability to read her

mind, or if she had accidently glanced toward the bay, but the major stiffened and his gaze followed her thoughts to the *Zephyr*.

"He is on board that ship?" With a string of curses, he shook her again. "Tell me!"

"Yes." Both Charles and Daniel were out of the major's reach.

"Unhand her." Like a dream enshrouded in nightmare, Daniel's voice sounded from behind her.

No! Lydia twisted to see him standing there, saber in one hand, cane in the other. "No, Daniel."

Instead of shoving her aside and charging Daniel, the major swung her against him and tightened his hold. He drew a dagger and laid it against Lydia's neck, its edge chill and so very thin.

"If you do not wish the lady to lose her head on your account," Major Layton hissed, "I suggest you drop your weapon."

Daniel's gaze deepened as he searched her face. Then his shoulders slumped. The saber dropped from his hand and clattered to the stony ground.

The blade eased away slightly from her skin while the major let go of her with his other hand and drew his pistol. He aimed the gun at Daniel. "I will take one victory today, even if I cannot have Selby or Marion. No quarter this time, Sergeant." A tight laugh spasmed in his chest. "Unless it is Tarleton's, as you call it."

A scream rose in Lydia's throat, but it wouldn't sound. *I will not be the one left behind. Not again.* Lydia spun, bringing her elbow into Layton's ribs as the other hand grabbed for the gun. She hardly felt the blade slashing into her shoulder as the pistol's discharge erupted in her ears.

The major stumbled back, and they both fell.

Momentarily the world hazed. Then Daniel appeared over her, wrestling the dagger from Major Layton's hand. The razor edge glistened with fresh blood and a wave of nausea collided with one of pain.

Lydia cried out as Daniel dragged her away from the British officer. She rolled onto her back. Blood poured from a gash running across her collarbone and shoulder, soaking into the cloth surrounding it. Her hand shook as she stuffed a fistful of her cloak over it, and then looked to Daniel.

One final blow to the major's jaw, and Daniel left him unmoving in the dirt.

"Is he dead?" Lydia could not hold her voice steady.

"I don't think so." Daniel crawled to her and gathered her into his arms. He laid a hand over hers, adding more pressure to the wound. Probably needed, but it only hurt worse. "What were you thinking? That blade could have as easily cut your throat. If his hand hadn't dropped that little bit when you struck him..." He nestled her head under his chin. "Next time just let him shoot me."

She tried to focus on his face when he looked down at her again, but it was getting harder to breathe as the pain worsened. "Does there have to be a next time?"

He shook his head, the concern never wavering from those wonderfully dark eyes. Then he looked up.

Someone approached. No, not just someone. A group. Scabbards slapping against thighs, boots on packed dirt.

~*~

Daniel tightened his grip on Lydia as the British soldiers advanced, Lieutenant Mathews leading. Hardness lined the man's face as he surveyed his fallen superior and then looked to where Daniel sat with Lydia stretched across his lap, his foot useless and her shoulder bleeding. No retreat or fight was left in them. Not against a dozen soldiers.

"Is he dead?"

Daniel shook his head. "No."

Mathews's face remained stringent as he motioned his men forward. "Private Taylor, find the surgeon for Major Layton and fetch him to the Reynolds' home." He signaled to two more. "Bring a wagon. It will make conveyance more practical."

They did as they were ordered, while the others waited for the next command.

Daniel didn't have to guess what was coming. He pressed a kiss to Lydia's head and began to lower her back to the ground. "Miss Reynolds also needs a physician. She's more seriously injured than the major."

The lieutenant circled in front of them, and then looked at his men. "I will guard the prisoner and lady. You finish patrolling the area."

A sergeant saluted and ordered the remaining eight after him.

As the area stilled, Lieutenant Mathews stepped near. "I can very well imagine what took place here," he said, his voice low. "And in this thing, I believe Major Layton's actions to be wrong."

The creak of an axle silenced him. He stood back while the first two soldiers returned and loaded the major, and then Lydia, into the back.

Major Layton groaned, but his eyes remained

closed.

The lieutenant extended his hand and pulled Daniel to his feet, before giving the slightest nod. "Climb up there on the bench where we can watch you."

Daniel did as commanded, pulse speeding. A pistol remained trained on him as the wagon crept along the shore road toward Lydia's home. There was still no sign of the surgeon when they arrived.

"Take the major inside and make him comfortable, and then come back for Miss Reynolds." Lieutenant Mathews made no move to climb down as his men disappeared into the house. He glanced behind. "Miss Reynolds, how does the situation stand with the deed?"

Lydia's breath hitched, and she glanced to Daniel. Her face appeared bereft of color, as though her usual rosy hue had leaked from the wound. "I told Mr. Hilliard to finish the documents. The cottage is yours. Your family's."

"Good. And...thank you." The lieutenant's stoic expression sagged and his voice crackled. "Hopefully this war will soon be over, and we can all go home." His ruddy complexion paled as he tossed his pistol to the ground and squared off to Daniel. "Your friends have not gone far, and I am now the only thing between you and your life."

Daniel only let himself hesitate for a moment. The other redcoats would return at any time, and the British officer needed an excuse for his prisoner's escape just as much as Daniel needed to escape. "Thank you." His fist caught Lieutenant Mathews square in the jaw.

35

Lydia flinched as the fresh bandage tightened around the deep gash on her shoulder. Pain resonated from the area, and already blood soaked the cream-colored cloth, but she focused instead on the man with his cane and halting stride as he paced the width of the modest living quarters. Gratitude flooded. Daniel was alive.

Thank you, Father.

"That is a mean looking gash you have, Miss Reynolds." Mrs. Cordes, their hostess on the small plantation, gathered the stained cloths that had bound Lydia's wound the long miles from Georgetown. "Rest yourself while I fix you and Sergeant Reid something to eat." She propped the basin against her hip and started down the stairs from the large loft of the house.

As soon as the door closed, Lydia pushed herself into a sitting position. "Daniel…" Maybe she shouldn't call him that anymore. After everything she'd done, such familiarity was probably no longer condoned. He had said little on the road to this Patriot home. "Mr. Reid, I…you have every reason to be angry and…I…" *I wish I could rewrite the past.*

Lydia shook her head as she pictured the first evening on the streets of Georgetown, her shin hurting and Mister Daniel Reid hefting her onto his pretty bay mare. The short conversation. She imagined letting him ride away. No secret meetings. No game of wits. No stolen kisses. Even if she lost him now, she couldn't wish all of that away. Just as she could not wish away the memories of her family. Despite all the pain, sorrow and loneliness, she could not regret the sweet moments of love—gifts from a loving God. A loving Father. A flood of moisture obscured Daniel from her view and she looked away from his steady gaze.

"Tell me why," he said.

She scooted back and sagged against the bed's solid oak headboard. "I thought England would give me a new life. I thought I needed to escape. I had no affection for Patriots when I first met you. My father was killed, his ship sunk by the Continental Army, and you were my passage across the ocean. Charles would not help me, though now I understand why. Deceiving you, convincing you that I—"

"That's not what I'm asking." He blew out his breath and perched on the chair beside the bed. "Why did you help Charles? Why did you bribe the lieutenant?"

He vanished behind a haze of tears. Lydia tried to blink them away, not caring if they fell to her cheeks so long as she could see the tenderness smoldering in his brown eyes.

His fingers brushed her arm below the bandage. "Why did you risk your life to save mine?"

Lydia slid her feet off the bed so she could face him. Her shoulder throbbed as she straightened, and the room momentarily faded to dark. "I already told you," she said when the haze cleared. "Somewhere along the way, in the midst of everything wrong, I fell in love with you, Daniel Reid. I love you."

He leaned forward, his fingers sinking into her hair fallen from its pins, and touched the tip of his nose to hers. "Lydia..."

"Yes," she whispered, closing her eyes. *Please kiss me.*

A chuckle rose in his throat and he pulled back. "I wasn't planning to ask this time."

Lydia looked at him as heat rose in her cheeks. "Then what—"

"I wanted you to say it one more time. That you love me. No more agendas, no more lies, no more pretend. Just the truth."

Ignoring his request and the sudden stab of pain across her shoulder, Lydia closed the inches between them and lifted her mouth to his. She moved her lips, letting herself become lost in the kiss and everything she wished to convey through it. Love. Hope. And even faith.

Thank you, Father.

Lydia touched his jaw as she opened her eyes to his. "There is your truth, Daniel Reid." Hopefully he would never doubt it.

From the grin spread across his face, it appeared he didn't.

~*~

Daniel fastened the cane to the back of the saddle. Not as nice as the one he had intended to take home, but it had served him well the past three weeks. He released the air from his lungs. His jaunt southward had cost him much. His horse with all his belongings, including the knife Pa had given him, several pairs of boots...and his heart. The corners of his mouth pulled upward as he hurried to fasten a bedroll over the cane. Only one thing remained before he could be on his way north. Daniel glanced up at the heavily laden footsteps upon forest debris.

"You ready yet, Sergeant?" Colonel Horry stepped over fresh proof of the horses' residence and drew near.

"Almost."

"Are you sure you do not want to stay? I could use another good man in my new light horse regiment."

Daniel shook his head and moved to the second mount to straighten the packs behind the saddle. Lydia would have little from her former life to take with her. Only her mother's Bible and a couple of novels Lawrence Wilsby had been good enough to bring from the Hilliards' for her.

"Well, best you hurry with that, or one of those men may make off with your bride before you have a chance to marry her. Even General Marion is in need of a good wife."

"And I'm sure he'll find one for himself one of these days." As much as Daniel liked the Swamp Fox, there was only so much he was willing to sacrifice for this war. His feisty Loyalist wasn't included. "Tell them I'll be along shortly."

"Yes sir, *Sergeant*." The colonel whipped out a salute, and then turned, chuckling his retreat.

Daniel finished with the last strap and followed Horry's trail back to the campsite in the back wooded area of the Cordes Plantation. Lydia sat at the fire, her bandaged arm nestled against her chest while she forked sweet potato into her mouth with her good hand. She noticed him and smiled. Maybe it was still too early to let her travel, but after imposing on the hospitality of the plantation owner for this long and being underfoot up at the house, Lydia insisted it was time to leave. Mostly, she wanted news of Eli, Charles and her niece.

Daniel promised her a month in Virginia with her family. That would give the weather a chance to clear and the snow to melt from the valley before they started up the Mohawk. He would be home in time to help Pa with the planting as he had promised.

Lydia held out the fork as he approached and nodded to the vegetable. "Would you like to finish it? I think I've had my fill."

"No, thank you." He lowered his voice and shot a glance to where General Marion stood with his officers, the Cordes family, and a patriotic clergyman. "I'd had my fill of those by the beginning of December."

She laughed and set the sweet potato aside. "Are we ready, then?"

"I am." He had no reason or wish to hesitate.

Francis Marion waved them over. "Let us finish here so we send you on your way before the morning is spent."

Daniel intertwined his fingers with Lydia's and they stood side by side while a simple ceremony was performed, binding them together. He took his bride in his arms and kissed her while men cheered. Easy enough to ignore the raucous with how good this woman felt in his arms...as his wife. Together they would face whatever remained of the war...and their lives.

Thank you

We appreciate you reading this White Rose Publishing title. For other inspirational stories, please visit our on-line bookstore at www.pelicanbookgroup.com.

For questions or more information, contact us at customer@pelicanbookgroup.com.

White Rose Publishing
Where Faith is the Cornerstone of Love™
an imprint of Pelican Book Group
www.PelicanBookGroup.com

Connect with Us
www.facebook.com/Pelicanbookgroup
www.twitter.com/pelicanbookgrp

To receive news and specials, subscribe to our bulletin
http://pelink.us/bulletin

May God's glory shine through
this inspirational work of fiction.

AMDG

Coming Soon

Don't miss the next book in the Hearts at War series

THE TORY'S DAUGHTER

Burying his wife is the hardest thing Joseph Garnet has ever done. Then he's called to leave his young son and baby daughter to fight Iroquois raiders. When Joseph tackles one of the marauders trying to steal his horse, the last thing he expects is to end up tussling with a female. The girl is wounded, leaving Joseph little choice but to haul her home to heal—an act that seems all too familiar.

Though Joseph doesn't appear to remember her, Hannah Cunningham could never forget him. He rode with the mob that forced her two brothers into the Continental Army and drove her family from their home—all because of her father's loyalties to The Crown. After five years with her mother's tribe, starvation and the rebels have left her nothing but the driving need to find her brothers.

Compelled by a secret he's held for far too long, Joseph agrees to help Hannah find what remains of her family. Though she begins to steal into his aching heart, he knows the truth will forever stand between them. Some things cannot be forgiven.

You Can Help!

At Pelican Book Group it is our mission to entertain readers with fiction that uplifts the Gospel. It is our privilege to spend time with you awhile as you read our stories.

We believe you can help us to bring Christ into the lives of people across the globe. And you don't have to open your wallet or even leave your house!

Here are 3 simple things you can do to help us bring illuminating fiction™ to people everywhere.

1) If you enjoyed this book, write a positive review. Post it at online retailers and websites where readers gather. And share your review with us at reviews@pelicanbookgroup.com (this does give us permission to reprint your review in whole or in part.)

2) If you enjoyed this book, recommend it to a friend in person, at a book club or on social media.

3) If you have suggestions on how we can improve or expand our selection, let us know. We value your opinion. Use the contact form on our web site or e-mail us at customer@pelicanbookgroup.com

God Can Help!

Are you in need? The Almighty can do great things for you. Holy is His Name! He has mercy in every generation. He can lift up the lowly and accomplish all things. Reach out today.

Do not fear: I am with you; do not be anxious: I am your God. I will strengthen you, I will help you, I will uphold you with My victorious right hand.

~Isaiah 41:10 (NAB)

We pray daily, and we especially pray for everyone connected to Pelican Book Group—that includes you! If you have a specific need, we welcome the opportunity to pray for you. Share your needs or praise reports at http://pelink.us/pray4us

Free Book Offer

We're looking for booklovers like you to partner with us! Join our team of influencers today and periodically receive FREE eBooks!

For more information
Visit http://pelicanbookgroup.com/booklovers